"No, you ce   "
Velvet's shoulder a snake, and then

"Every instinct tells me to pack you up and take you home."

This time she moved to take Talgarth's lapels in her hands, and her green eyes held a plea as she looked up at his handsome face. "Oh no, my lord. Please do not. I will try and behave as you like, I do sincerely promise."

She was a beauty. Her green eyes melted him in a way he could not explain to himself. Her touch very nearly thrilled him in a way he would not acknowledge. "Do you, little one?"

"Oh yes, yes, I shall not flirt with anyone you cannot like, and I shall be very circumspect with Edward Martin, though you can not object to his courtship."

"Object to his . . . Velvet, do you want Edward Martin to court you?" He waited breathlessly for her answer, not understanding why it was so important to know.

"I . . . no . . . not really."

He took hold of her all at once. He didn't understand what he was doing, how he could allow his body to move in direct contradiction to his mind, but he was bending her to him, and all at once he was discovering the sweetness of her lips . . .

Lady Velvet

Claudette Williams

ZEBRA BOOKS
KENSINGTON PUBLISHING CORP.

Dedicated to my parents with adoration.

ZEBRA BOOKS are published by

Kensington Publishing Corp.
850 Third Avenue
New York, NY 10022

First Printing: July, 1994

Printed in the United States of America

One

The dignified butler, who felt himself embold-ened to take a liberty his many years of loyal service had won him in the house of Salsburn, ran his dis-approving eye over the Marquis of Talgarth's tall and lanky form.

This blatant appraisal won him a sheepish grin from the young marquis, who then scanned himself and agreed, "A bloody mess, ain't I?" The marquis then removed his muddied greatcoat, his well-worn beaver top hat, his damp kid driving gloves, handing over the suspect bundle to the stately servant.

The butler objected with a cluck of his tongue, and the young marquis laughed, "Mud, you know. Can't be helped." Lowering his voice conspiratori-ally, he added, "My grandfather about, eh?"

The butler's brow was up, but he had a great af-fection for his Grace's only grandson. He sighed, and his gaze went pointedly toward the library doors as he whispered, "He is, and he is not very pleased."

"Uh-oh. Methinks I should take back my great-coat and make good my escape before the ol' boy finds out I've arrived. What say you, Jarvey my man?"

The butler's eyes twinkled, but he replied gravely that he did not think that would answer.

The marquis laughed, "Right then." He looked himself over and sighed. "Scraped off most of the dirt, you know. Didn't stop at my lodgings to change m'clothes. Had a notion m'grandfather would want me to come here immediately. Never mind, I'll tread carefully."

The elderly retainer had watched the marquis from infancy to his present eight-and-twenty years. This rough-and-ready behavior was to be expected. "Yes, my lord," he answered and started off.

"That's a good fellow," beamed the marquis, pleased to have passed this first of many hurdles in his grandfather's house. "I'll just show myself in then."

The Duke of Salsburn had been at his library door listening to this exchange. Quietly he quickly closed the door and hurried to take up a position in his favorite chair by the fire, where he pulled a knit shawl round his shoulders. The duke was seventy years old and still considered by his many acquaintances and friends to be the very broth of a man. His thick mass of white hair was tinged with silver and made a startling frame for his still very handsome features. His height was considerable, and age had not bent him. He was full of spirit, wit, and humor and took pride in managing his own affairs in his own inimitable style. However, at the moment he had a part to play!

The duke had been anxiously awaiting the arrival of his only grandson, not only because of the deep affection he had for him, but because there was something he wanted his grandson to do, and trickery was the only way to accomplish this end. He set the wheels in motion by drooping his weathered head and coughing into his fist.

Upon entering the room, the marquis took in the scene and became immediately concerned. His grandfather was a robust man who had never donned a shawl in his life. The marquis approached, a frown of concern darkening his blue eyes. "Grandpapa, what is this? What the devil is going on? Are you ill?"

"Dustin . . . is that you?" replied the grandfather in weak accents.

"Well, who the deuce do you think it is? Of course it is I," replied the marquis, striding forward to take a better look at his only surviving grandparent.

For as long as Dustin could remember, his grandfather had been everything to him. He had lost his mother at birth, and his late father had rarely been around. "Damnation, ol' fellow . . . you never mentioned being ill in your note!" accused the marquis with some distress.

"Didn't I?" returned his adoring grandfather in a tone meant to convey confusion.

"No, you did not! So then, has the doctor been here?" demanded the marquis, now taking charge and feeling just a bit frightened.

"No . . . what do I want with that bloody leech?" retorted his grandfather with a snort, forgetting his supposed weak state. "I have been waiting for *you.*"

He eyed his grandson then and added, "And you have taken your bloody time getting here as well!"

"Eh?" Dustin's clear blue eyes narrowed with sudden suspicion. His grandfather was not above hoaxing him to get his own way. "All right then, Salsburn," the marquis crossed his arms over his chest as he took an opposite chair, "just what is going on here?"

His grandfather countered immediately, "Don't take that tone with me, lad." Feeling a little guilt-brushing was in order, he said, "I needed you. I sent for you. I'm glad you've come."

"As fast as I could," returned the marquis with a glimmer of a smile, for he had in his young adulthood learned the knack of dealing with a dominant grandparent.

"Two days?" sputtered the duke. "You call taking two days getting here as fast as you could?" The duke wagged a finger. " 'Tis but a three-hour drive from Gilly's box, and well you know it!"

"Salsburn, do but consider," urged the marquis. "By the time I received your note, my hunter was done in. We had a hard day in the hunting field, you know." He shook his head. "I had to rest him a day before I could bring him in tow behind my phaeton." The marquis was grinning now, for his grandfather was an avid horseman and would not argue this point. "Now then, Grandpapa, here I am at your command; what is it that needs my attention?"

"Paris, lad," answered the duke, sitting up straight to take his grandson's measure. "I need you to run to Paris for me." The duke's light tone indicated that he thought this was nought but a minor task, no more than going round the square in town.

"Paris?" Clearly the duke had succeeded in startling his grandson.

"Aye, then, Paris." Salsburn frowned over the problem. "Don't really like sending you there, what with the talk of war, but there you are."

"War? Damn, it's only been a year since we signed that deuced treaty! What can Napoleon be thinking of?"

Salsburn had friends in the Home Office. He knew that Napoleon was not quite ready, but here was his only ace. His grandson would not let him go in the face of danger. He lowered his eyes to his Oriental rug and rounded his shoulders into his shawl. "I would go myself but for this dratted quinsy . . ." Thus he attempted to give truth to the word by coughing roughly into his hands and with some resonance.

The marquis was no fool. He waited for the coughing to stop and asked pointedly, "Why must either of us go to Paris?"

"Ah, 'tis poor little Velvet. Stranded there, you know."

"Velvet?"

"Don't tell me you don't remember Velvet?"

"Aye, I remember her, but what has she to do with all of this? Why is she in Paris?" The marquis remembered Velvet very well. She was the very imp of a child, full of pluck and spirit. He had always liked the little thing.

"Sad to tell. You remember her grandfather, Lord Colbury, took her with him when her mother died some years back? Well, then my old friend decided he would take her round Europe. They were staying in Italy, some confounded place, I don't know—I think it was a villa on Lake Como. They were there with their French connections when he died."

Talgarth considered this between knit brows.

"I know you never liked Colbury, but he was a dear old friend. The thing is, he left me in charge of the girl's fortune until she marries. Till now she has been in Paris with her French relatives. She spent her year of mourning there with them and has just been brought out into French society. With politics such as they are, 'tis time she came home to England. Besides, don't want her marrying any Frenchie. Colbury wouldn't have liked that."

"Why the devil can't her guardian bring her home?" The marquis was beginning to feel trapped.

"I am her guardian," said the duke softly. "She has an uncle on her mother's side, but Colbury never liked the fellow. The thing is, I left her with her French cousins because she was comfortable with them and I did not wish to cause her further grief after her grandfather's death. However, the Comtesse de Condé, Velvet's cousin, writes that Napoleon seems to be hinting at war, and she thinks Velvet, who misses home, would be better served in England. Duty, my boy, must fetch the child home."

"Damn," answered the marquis, roughing up his ginger-tinted hair.

"Precisely so," sighed the duke. "You must leave

in the morning. I have already written to them, so you are expected."

The marquis once again narrowed his blue eyes as he scanned his grandfather's sweet expression. "When, Salsburn, did you write to them?"

"Two weeks ago." A slip, thought Salsburn, as soon as the words were out. Nothing for it, brave it out.

"You, my beloved, were not ill two weeks ago. We were together at the Rothman's rout!"

"No, but I am too ill to go now." Hurriedly the duke added, "Dustin, the child is nineteen. She will be more comfortable with someone your age. Her maid will travel home with her. She will be in a coach; you may travel on horseback. So you see, you won't be bothered. She is just a child."

"Velvet . . . nineteen already?" The marquis recalled her last visit to Salsburn Park. She had been no more than fifteen and a wild scamp of a girl, a veritable minx, and he had liked her well enough.

"Aye, 'tis time she were brought home and presented in London," said the duke.

"Devil a bit . . ." complained the marquis. "If she has a companion, we can get her to our yacht—have it wait for her in Calais."

"No, Dusty. It would not do. With conditions such as they are between our two countries, I cannot allow my ward to travel unescorted. You must see that."

He did, and it infuriated him. "Oh no, that would never do. But I am still not rushing off to Paris to play nursemaid for some chit of a girl! Grandfather, beloved you are, but you will not drag me willy-nilly into your wild scheme."

"Duty calls, Dustin," the duke said gravely, and this time he was not play-acting. "Her guardianship is now in my hands. Colbury was my dear friend. I know what he would want. She must be brought home. I have asked your aunt Harriet to stay here and be our hostess for the Season. You like Harriet . . . ?"

"Like Harriet . . . ? Well as to that, aye, that I do, but what has that to do with me? You want to give Velvet a Season with Aunt Harriet in tow? Well then, so be it! It has nothing to do with me. As for Paris, no and no again. I am not going to run amuck with some chit in Paris! Why can't a servant be sent?"

"You know that would not be seemly." The duke shook his head. "I did not realize you would be so resolved against doing me this little favor. Never mind, lad. I shall do it myself."

"You shall, eh? Do you think you raised a fool?" The marquis was in desperate straits, and he knew it. He was on his way to Paris. There was nothing for it, but to understand that it was so.

His grandfather was seized by a coughing fit, and his grandson threw up his hands in capitulation. "Right then, Salsburn. You have won this round. I shall fetch the chit for you and then be done. Mark me on this. When I deposit her on your doorstep, I walk away a free man."

"So good, Dustin. I knew I could count on you in this matter," returned the duke in meek accents. The marquis shot his grandfather a scathing glance. "You are an impudent old fellow, strike me if you're not! Here I am nearly thirty and you still manage to order me about!"

Two

Lord Farnsworth was an English rake of no mean order. He had every attribute an Englishman of noble birth needed in the year of 1803, every attribute save one.

His lordship had height, style, boldly handsome features, and wealth. However, though he was considered a top sawyer, a great gun, and there wasn't an English hostess that felt her invitation list complete without his name on its page, the one thing he lacked was a soul.

Lord Farnsworth had loved many women, but he had never been in love. He did not understand compassion, and therefore had none to give. He was too busy with his needs to recognize needs in others. Even so, he thought it time that he married and delivered another Farnsworth to the World.

Thus, he set out to find a suitable wife. She must be a beauty. She must be a society miss. She must be clever enough to carry on a mildly interesting conversation with him when he wished to speak to her. She must be wealthy enough to at least match his own fortune, and she must, of course, adore him.

Oddly enough he found that no one in the last year quite fitted the bill.

There was Arabella Billings. Attractive girl with fortune enough, but when she opened her mouth to speak, her voice ruined it all. No, no, never Arabella. He looked further and discovered Elizabeth Rushpole. She was a buxom blonde with flirtatious twinkling eyes, whose kisses were most enjoyable. The problem was, too many of his friends were enjoying those kisses. No, no, never Elizabeth Rushpole. Then there was that dark tall beauty, Fancy Hastings, but unfortunately Fancy had eyes for only one man. An odd thing that she should prefer someone other than himself, but he reasoned, there one was. Since London was sorely lacking, there was only one solution: Paris!

He had relatives enough in Paris, and their Season was always scandalously good fun. He would look among the French beauties for his future bride. Indeed, it would be great good fun to have a little Parisian bride giggling in his bed and flitting about his home. Hence, it was a week later that he found himself at the Davenant Ball in the City of Light.

He was bending over some lovely young Parisian's hand when his cousin Henri tapped his shoulder and whispered, "Ah, there she is, the one I have been telling you about. She is English and every Frenchman in Paris would die for her . . . look there!"

Farnsworth looked in the direction of a light, musical laugh to discover one of the loveliest creatures he had ever clapped eyes on. She was from head to toe a perfection of color and curves. Her hair, the color of sun-dried wheat, was nearly white in its blinding shafts of light. Her brows were dark and winged; her nose, small and pert. Cherry lips pursed in a pout as she teased her escort.

"Who is she?" Farnsworth demanded.

"She is Lady Velvet. Is she not ravishing?"

"She is exquisite."

"*Eh, bien.* It is so. Come, I will introduce you to her. All of us grovel at her feet, and she is unaware." He shook his head. "She knows not how beautiful she is."

"Who is her family?"

"She is Colbury. She stays with her cousin the Comtesse de Condé."

"Ah, she will do," said Farnsworth, thinking out loud. "Introduce me then, my dearest Henri. Introduce me, for I tell you at once, this one is mine!"

Lady Velvet Colbury was an innocent, ignorant of the impact her natural beauty had on a room filled with appreciative men. Her green eyes sparkled with ready humor and gentle sweetness, and she was pleased to meet a fellow Englishman as Lord Farnsworth was introduced.

His lordship bent low over Velvet's satin-gloved fingers, saying, "I am enchanted to find one of my own here in Paris. You must promise not to leave my side."

Velvet laughed delightedly as she withdrew her fingers. Eyeing him openly, she whimsically advised him, "La, but, my lord, you should first know the person from whom you extract such a promise;

otherwise you might find yourself in tedious circumstances."

Farnsworth was amused. The chit was no shy miss! "You mistake," he answered smoothly. "I knew you the moment you walked into the room."

"Did you indeed?" countered the lady saucily.

"Absolutely. You are an angel, and mark me, I mean to make you *my* angel."

Velvet laughed. " 'Tis you who mistake, my lord. I am no angel."

She was claimed at that moment by one of her numerous French male cousins. Dropping a quick curtsy to Farnsworth, she allowed her relative to drag her to a lively group of young French people.

Farnsworth watched her departure. She was beauty; she was grace and wit; she was well-connected. She had certainly learned the art of dalliance. She would make him a perfect wife. Indeed, this one must be his!

"Damnation, Gilly, stop your complaining. The hunting season is nearly over anyway, and you like Paris." The Marquis of Talgarth ceased to berate his friend as he pulled his horse to a complete stop on the French road and stood in his stirrups to turn and look for their traveling coach.

Sir Harold Gillingham was a good-natured fellow always ready to lend a reasonable hand to a friend. The Marquis of Talgarth was his dearest, closest friend. They had spent their youth at one another's side both in and out of school.

Thus, when Talgarth called on him for company he usually found that it fit nicely with his own plans. Not this time, however, for it was nearly the end of hunting season. There were fox out there, there was the chase, and there were the hounds. Gilly was an avid fox hunter. It was unthinkable to ask him to give up his last two weeks. Unthinkable. "Most unreasonable, Dustin," Gilly advised him not once but several times during their journey to Paris. To add to his injuries, the voyage over the Channel was bumpy, and Gilly had never been a seaworthy fellow, as he had told Talgarth at every opportunity.

"Ah, but, Gilly, think of the French lovelies awaiting us." Talgarth attempted to assuage his friend's bristling fur.

"French women are delicious, but they also take a damn deal too much romancing for my tastes!" snapped Gilly. "And we should have taken that shortcut. Would have been at the hotel by now enjoying a bit of nuncheon."

"If we had taken that shortcut, we would now be in Dijon, you madman," replied Talgarth testily.

"Humph!" returned his dearest friend.

They entered Paris some ten minutes later, for indeed Talgarth's sense of direction was always without fault. Another twenty minutes found them at their hotel. An impeccable meal followed by a soothing hot bath and a change of clothing did much to even out their frazzled tempers. Thus, they found themselves making their way to Dubois's Gaming Club for an evening's entertainment.

It was at Dubois's that they encountered Lord

Farnsworth, who had just left Lady Velvet at the Davenant Ball and was in the best of spirits. Talgarth and Gilly were recovering from an uncomfortable journey, but otherwise were pleased enough to be out for a night's entertainment. This particular meeting was a setback for all three gentlemen.

Farnsworth managed to drawl sneeringly, "Talgarth, here in Paris? The senses must surely be distracted."

Stepping forward, Talgarth said heatedly, "Shall I show you how *my* senses are distracted, Farnsworth?"

Farnsworth answered warily, for he knew the marquis was in earnest. "I, sir, have matured past the age of blood sport. You, I see, are ready, as ever, to lower yourself to the vulgar!" A double meaning was intended.

A double meaning was understood, and had Gilly not held his friend in check, the marquis would have swung at Farnsworth. Instead his eyes blazed deep with dark hatred. As there was a crew of Frenchmen all gathering in great interest, he only said lowly, "Watch your back, Farnsworth. Remember, always watch your back."

A jovial and familiar voice at their side dispelled the moment. "What is this? *Vraiment*, it is wonderful! My old friends, Dustin . . . Gilly!"

The marquis turned to find a tall, lean, hazel-eyed Frenchman and grinned, "Armand! Well, damn, it is good to see you!"

"Here you are as ever stirring up the pot. Come, we will drink together." Armand managed to kiss

Talgarth on both cheeks and then turned to do the same to Gilly.

"Armand, Armand . . ." objected Gilly distressfully, "save your damned kisses for the ladies. That's a good fellow. Happy to see you, ol' boy, but don't want you kissing me, you know."

The three men went off in a bluster of questions and laughter, and left Farnsworth to watch after them contemptuously. As his was a large circle of acquaintances and relatives in Paris, he was easily able to find his own quarter within the company of men at the club.

It wasn't long before Comte Armand de Beaupré requested to know why Talgarth was in Paris. Talgarth explained he was acting as his grandfather's agent. Armand turned to Gilly. "And you, *mon ami*? What tears you away from your precious hounds?"

Gilly pulled a face. "*He* does. Wants me to help him play nursemaid."

Armand laughed. "Ah, friendship? *Mais non*, even friendship has its limits."

"Tell him!" returned Gilly ruefully.

"*Diable!* The truth now, if you please. Can you really be here to play nursemaid?" said the comte.

"Aye, m'grandfather was ill," replied Talgarth. "He has a ward staying here with her maternal relatives, a cousin, Comtesse Marie de Condé—"

"*Mon dieu!*" Armand rolled his hazel eyes. "Why did I not realize? I knew of course that Marie had written Salsburn, but I had forgotten your connection." Armand shook his head and burst out laughing. "The rogue Talgarth to play protector of that which he hunts. *C'est très drôle!*"

"Stubble it, Frenchie," retorted the marquis amiably. "I am duty-bound to do this for m'grandfather. Besides, Velvet is nought but an innocent chit. I don't play with innocents. Besides, all I am doing is seeing her safely to England," he winked then, "just in case the Frogs mean to start trouble."

Armand's smile vanished. *"Ah, la politique. C'est barbare. Hélas! Mais non, non,* we will forget it now. Dusty, beloved, it has been what? two, maybe three years since we all were together in Italy. Ah, but such a spring and summer that was," sighed Armand. "And now you are here for my Velvet. She is my cousin, you know, though she calls me uncle, and she is very good friends with my two sons."

"What? Damn!" ejaculated Gilly. "The chit is related to all of Paris!"

"No, no, she is de Beaupré. She stays here with my sister Marie, who is a Condé by marriage. Dustin, for shame! You cannot have forgotten my sister Marie? As I recall, you danced with her much more than was allowable."

"Marie! Lovely Marie. Of course I have not forgotten; you nearly called me out on that one," grinned the marquis. "When was she married?"

"Last year." He shook his head. "And now, you, rogue Talgarth, no more than a nursemaid . . ." Armand smiled. "Ah, but to my Velvet, who is *très jolie.*"

"Is she?" Talgarth recalled her in his mind's eye;

she had been a minx of a tomboy, riding her horse astride with her flaxen curls atumble.

"*Oui,*" grinned Armand. "Ah, but you will see. . . . You will see."

Three

Lady Velvet was considered an extremely independent miss. Though she had been petted and cosseted first by her parents and then, after their deaths, by her only surviving grandfather, she had grown to young adulthood totally unspoiled and unaware of her arresting beauty.

Velvet, in her finery, was a work of art whose smile and glittering, twinkling eyes brought life into every room she entered. However, she despised flattery and often, to the annoyance of her French relatives, shunned it for no other reason than she found it tiresome. She did not give a good fig for jewels, gowns, and polite society's latest *on-dit*. Instead she yearned to be riding her horse across the English moors, through the fields of her home, following the hounds on their chase and dashing about with the freedom of earlier years.

Thus, her French relatives sadly realized they could detain their dear Velvet no longer. She missed her English life—a thing they could not understand—so they wrote to her guardian, the Duke of Salsburn, regarding her future.

While Velvet awaited the day she would return

home, she found herself besieged with suitors, admirers, and roués attempting to seduce her in one fashion or another. She found their antics laughable and longed for something else. "What, *ma chérie*," her cousin would ask, "what else is there?" Velvet did not have the answer to this, but she knew there had to be more to life than forever attending fêtes simply to eye one another's gowns and jewels!

Velvet's spirit longed for excitement. It was inevitable, therefore, that she and her two male cousins, Jacques and Louis de Beaupré, would end with their heads together. Jacques and Louis were her age, too wild to pay serious tribute to the ladies, and at an age where they were itching for sport. Propriety was important, indeed, and when one's parents were watching, propriety must be observed. But when one's parents were not watching . . . ah, that was another matter! Each was ready for a lark, and thus they began hatching a plan.

Somehow talk of Paris and all its secrets, particularly its dark side, which was withheld to them, came up in conversation. Speculation fed on itself until there was nothing in the world they wanted to do more but to explore Paris in the middle of the night and without any chaperon! There were gaming halls, there were ladies of the night, and there was the freedom to go about unhampered by convention. They must dress the part, all of them. They must look like bourgeois instead of young aristocrats, and no one must suspect that Velvet was a girl! This made them all laugh, and Louis thought it quite beyond their means to disguise Velvet's gender, but she insisted it could be done. Finally it was decided that the boys would smuggle her a pair of breeches and a neatly cut vest to hide her femininity, a dark cloak, and a low-brimmed hat. They were young and heady with the desire for adventure, and this outweighed reason.

Thus, directly after the Davenant ball, the young vicomte and Louis called for Velvet beneath the railed balcony of her bedchamber. She was ready and waiting, and rushed to the sound of their voices. Hushing them as they whispered advice, she told them she was quite capable of managing the trellis.

She did, in fact, climb down most of this edifice without a hitch. However, on the last niche of the intricate woodwork, her half boot caught. With a gurgle, she found herself pitching forward.

Jacques planted himself to catch her, and then they found themselves thumping heavily to earth. Louis thought this spectacle hilarious and doubled over as he attempted to quiet his mirth. Jacques grumbled, Velvet giggled, and the three were off!

They reached the corner of the Condé residence and held each other's hands. "Well, we have done it!" announced Velvet breathlessly.

"*Hein!* We are wonderful," agreed Louis, who was just eighteen and the youngest of the three.

"*Mais non,* puppy," stuck in his brother. "The time is not yet for celebration. We first must have our evening. Then we must return our Velvet safely to her room. Then we must return safely to ours. And then, Louis, then we may congratulate ourselves! For if we are caught, there will be hell to pay. Our father will kill us, surely he will."

This put a momentary damper on the three, but they were spirited youth in the mood to believe they were invincible. Velvet reminded them of this: "Voyons! He has spoken, and now, my lads, there is a hackney. We have begun."

Had Armand de Beaupré known that his two sons were on the town, he would have hoped that at best they would only be high-spirited. They were already in disgrace as they had been sent home from school for putting a monkey in the dean's office and causing something of a near riot. He adored his sons and forgave such antics as the follies of youth. Had he known, however, that they had taken Velvet and gone into the forbidden quarters of Paris, he would have been sadly disappointed and highly outraged at behavior he would have considered unforgivable.

His sons, especially Jacques, knew this and were uneasy with Velvet, even in her male attire, at their side. They shouldn't be on this dark corner with a painted lady of the night, and Velvet had absolutely no business here with them whatsoever. It was certainly becoming apparent more and more each minute as the prostitute continued to accost them.

"Ah, messieurs, look here. Am I not created to give you pleasure?" So asking, she opened her cloak to reveal her body in a gown Velvet was sure was completely transparent.

Velvet cleared her throat and said huskily, *"Mais non, ma chérie.* We *must* be going!"

The whore looked Velvet over. Here was just a boy. She found his features, although nearly hidden by his hat, to be almost pretty . . . too pretty. She looked closer. "Ah, I can see you are young—perhaps too young, my little one—but there are things, such delightful things, I can teach you."

Velvet eyed her curiously and wondered for a moment just what women like this one taught young boys. She did not have a chance to inquire, however, as Jacques stepped in and said in sophisticated tones, "You are very beautiful, and one can only dream of being with you, but tonight we have another engagement."

"Ah, but wait, *mon cher.*" She sidled up to him, took up his gloved hand, and put it within her cloak. "You see . . . such pleasure I can offer all three of you," and then with a laugh, "for the price of one."

Jacques took out a coin and put it between her teeth as he removed his free hand from her full breast. "There, *amante,* for bothering with us at all, but we must go." So saying, he hurriedly led the other two away while the woman called out endearments behind them.

"Jacques, that was very well done of you," said Velvet admiringly. "I rather thought she would not let us go."

"It is too bad, Velvet, that you were there," Louis laughed, "otherwise she might have had her way with us."

"Oh pooh. You wouldn't have wanted that . . .

not with her," said Velvet candidly. "I may be
only a green girl, but there are some things I
know." She glared at them as they chuckled and
then said, "Well, that was very interesting. I always
wondered how such women lure the men to their
dens. It is very different than the flirting we do.
Come, Jacques, what are we about now?"

Jacques had heard about a place, a wonderful
place, where one could, with but a small investment,
make a fortune if one were smart. They did not have
enough of an allowance to be able to enter the more
respectable gaming houses, and besides, their father
had not yet given them permission to enter these
establishments. So when they arrived at Picard's
House of Pleasures, they discovered a dark, dingy,
sordid hole.

Velvet wrinkled her nose with disgust and made
an immediate decision. She would never return to
such a place from choice. 'Twas dreadful and not at
all what she had imagined. Louis seemed nervous
and did not say very much, but it was obvious that
Jacques was most intrigued. A croupier called to
them to join the play of the dice, and Velvet watched
as the man took up the painted ivory cubes and held
them high, taunting all to become rich in but a
moment.

Jacques took out a coin and hurriedly joined the
table of ill-bred, dreadful-smelling men, and Velvet
whispered to Louis, "I don't like this place."

He agreed. "Perhaps we should leave." He shook
his head. "If Papa ever finds out . . . Jacques, Jacques,
I think we should go."

However, Jacques was not about to leave. He had won his first throw of the dice. He told his brother not to be a baby and continued to play. Velvet and Louis stayed close, and Jacques's winnings began to add up considerably. It was only twenty-five minutes later when Jacques was gathering a crowd and jovially announcing his good luck. Louis stared at his brother who was usually so level-headed and wondered what was wrong.

"Louis," Velvet said softly, "Jacques is in trouble. He has caught the fever, the gaming fever. I heard about it often from my grandfather. He said that when a man has it, he will lose everything. He often warned me against falling in love with such a man. He said you can see it in their eyes when they hold the cards or the dice . . . and there, look! Jacques has such a look. We must get him away from here at once!"

"Oui, oui . . . I, too, have heard of such things." Louis was frightened now. His brother was not himself. However, even as he and Velvet spoke, Jacques began to lose, yet he still would not leave the table.

Velvet and Louis hounded him to go, but he became angry and told them to leave without him. "No, I will not leave without you, Jacques," Velvet replied, "and it is growing quite late. We will be found out. You must come at once!"

"No, not yet. Let me recover my losses," Jacques pleaded.

"No. If you do not come with us now, Louis and I will go and confess all to your father. I swear this to you."

Louis's eyes rounded. He said strenuously, *"Non, non,* Velvet knows not what she says, but, Jacques, we must go."

"Listen to me, both of you, for I mean this. If we do not leave this minute, this very minute, I will go straight to Uncle Armand and confess everything!" Velvet would have said anything at this point to get Jacques away from the gaming table.

He turned to stare at her disgustedly. *"You,* my dear friend, would do this to me . . . to Louis?"

"I would, and it is because I am your friend."

Suddenly Jacques pulled himself up as though he was shaking off a spell. He shrugged, and his eyes seemed to lose the glitter that only a moment before was so intense. Velvet saw all this and shuddered.

Jacques laughed, "Well, well, come then, children. Come, take me away while I am still a winner." He drew out his pocket watch and exclaimed, *"Mon Dieu,* we must rush if we are to be safely in our beds before the sun shines on Paris once more!"

Louis and Velvet both breathed a sigh of relief, and the three hurriedly made their way out of the gaming hall into the night's cool air. A passing apple cart gave them immediate transport, though its driver did not know it, and it was not so very long before they were hopping off to make their way to more familiar quarters. Laughing and jesting, they turned a corner, and Velvet sighed, then asked just where they were and how much longer it would take.

Jacques looked round and exclaimed, "Impossible!"

"What? What is it?" Velvet's emerald eyes widened.

"We are near—too near—Father's club. Someone may see us."

Out of nowhere they heard a man's outraged shout: "Stop, thief! *Sacrebleu!* Stop him!"

The whistle of a passing beadle alerted several men just round the bend, who began shouting, and then a hurtling urchin came upon them like a storm, bumped them severely, and vanished into the night.

Jacques shouted, "Run! Run quickly!"

So saying, he and Louis separated, and Velvet hesitated, not knowing where to go. She made up her mind and started off when all at once a strong hand had her by the shoulder. She felt as though she would break under the pressure of the grip and turned indignant green eyes upon her attacker. "Ouch! Just what do you think you are doing?" she inquired in her native tongue, which always came naturally in moments of stress. She then called to her cousin for help: *"Jacques, à l'aide!"*

Jacques was, of course, by now quite out of earshot. However, Talgarth gripped her tighter, for although his mastery of French was not great, he understood enough to know she was calling for help. He looked round, but no one appeared, and he remarked in English, "All flown the coop, my lad." It was an oddity that the boy had first spoken to him in English and then reverted to French, but no mind.

Velvet went into shock. She looked up and found an all-too-familiar face. That voice! How many times had she dreamed of that face, that voice? Faith!

What was she going to do? Here was the Marquis of Talgarth! However, he did not know her. Of course he would not, she told herself. Why should he? He had not been dreaming of her for years!

Talgarth was calling for Gilly and the beadle. Oh no, thought Velvet. If she were exposed now, all would be ruined. She had to get away. As Talgarth turned round to the sound of Gilly shouting for him, Velvet did what she could. She aimed a very sound and substantial kick to his shin. Talgarth shouted with pain and held her tighter. With a shake he declared, "Little devil! Here I was just feeling sorry for you. Well, no more of that! Where is the monsieur's purse? Tell me that!"

Velvet answered him in French and in as deep a voice as she could muster, "I took no purse, monsieur. This I swear."

He shook her. "What then, lad, did you give it to your friends already?"

"I took no purse." Out of desperation she added, *"Grand Dieu,* release me, please."

"Release you? Ha! Why should I do that?" Talgarth had planted the boy against the brick wall. "No purse, eh? Well, my boy, we shall just see." He turned the boy to face the wall, slapped the lad's hands spread-eagle, and began to search him.

Velvet quickly stopped this, spinning round. She found herself planted against the wall again with the marquis's arm pressed against her neck. She thought she would die if she did not get some air, so hard did he have her pinned.

"Very well, little beggar, we shall see just where

monsieur's purse is." Thus, with his free hand the
marquis did a search of her person only to bring
himself upright in some shock. "Damnation!" he
ejaculated as he stared at the urchin's little piquant
face. "You are a girl!" He stepped back.

"Voyons!" breathed Velvet as she regained her
voice. "How very clever of you, sir." Her sarcasm
dripped, but it was only to throw him off. She could
not allow him to stare at her too long. He stood
confounded by this new development as Velvet suddenly came to life and went into action. She dashed
beneath his arm and ran as fast as her legs would
allow. She never bothered to look behind her. Had
she, she would have realized that the marquis made
no attempt to follow. She ran straight into Jacques
and Louis at the end of the dark narrow lane.

"Tiens, you are here," said Jacques. "What took
you so long?"

"No time. Quick . . . to home," declared Velvet,
pushing at them to proceed.

"Bon. It has been a grand evening, has it not?"
said Jacques.

Velvet and Louis laughed in unison, "Grand, but
the clock, young Vicomte, it is ticking!"

Four

Later that day Talgarth grimaced at Gilly as they took the stone steps to the front doors of the Condé residence, "Look, Gilly, for the tenth time, I didn't let the little thief go. She got away, and the little beggar didn't have Monsieur Peckard's purse on him! Couldn't have been the thief."

"Well as to that, he could have had an accomplice. Think you should have held him for the beadle to question." Gilly then leveled a frown on his friend. "And you did it again."

"Did what again?"

"Referred to the thief as a she, you know."

The marquis cut him off. "Did I? Can't think why. Never mind. Let the matter drop."

The front door opened then, without either gentleman having knocked. The Comte de Condé stood before them, and it was obvious from his attire that he was about to go out. He smiled a welcome and quickly explained, "Ah, *bonjour*, gentlemen. How good it is to see you again in Paris. I regret that business calls and I am already very late, but my dear bride awaits you in the study."

He was an older gentleman of considerable pres-

ence, in spite of his slight size. His smile was genuine
as he shook their hands and waved them inside.
Both Talgarth and Gilly were only slightly acquainted with the comte, and thus only the amenities were exchanged before a neat butler led them
to the study.

The Comtesse de Condé turned from the window
box where she was readjusting an arrangement of
hothouse flowers. In contrast to her husband, she
was tall and young. She was, in fact, twenty years
younger than her forty-five-year-old husband.
Though not a classic beauty, she was certainly a vi-
brant, attractive woman of easy style. Her chestnut
waves were neatly tied at the very top of her well-
shaped head and cascaded down about her ears. Her
eyes were hazel and warm with welcome as she
greeted the two Englishmen. She laughed as she exclaimed their names and went hurriedly forward,
her hands outstretched.

The marquis grinned at the tall lithe lovely as she
rustled toward him and thought that pale green silk
became her. After he caught her hands in his, she
was pulled immediately into his arms for a hearty
hug. "Marie, beloved woman, finally to hold you,"
he then bent her backward into a graceful dip, "to
kiss you," he dropped a friendly buss upon her neck,
"to ravish you!" he growled.

"Release me, rogue!" she laughed. "My husband,
what will he say?"

"I will tell you what *I* say," put in Gilly, beaming
happily. "Hand her over to me! I should like to ravish her a bit as well."

"Never, she is mine!" answered Talgarth jovially, but made no real attempt to stop his friend from taking over.

Gilly set her upright, took her into his embrace, and gently planted a kiss upon her poised lips. "Ah, once more I live," said Gilly dramatically. He was rewarded with a mild slap to his arm.

"Naughty boys! When you left me years ago, I was broken-hearted."

"Fie, deceitful woman! You became engaged to the comte one month after our departure. You see, we were with your brother last night," retorted the marquis with a wagging finger.

She caught his hand, for they had been good, good friends during her first wonderful time in Italy. "So you are here. Your grandfather writes that you mean to take my dear Velvet away with you to England." The last was said sadly.

"Marie, Grandfather told me that you thought it best." Talgarth looked puzzled.

"Moi? Non, non, et non!" She sighed. " 'Tis Tante Louise. She is such a stick. Pooh! She says that Velvet must go to her own country before war breaks out between your country and ours. She says that, but *moi? Non, non.* Oh, Dusty, I do so love to have Velvet with me here. *Mais non,* Tante Louise and my own dearest comte say she must go, and Velvet says so, too."

"Aye, I suppose 'tis the right thing for the little scamp," agreed Talgarth.

"Scamp! Indeed, she is that. Oh, she has done

some outrageous things, but they love her here."
Marie smiled fondly.

"Where is she?" Talgarth looked round as though
expecting her to walk through the open doorway at
any moment.

"Naughty puss. When I sent up her chocolate this
morning, I sent a note reminding her that you were
coming by this morning. I can't imagine why she is
late." Marie looked past the marquis's shoulder and
then said softly, "Well then, my dear Dusty, here is
my little cousin now."

Talgarth and Gilly turned, expecting to see the
young hoyden tomboy they had known four years
ago. What they saw caused Gilly to suck in air and
the marquis to be surprised into exclaiming, "By
Jove, Velvie, girl!"

In her heart Velvet was still the young girl the
Marquis of Talgarth had captivated and filled with
dreams. She had been fourteen, he had been three
and twenty at their first meeting, and she had fallen
madly in love with him. She had only just begun to
blossom then. He was a sophisticated Corinthian,
full of wit, sparkle, fashion, and more. He had compassion, and it had extended itself to Velvet. He had
not ignored her as some might have done, but he
had taken her under his wing and actually enter-
tained her during her visit. She had worshiped him.
He had found her hoyden spirit charming.

They had met only once or twice in the year following, and while he had gone merrily on his way,
Velvet had remembered every moment they spent
together. He had filled her dreams. He was her

knight in shining armor. He had become the example she compared all other men to, and all others fell sadly short of her marquis's many outstanding qualities. Now, here he was! Would he recognize her from last evening? Would he think it possible? Her knees began to shake.

Marie watched her usually confident, lively cousin turn into a shy retreating miss, and her eyes widened. What was this? "Velvet, *ma petite*, come. Here are two old friends of yours."

Velvet amazed her cousin further by shyly smiling as she stepped forward. As her vision had slightly blurred, she did not notice the footstool. She walked into it and flew directly into the marquis's capable arms.

Though Talgarth had been momentarily taken aback by Velvet's emergence into lovely womanhood, her shyness reminded him of when they had met. When she had tripped, he chuckled, then caught her.

Velvet blushed and stammered something incoherent. The marquis pinched her pert nose easily and set her upright. "There, there, puss. The blasted stool had no business being there!"

Velvet giggled and turned to Marie's clucking tongue. "Ah, my naughty cousin uses the stool to fall into the arms of a handsome marquis. An excellent trick, I think."

"*Oui*, it is a certainty!" teased Velvet. "'Tis only what I have learned so well from my dearest, most experienced cousin Marie, yes?"

"Dreadful child!" exclaimed Marie with a smile.

Both women giggled before giving their attention once more to the amused male guests. Some moments were lost in deep conversation about the past, Velvet's grandfather, her days in Paris over the last fourteen months, then Talgarth got to his feet and announced, "Well then, my ladies, fetch your cloaks. We mean to take you out for some fresh air. 'Tis a perfect day."

Velvet looked to Marie hopefully and urged, "Oh yes, please. Marie, do say yes." She had passed the test. He did not know her from the night before!

"I say yes, and yes again," returned Marie, getting to her feet.

Lord Farnsworth crossed the avenue. His steps were light, his head was light, and his heart was merry! He had chosen a bride. She was Lady Velvet Colbury. She came from an excellent family. She had beauty, she had wealth, and she had wit. Indeed, Lady Velvet and no other!

He was on his way to the Condé residence to pay Lady Velvet a morning call and invite her to take a walk in the park with him. Farnsworth was quite pleased with himself. His soft beaver hat just barely hid his shining waves of chestnut hair, and he knew his coiffure was styled in the latest fashion. His cravat was tied with perfection, a perfection he told himself even Brummell would applaud. He rather liked the high starched shirt points of his collar although he knew some might not dare their extremes. His embroidered waistcoat beneath his blue superfine was exquisitely moulded to his lean torso. His greatcoat covering all this was made of the finest dark wool and cut by none other than Weston. Its many tiers proclaimed his style, his wealth, his status, and he rather thought himself a prize!

Following this trend of thought, he knew that Lady Velvet must swoon at his feet. How could she not? He meant this to be a quick courtship, for she would have many suitors, and he wanted no other to do more than even look at her. He sighed contentedly as the soft breeze tickled his neck, for it held a promise of spring. He could see crocuses peeping up in the flower beds he passed, and it would not be long before they bloomed.

In this mood Farnsworth reached the curbing and made ready to cross the mildly busy avenue to the Condé residence when a shock wave swept through him. His eyes could not deceive him. There, leaving the Condé residence, was the Marquis of Talgarth and on his arm Lady Velvet!

How was this? There, too, Marie de Condé and that dratted Gillingham! What was going on? How had Talgarth already found Lady Velvet? Did Talgarth know? Was it possible that Talgarth had already discovered his interest in Velvet? How? Damn Talgarth's eyes! How in bloody hell had he managed to get to Velvet already? How had he beat him in this?

Farnsworth stood for a moment, a welling of hatred in his bosom. He knew, of course, that he had made an enemy of the marquis some years ago. So much time had passed, he assumed retaliation would not be forthcoming. Now, it was obvious that Talgarth still intended vengeance. Had he not declared it all those years ago? Damnation!

Farnsworth shook his head. He had been in his last year at Cambridge with Talgarth, and the marquis had bested him at one thing too many. He had meant to repay him with a prank. It had been a lark, only a lark. He had not really intended it to go so far, but once caught up, he had not been able to stop. Hell, bloody hell, it had been the culmination of so many humiliations at Talgarth's hands. They had been rivals at so many things, education, sports, friends . . .

Well, well, evidently Talgarth meant to seek out his revenge still. Did he mean to steal Lady Velvet? Damn, it wasn't fair! He had been a boy, twenty years old, and he had not meant things to get so ugly. The girl had been nothing . . . nothing—what was all the fuss about anyway? Did Talgarth mean to repay him in a similar fashion? No, he wouldn't dare, not with Velvet; she was, after all, a Colbury!

Right then, so be it! Quietly and in a far different mood than he had been all morning, Farnsworth adjusted his plans. He would send her a posy of violets this afternoon and then present himself for an afternoon visit. Perhaps he would invite the comte, his lovely wife, and their cousin to the Opera. Indeed, he might just do that. However, he must not allow the marquis to know that he was in earnest over the Lady Velvet!

Five

Paris and its beau monde sparkled with laughter and fashion as the Marquis of Talgarth and Gilly walked the ladies through the ornamental park. It quickly became evident that not only was Marie de Condé considered *Haut Ton,* but Lady Velvet was well-known and highly thought of, as well. Velvet had developed her own circle of friends and admirers. The marquis leaned over to his new charge and mentioned this without hiding his surprise.

Velvet rounded on him with a touch of indignant, but good-natured humor, "And you did not think it was possible?"

The marquis had a habit of working out problems out loud, and at times he did not think to hold his tongue. "Well, Velvie, you were a rough-and-tumble hoyden when *I* knew you, and . . . well, there are beauties enough in Paris, but I suppose your fortune weighs in."

The good humor left Velvet, and she leveled an insulted look at her escort. "My fortune? Is that what you think? What of my character? Does that not count? Or do you not think I have any?"

He eyed her warily; a warning sounded in his

brain. He had stepped into murky waters. "Well, as to that, I'm sure your character is very nice, but—"

"But? But what, sir?"

His lordship did not have time to extricate himself from this sudden difficulty as a shout was heard ahead. Both he and Velvet looked up to find a riderless horse with reins flying and saddle askew charging right at them. Velvet immediately put out her arms at her side. It was an instinctive act, born out of her many years of raising horses with her grandfather. The marquis had been about to shove Velvet roughly out of the way when he saw her in action, smiled to himself, and did much the same. He waved his arms to catch the panicked horse's attention.

The animal saw an impossible obstacle ahead. Two humans directly in his path. The horse slowed in order to go around them. However, a tall wide oak was yet another object to be reckoned with, and the frightened gelding screeched to a halt that sent him backwards on his hind legs and nearly caused him to fall over.

Velvet and the marquis were at the poor animal's head almost immediately. The marquis reached for the broken leather reins and held them fast as the horse righted itself and snorted its confusion.

"Easy lad . . ." soothed the marquis as he held the reins firmly, drawing himself closer to the horse's head.

Velvet cautiously reached up a gloved hand to pat the animal's sweating neck, and the gelding jerked upward and away from the motion.

"What do you think you are doing?" snapped the

marquis and then back to the horse, "Easy there
boy. . . . No harm. . . . No harm . . .''

Velvet felt herself seethe. Ignoring the Marquis
of Talgarth, she touched the gelding and softly
cooed, "Sweet thing, where is your rider, then?"

"Well, looks like we won't have long to wait for
that answer," said the marquis with a lift of his chin.

Velvet saw a handsome man riding toward them.
The rider was causing something of a scene as he
had spotted them and, without thinking, took a
shortcut across the fine green lawn. One of the head
gardeners witnessed this with resonant outrage.
The rider ignored him as he cantered across the
turf, and the incensed gardener took chase on foot.
All this under the amused eyes of many of the fash-
ionables.

Marie de Condé giggled as Gilly grinned and
softly said, "I say, bold fellow, don't you think? I
should listen to that fellow with the rake, wouldn't
you?"

Velvet felt sorry for the fellow, for as he slowed to
approach, it was obvious to her that he was seriously
concerned for the horse. He managed to nimbly
jump off his mount and hurry to them, exclaiming
in English, "However did you catch Sinbad? He is
the devil of a fellow when he panics." As he reached
them, he said hurriedly, "Thank you. I hope the
stupid fellow hasn't gone and done himself an injury." He was already bending to inspect his horse's
legs.

"You're English," ejaculated Marie de Condé.

The gentleman came up with a sheepish grin and

admitted the fault. "Why, yes, and," he looked round at the little gardener who was berating him, "apparently I have committed a solecism. I am sorry."

The gardener continued to rant. Gilly, rather annoyed, went forward and in fluent French said, "There, there . . . Runaway horse, you know."

He dove into his pocket and came up with a substantial coin. He showed the coin to the French gardener, who eyed it, but continued at a slower pace and in a softer voice to berate them all. Gilly began to put the coin back in his pocket, but the Frenchman snatched it, wagged a warning finger, and left them to their own English madness.

The assembled group laughed over these antics before Velvet returned them to the question at hand. "Where, sir, is the rider of this wonderful horse?"

The newcomer grinned. "No doubt she is still fuming behind a bush."

"You mean a female was riding this hot blood?" said the marquis, surprised.

Velvet rounded on him. "Why couldn't a female ride a hot blood?" She was quite a horsewoman and had been thrown up on prime blood by her grandfather many, many times over the years.

He eyed her ruefully. "I have no doubt that a spitfire could manage a spitfire."

"Ah, then you don't attribute it to skill?" Velvet's hands went to her hips. " 'Tis not whether the rider is a male or a female, sir, 'tis whether or not the rider is skilled at the sport!"

Talgarth eyed her for a long moment. There was

something about her voice, about the way those green eyes of hers sparkled that reminded him of someone. It was a ridiculous notion, he told himself. Yet . . . ?

Velvet saw it at once. She saw the look in his blue eyes. Had he recognized her? Did he realize it had been she last evening?

Marie de Condé waylaid their thoughts by inquiring in shocked accents, "Sir, never say you left some poor woman alone in the bushes?"

The newcomer took out his card and handed it to the marquis as a way of introduction. He grinned sheepishly at Marie and explained, "No, no, 'tis only my sister." He could see Marie was about to lecture him, and he hurried on. "Allow me to explain. You see, Leslie and I were out riding this morning, taking a shortcut back to our livery, when she remarked how good Sinbad was behaving. She wanted a go with him, you see. We dismounted, and I was about to change the saddle so that she could ride him, when he spooked. Leslie was holding both the horses at that moment while I was taking off her saddle." He nodded to the mare at his back, and everyone noted for the first time that the horse was without a saddle. "She couldn't hold Sinbad, I hopped on the mare, and, well, here we are."

"*Tiens!* So you are, but your sister, she is alone," Marie returned pleasantly. "Go now before something dreadful happens to her." She waved him off.

"Yes, but I don't even know your names. Where I may find you to properly thank you?"

"This poor sister of yours, she is subject to thieves

and thugs while you stand and socialize. *Mais non,*
it is unforgivable," laughed Marie.

"Had a thief or a thug approached Leslie, there
is no doubt we would have heard *them* screeching
for our help, but here, you are quite right. Please,
may I have your names before I ride off to my sister's
rescue?" The gentleman was already putting himself into position to mount his saddleless horse.

"Here, I'll give you a leg up," stuck in Gilly, going
forward as the marquis quickly made the required
introductions.

"Enfin!" declared Marie. "You, M. Edward Martin, go to your sister and do not switch horses again
in the park. It is most unwise."

Laughingly they watched him depart before
Marie turned to Velvet and nodded. "That one will
come quickly to call. Do you not think so, *ma petite?"*

Velvet eyed her cousin. There was no doubt of
Marie's meaning, but she did not note any marked
attention from Mr. Martin. She shook her head.
"Monsieur is definitely coming to call, Marie, but
he is drawn by your hazel eyes, and methinks,
Comtesse, your comte will not be pleased!" With
this Velvet laughed saucily and received a tweak of
the nose.

"Naughty puss," returned Marie.

"I had no idea they were in France," said Gilly, a
faraway look in his eyes.

"You know this Martin fellow, Gilly?" inquired
the marquis.

"In a manner of speaking." Gilly suddenly blushed.
"Know his sister. Well, don't really *know* his sis-

ter . . . only met her once, a month ago at a rout. She was leaving the next day with her brother for Italy."

His friend's heightened color was not lost on the marquis. With some curiosity he nudged him. "So, you know *Miss* Martin, eh? Holding out on me, ol' boy?"

"No, no, don't know her. Only danced with her . . . one dance," Gilly said idly. "That is all, really."

The Marquis of Talgarth grinned widely. Well, here now was something of a mystery. Why the deuce was Gilly turning red? "Right then, Gilly, no reason to blush. You know lots of women."

"Ah, but the other women are not Miss Leslie Martin. Are they, Gilly?" teased Velvet lightly.

"No, no, you are being absurd," retorted Gilly, now going white. "I don't know her, honestly. She probably doesn't even recall taking a waltz with me." He found his friends staring at him and frowned. "Now really, I only mention it because it seems a bit of a coincidence meeting her brother here in Paris when I had no intention of coming to Paris and had no idea they were here."

Velvet and Marie put their heads together and giggled over Gilly's discomfort. However, their amusement was cut short when the marquis slapped his friend on the shoulder and remarked, "Never mind, Gilly, let the silly chits giggle. 'Tis what chits do!"

Velvet again rounded on the marquis. Her green eyes glistened, and forgotten was the knight in shining armor. "How dare you?" breathed the lady. "We won't be called silly, and we do a great deal more than giggle! What, if laughing comes out like a man's roar, then it is fine and noteworthy entertainment?" She shook her head. "It's like saying only a man can ride a hot-blooded animal. Absurd!"

"As a rule, that is a fact. It isn't a female's fault. She is the weaker, gentler sex."

"Ah, allow me to understand you, my lord," Velvet said heatedly. "You are saying it takes only brawn to handle a horse, a spirited horse?"

"Well, not exactly . . ." The marquis felt himself in dangerous waters, but pride kept him from swimming to safety.

"Well, I will wager you that I could ride Sinbad . . . or any other spirited prime blood."

"Done! You are on, my girl, you are on!" snapped the marquis, and his blue eyes glittered.

The blue sparkle caught her attention, and she felt breathless for a moment. Here again was the knight in shining armor, and he was absolutely magnificent.

Marie put a gloved hand on each of them. "*Non,* my beloveds. You cannot."

"Yes, we can . . ."

"Monsieur Martin . . . he has not agreed. You cannot do such a thing without even asking him."

"Then we will ask him with all great speed," said Velvet softly.

Marie de Condé put her hands heavenward and turned to Gilly. "This, this is scandalous!"

Six

Velvet took a long look at herself in the long gilt-edged mirror of her bedchamber. She was not as tall as she would have liked to be, but the little green satin pumps helped. Her long golden hair was styled in a waterfall of cascading curls from the top of her head, but she didn't feel she looked old enough. The Marquis of Talgarth was nine years her senior. It was no wonder he treated her like nothing more than a schoolgirl.

She studied herself. Her eyebrows were dark and finely shaped as they winged above almond-shaped emerald green eyes. Her lashes were thick, curled, and dark against a complexion that was an enviable smooth peaches and cream. Her nose was small and pert, and her lips, enhanced with the latest Parisian rouge, were full and inviting. Still, she saw the tomboy all rough and ready.

Velvet sighed over the cluster of emerald and pearls ornamenting her ears, thinking them too missish, as was the matching pendant at her fine soft neck. She looked at the bodice of her emerald green gown with its white trim of lace and thought it was not provocative enough. But she was wrong. The dark emerald velvet gown displayed to advantage all her enchanting curves. Velvet could not see it, but she was a beauty!

Marie entered the bedchamber with a soft knock and was struck by this fact. It was to her credit that she did not feel more than a touch of jealousy. Marie had always been attractive and pursued, but more than this, she had made a love match with a man twenty years her senior and was content, very content. She looked a picture herself in her light blue satin with silver sarcenet.

"La, *ma petite,* you will get wrinkles before your time if you frown like that," she clucked. "Why do you frown when you look absolutely ravishing? I think perhaps, Dustin, he is right and you are nought but . . . what do you English say? *Oui, oui,* I know, a silly chit!" Marie laughed and hurriedly ducked with a scream the lace-covered pillow that Velvet threw at her head.

"Really, *ma belle,* is it true? Seems to me that Lord Talgarth called us *both* silly chits earlier today, so I shouldn't be so very complacent if I were you!" retorted Velvet good-naturedly.

"Well, and so we must be if we are forever preening and fussing just to have the men admire us." Marie wagged a finger and then sighed happily, *"Moi,* I like it!"

Velvet laughed, and went forward to take Marie's hand. "Well then, it's early. Let's go down and enjoy some nice hot tea. In England, we would do that just about now . . ."

Marie stopped and pinched Velvet's nose. "You

miss your England, your damp, cold, staid England? I wish it were not so. I should like to keep you with me always."

Velvet gave her waist a hug. "And I should like to take you to England and keep you with me, but I fear your dear Condé might object."

"*Oui, oui,* he would," laughed Marie happily. "He is very attached to me, you know. He will join our dinner and theater party tonight. It will be lovely with Armand, his boys, Gilly, and Talgarth. All eyes will be on our box—we are *très haute,* are we not?"

They had reached the long dimly lit hallway when Marie's chambermaid approached, a silver tray held out toward Velvet. The servant offered this with a bob, and Velvet turned surprised eyes to Marie as she took up a posy of violets and a sealed card. Marie thanked and dismissed her elderly maid with a smile before turning excitedly to Velvet and saying, " 'Tis from Mr. Martin, is it not? I knew it. Ah, *oui. Moi,* I knew as soon as he looked at you that—"

"Marie, do stop babbling. 'Tis from Lord Farnsworth," Velvet said with a frown as she attempted to put a face to the name. "Ah, yes, I remember. Well, how very sweet . . ."

"Farnsworth?" Marie took the card from Velvet's fingers. "He is English. *Oui, oui,* I know his family—Mornay, *Haut Ton. Mais oui,* I like this."

Velvet laughed, "Content yourself then, and leave me be."

They linked arms and in very good spirits took the wide stairs to the marbled central hall where Velvet laid Farnsworth's card on a nearby Sheraton wall table along with the posy, thinking to take the violets up to her room later. They entered the French study to find Armand and his two sons poking at a roaring fire and vivaciously debating who was better qualified to do the poking.

Armand turned and greeted his sister, taking her hands and kissing both cheeks before giving Velvet a bear hug. "Ah, *ma petite,*" he teased her fondly, "if neither of my sons snatches you for a bride, it will be left to me." He sighed. *"Mais non,* you will say I am too old."

"Absurd creature, you are no more than—what are you? *Oui, oui,* I know," Marie giggled. "Seven and forty! Why there, you are a bit older than my Condé. He turned five and forty last month." She shook her head. "There, you are not so *very* old for Velvet, but you two are not a match, *non, non."* She turned as her husband entered the room and went to him, hands outstretched.

Velvet watched the two with a soft smile. Condé was not a very tall man, but there was an aura of authority about him that called one to order. He was masculine, athletic, stylish, soft-spoken, and had eyes for no one save Marie, whom he spoiled lavishly.

Her attention was caught then by Louis, who drew her to one side. "Velvet, we must talk," he whispered.

"Very well, about what?" Velvet smiled.

"It is Jacques."

Velvet's brows went up. "Whatever do you mean?"

The lad ran a hand through his hair. "I am worried—"

"What?" said Jacques, coming up behind them

and touching their shoulders in camaraderie. "Are you planning our next outing?"

"Indeed," said Louis. "Velvet thinks we must go to the fair tomorrow—all day."

"Tomorrow?" Jacques was frowning. "Hmmm . . . I rather thought I would—well, I can always go off in the evening . . ."

"No, no," retorted Louis swiftly. "Tomorrow evening we are promised to Papa. You cannot."

"Right you are. Well, no harm, I can always put off my plans to the next day." He grinned warmly at Velvet. "The fair it is."

"Splendid," said Louis. He nodded happily to Velvet. "We go to the fair tomorrow."

"Louis?" whispered Velvet as Jacques moved off to converse with the Comte de Condé, "what was all that about?"

"Hush, we cannot talk now," returned Louis.

Velvet could see that something was wrong, very wrong, but she could not imagine what it could be and was anxious to know. She tugged at Louis's sleeve, "Louis, just tell me!"

"Shh, I cannot. Tomorrow at the fair. Somehow we will find a moment, and we *must* talk. Perhaps it is nought, perhaps I am wrong . . ."

Sir Harry Gillingham and the Marquis of Talgarth were entering the Condé residence at that moment. The well-dressed diminutive butler had opened the door, and another well-dressed servant, a footman, came forward hurriedly to receive their cloaks, hats, and gloves. The marquis grinned as Gilly leaned over him and whispered, "Careful you don't trip over one of these damnable frogs; they're all over the place."

The butler preceded them to the wide double doors, but the marquis had not followed. His eyes had strayed to a posy of violets and the card next to it. Lord Farnsworth's name fairly leapt out at him and sent a chill through his blood. "I don't believe it!" So saying, he took up the small lace-trimmed posy of violets in one hand and the card in the other. "I just don't believe it!"

"Neither do I," said Gilly, much shocked. "What are you doing? You can't go about reading the Condé mail. I mean, Dusty, really!"

"This isn't Condé mail. This posy is from Farnsworth to my ward!" snapped the marquis.

"Your ward? Who is your—oh, are you speaking of Velvet?" Gilly shook his head. "Mistaken there, ol' boy. Not *your* ward . . . your grandfather's."

"In his absence, she is mine, and as her guardian, I won't have Farnsworth sending her flowers or anything else!" The marquis strode forward, for he and Gilly had already been announced and the butler stood patiently awaiting them as he held open the door.

Talgarth entered, posy in one hand, card in the other. He sent a perfunctory greeting round the room, leaving his friend to cover his tracks with amenities. Talgarth took Velvet's elbow and, with a quick apology to Louis, drew her aside to demand, "What the deuce is this?"

Velvet studied the flowers and offered, "Violets?"

"Violets! I know they are violets. What I want to know is why are they here, addressed to you from Farnsworth?"

"They are here because Lord Farnsworth sent them to me," Velvet answered simply. By now her feathers were ruffled.

"Deuce take it, girl! I am not playing games. I haven't the time or the inclination."

Lady Velvet's hands went to her hips. "Nor do I."

"What, then, are these doing here from Farnsworth?"

She was puzzled enough by his behavior to attempt to assuage him and answered reasonably, "My lord, I don't know what all the fever is about. I met him the other night; he sent me flowers. Why I should find myself explaining this to *you* is beyond me!"

"Is it, my girl?" The marquis's blue eyes blazed. "Well, it isn't for you to wonder about such matters. These things are better left to me!"

"You are *not* my guardian!" retorted Velvet heatedly.

Marie went to her and put a comforting arm about her shoulders. Everyone's conversation in the room had come to a halt as they listened to Velvet and Talgarth's exchange. The Comte de Condé softly attempted to take control of the situation, "Well, my dear," he offered Velvet gently, "Lord Talgarth stands here in place of your guardian, the Duke of Salsburn; therefore, I am afraid that you do owe your filial loyalty to him at this time." He turned then to the marquis, lest the Englishman become too smug, and quickly added, "However, I do not, my lord, quite understand your objection to this Farnsworth sending a posy of violets. The gentleman is English *Ton*. Apparently he admires Velvet, as well he must, and has sent his compliments. Quite acceptable."

Talgarth gritted his teeth. "You may trust me in this, Condé; English *Ton* he may be, but not by *my* standards! I won't have him coming near my Velvet, and that is final!"

Gilly cleared his throat. "He is right, you know. Farnsworth is *Ton*, but has a bad, bad heart . . ." He shook his head and turned to Velvet. Gently he said, "Talgarth knows what's good for you, my dear. Forget Farnsworth and his posy."

Velvet would have giggled under ordinary circumstances, but something she could not name had irritated her terribly, and she snapped at poor Gilly, "I am old enough to know what is good for me, and I rather like Lord Farnsworth and his violets!"

Marie went to the marquis, who was about to bluster out something she was sure would be dreadful, and put her slim arm through his to draw him aside from the assembled company. "*Non, cher.* Why all this heat? 'Tis nought, after all. Velvet," she lowered her voice to a scarcely audible whisper, "cares not a fig for this English fellow. Do not make of him the forbidden fruit." She winked coyly at him for emphasis. " 'Tis unwise, *oui*? You must know that."

She patted his hand. "We all must observe the proprieties, though. Farnsworth is not only English

Ton, but his family is very well-connected to our First Consul, Napoleon. One does not wish to make enemies in our so uncertain times, does one?"

He shook his head. "Forgive me, Marie. Of course not. I will immediately make arrangements to return Velvet to England and put her safely in my grandfather's hands. I did not mean to embroil you in this."

"*Non, non*, you distress me greatly," Marie replied, horrified. "You cannot. When we wrote your grandfather, we did not realize how very quickly you would come for Velvet. We have planned a ball in her honor next week. You may not take her until after the ball."

He touched her chin. "Your wish, my enchantress, is and must be my command. Next week then, but believe me in this matter: Farnsworth must be kept at arm's length. I will trust in you to manage it."

"*Oui*, as you wish, but, Dustin, darling, why is it so?"

Talgarth's eyes grew bleak. No one, save Gilly and his grandfather, knew what Farnsworth had done, what his wickedness had cost so many. He shook his head. "There is just cause . . . and it is unspeakable."

"*Mon cher*, this I do believe, for your eyes tell me this is so. I tremble to think what it could be, but I will keep my Velvet safe from this man."

"Tante Marie," Louis called to his father's sister, "your people tell us that dinner is served, and, me, I could eat a horse!"

"*Non, non*, you are a terrible boy," laughed Marie,

clapping her hands. "Come, we must not allow our dinner to grow cold."

Velvet defiantly snubbed the marquis as she went before him on the young vicomte's arm. Gilly coughed into his gloved hand and whispered, "You were no better than a bull in a china shop, ol' boy."

"I'm glad I was no worse," grimaced the marquis. "You know, this is my first time playing at nurse-maid!"

Seven

The Condé party was taken to their box in the opera's wide, high balcony. Gilly squirmed as he looked about and whispered to the marquis for the tenth time that this sort of music was not to his taste. He was worried at what lay ahead as his tastes in music ranged from bawdy ballads to English country tunes. The marquis laughed at his friend's fidgeting and told him to calm himself. "Look there, Gilly, ol' boy. Beauties to behold!"

The opera house sported the new gaslights, and many were gracefully ornamented with crystal. Fashionable women, many of whom were quite scantily dressed, caught and held a man's roving eye. One in particular moved even Gilly to exclaim appreciatively, "I say, Talgarth, have a look there."

Gilly's chin directed the marquis to a box opposite, where a young woman, tall, lithe, beautifully proportioned, wore a gown that was acceptable in Paris but would have been scandalous in London. The pale silver gossamer-thin muslin, quite prettily spangled with silver embroidery, hugged the young woman's body. The bodice of the gown was very low cut, so low as to display her full young breasts. Gilly grinned wickedly, and Talgarth laughed to agree, "Damn! Lovely, quite lovely!"

Velvet had been watching the two, and their quiet exchange of glances was not lost on her. She studied the woman in question and blushed as she realized just why the men were grinning. Even Louis was saying to his brother, *"Eh, mon frère . . . Très belle, eh?"*

"You are all quite odious!" pronounced Velvet with half a smile.

However, this did not deter the gentlemen, who, led by Armand, announced that they must go pay their respects to such outstanding beauty. Marie waved them off with a laugh and turned to her husband with one fine brow raised. "Do you itch to be off with them as well, my dear?"

Condé chuckled and took up his wife's gloved fingers. "Need you ask, beloved?"

Velvet smiled to see Marie lower her lashes and smile contentedly. However, sensing someone behind her, she then nearly jumped. Velvet looked up and found Farnsworth's handsome features smiling warmly at her. He stood back and made her a quick bow, apologizing for startling her, "Please, forgive me, Lady Velvet. I did not mean to make you jump."

"Of course you did not," Velvet quickly returned. Independence wanted out as she knew an urge to invite him to be seated. She could not do so, however, without Marie's leave. She blushed her confusion. Farnsworth noted the blush and mistook it. Happily he understood it to mean that she was already forming a *tendre* for him. Velvet eased her discomfort with polite conversation. "How very nice to meet you here. Do you enjoy the opera?"

Farnsworth made a formal greeting, bowing low and gallantly toward the Comtesse de Condé and then exchanging a nod with the comte. He then smiled confidingly to Velvet. "No, I do not. I am not interested in the opera."

Velvet laughed, "Ah, then you would get along famously with Gilly."

There was a moment's hesitation as Farnsworth considered the meaning of such an odd remark, but then, of course, she would not know of his feud with the marquis. He smiled and answered her softly, "It is not Gilly's company I seek.

Velvet laughed again and thought Farnsworth a delightful gentleman. "Now I must ask why you are here, my lord."

"You know the answer, do you not?" he returned boldly and saw the comtesse's brow go up.

Velvet ignored this and sincerely said instead, "Thank you, my lord. The violets you sent are just beautiful."

"Sent for the same reason I am here tonight," he answered quietly.

The conversation was interrupted as Marie spotted Edward Martin accompanied by a young lady. Pleased for this welcome interruption, the comtesse greeted him with great enthusiasm. "Mr. Martin! Well, how nice!"

Velvet looked up and smile warmly. "Mr. Martin." She looked toward the tall, elegantly dressed young woman beside him and noted that the woman was perhaps closer to Marie's age than to her own.

Edward Martin beamed brightly and hurriedly introduced his sister, Leslie. Some moments passed before they left the box and as the comte was informed that these were the people in the park with the runaway horse. During this time, Farnsworth assessed the situation and decided from the way Edward Martin had gazed at Velvet that here was a certain rival. He did not have time for more, as suddenly the marquis and Gilly were on the scene.

Gilly had seen with surprise the marquis's face change expressions. They had all been enjoying a hearty flirtation with the scantily clothed Parisian beauty when all at once the marquis sucked in air and gritted his teeth to curse, "Damn his eyes!"

All at once and without even a backward glance, the marquis was off. Gilly turned to the French beauty and saw that, although she was slightly surprised to so unexpectedly lose one of her admirers, Armand and his sons had already taken up the slack. With a boyish grin Gilly bowed himself off to hurry after the marquis, for he had seen what had enraged Talgarth. Farnsworth was in Velvet's box, bending over Velvet's fingers. Gilly caught up to Talgarth to hear him curse under his breath, "I mean to cut out his heart and serve it to the devil; mark me on this, Gilly."

This did not really surprise Gilly, for he knew well enough what Farnsworth had done, but there was something else in the marquis's face. Something more than his usual hatred of Farnsworth glittered in Talgarth's blue eyes. Gilly could see the outrage there, outrage that Farnsworth had dared to look Velvet's way. No, no, thought Gilly, now the marquis was out for blood.

Surprisingly enough, though the marquis's purpose was deadly, he was in complete control and his mien commanded attention. All eyes looked his way as he entered the Condé box. The marquis's sneer altered his face, and a blast of frigid air permeated the space.

"My lord," the marquis made a showy bow, "I see you mean to go on taking ill-advised chances." There was no doubt as to the marquis's meaning.

"Chances for some, certainties for others," Farnsworth drawled.

"Agreed. Some do, in fact, have a fate that is most assuredly a certainty," returned the marquis as his blue eyes raked Farnsworth and dared him to answer the challenge.

Farnsworth hesitated at that point. He genuinely did not wish the marquis to discover his intention to court Velvet—at least, not now. He needed to bide his time. He decided to ignore this last remark and turned to Velvet. "I must bid you a good night, my dear."

"And I hope that you enjoy the music more than you think you will," returned Velvet sweetly.

"Darling Talgarth," cried Marie, suddenly finding her voice, "come. You must sit yourself between Velvet and me. . . . Here."

Talgarth was being called away from his purpose. So be it. This was not the time. He and Farnsworth would have to meet, but not now. He wanted Velvet well away from Farnsworth's wiles. Smiling at Marie, he then turned and attempted to win a smile from Velvet as he knew she was still angry with him.

Velvet eyed him for a moment and then gave in to his twinkling eyes. Such blue eyes, she thought before her mind drifted into curiosity. Just what was the problem between Farnsworth and Talgarth?

"There now," offered the marquis as he tapped her nose, "that smile so becomes you. Is it for me?"

"Men," retorted Velvet, still smiling whimsically, "take so many things for granted. They really should not."

The marquis laughed and let it go. Across the way he saw that Farnsworth was taking up his place with his relatives, relatives who were so very intimate with Napoleon. Marie was right on that score: it would not do just now to offer that crew insult.

Farnsworth glanced toward Velvet as she sat looking like a goddess. He had had no choice earlier but to bow himself off. Velvet had eyed him curiously, and it was clear to him that Talgarth had filled her head with some remarks about his unsuitability. Never mind. Even Talgarth could not fault his *Ton*. He would pay Velvet a morning call. Surely the marquis could not be with her all of the time? This was going to need careful handling.

Eight

It was a fine spring day. The sun's rays lit the Condé salon in shafts of rainbow colors. Marie lounged with her coffee, Velvet with her tea and crumpet cake, and both appeared happily engrossed. This was not perfectly true, for Velvet was restless to be off. She was dreaming of a ride across the moors, picturing the beloved English scenery, imagining the scent and feel of the English countryside she loved so well. She sighed to herself; what she needed was a lark. Well, the Beaupré boys would come by for her in an hour or two and take her to the fair, but until then she was stuck in the salon, awaiting at Marie's insistence for their morning callers. Dull work, indeed!

Some moments later, however, the first visitors arrived and were announced. Velvet looked round with keen interest and whispered under her breath, "Marie, he is here! Edward Martin has come to gaze into your magnificent eyes!"

Marie laughed and hushed her as Mr. Martin and his sister entered. Greetings and introductions were exchanged before Leslie Martin exclaimed, "I don't know what you must think of me engaging in such odd behavior, for I don't think I should have dared in Hyde Park, London." She sighed. "There wasn't anyone about, and I thought we could do the thing quickly and without trouble." She smiled ruefully. "But, there. One's sins are forever catching one up!"

"Surely you make too much of it," laughed Velvet easily. "For my part I would have tried it if only to set the dowagers' tongues to wagging!"

"Ah!" ejaculated Marie. "This one, my dears, is a veritable minx and cares nought for the proprieties. She is a sad trial but, oh, so beloved."

"Indeed," declared Leslie, "I love her already, for she is quite after my own heart."

They took seats then at Marie's invitation, and as Marie poured the coffee, Velvet had a moment to take Leslie Martin's measure. She found her to be a tall, sturdy girl with more presence than real beauty. Everything about Leslie Martin appeared to be straightforward, and she had such expressive dark eyes. Beneath her chip hat she wore her dark hair cropped short with curls that framed her face. Her walking ensemble of dark green velvet had been made by a modiste of the first stare and displayed Miss Martin's figure to advantage. Indeed, Velvet felt an instinctive feeling of friendship when she looked at Leslie Martin.

She turned then and found Mr. Martin's hazel eyes resting on her profile and felt herself blush ever so slightly. He leaned toward her and said, "Do you know a man should not be required to look at you too early in the day?"

"What? I must say, Mr. Martin, that is not a very handsome thing to say," giggled Velvet.

"No, no . . ." Mr. Martin hastened to repair his words. "What I am so clumsily trying to tell you is that once a man has looked at you, it quite destroys his ambition to do anything else."

"Ah, now that was quite pretty," said Velvet, "but, as you said, 'tis too early in the day, and a lady should not have her head turned before her day begins."

Lord Farnsworth was announced, and both Velvet and Marie looked at one another before they turned their heads to the new arrival. His lordship was looking exquisite in a walking coat of gray superfine. His waistcoat was pale yellow embroidered with silver threading, and his cravat was tied with delicate expertise. He took the comtesse's soft white hand and kissed it perfunctorily before turning to reach for Velvet's. She had no choice but to offer it, and he first caressed her fingers before he bent low and kissed her wrist. When he brought his eyes up to look into her brilliant green gaze, she felt something almost frightening and withdrew her hand. Farnsworth sensed that he had gone too far too soon and determined that he must move slower, which he would do if only he could keep Talgarth at bay.

As Farnsworth took up a chair beside Velvet, Leslie Martin was in lively conversation with Marie. Edward Martin again attempted to regain Velvet's attention. He was vaguely aware of Farnsworth's eyes on him and glanced his way once or twice with a frown. Velvet's banter, however, captured him, and Farnsworth was forgotten.

"Oh, and what say you to this, Mr. Martin?" said Velvet. "If I were—"

"Yes."

"You cannot say yes. You have not heard what it is I mean to request," laughed Velvet.

"It doesn't matter. I would refuse you nothing," returned Mr. Martin gallantly.

"Ah, but wait. What if I told you I should like to ride your Sinbad?"

"Don't do it," put in Leslie with a laugh. "He is a brute—not a bit of fun, I promise you. Wants manners, you see. My brother likes to keep him hot and prancing, so he does nothing to train him out of his fidgets."

"Yes, but some men think that a woman cannot manage such a creature," retorted Velvet.

"Well, my girl," said Farnsworth unwisely, "a woman shouldn't have to deal with a spirited horse."

"See," said Velvet, looking from Leslie to Farnsworth.

"My lord, you don't seriously think that a skilled horsewoman could not manage a highly spirited horse. That is quite absurd," reprimanded Miss Martin.

Her brother laughed and teased, "Well, as to that, you aren't ham-handed, sis, but you can't manage Sinbad!"

"I certainly can. I choose not to do so when he is particularly bad-tempered, but should the occasion arise, I think that I could ride him tolerably well," she snapped.

"I should like the opportunity," put in Velvet quietly. "In fact, give him to me for a week—every day, for one week—and I shall give you back a nicely mannered animal."

"No, no, I could not in good conscience take such a wager," chuckled Mr. Martin.

"Mr. Martin, if you do not wish to lend out your horse, I would perfectly understand. If you mean to protect me, I would be horribly insulted," returned Velvet.

"Darling, this is absurd." Marie waved her delicate hand at her cousin. "You must not tease Mr. Martin in this fashion."

"I will make a deal with you," said Mr. Martin thoughtfully.

"You can't mean it?" stuck in Farnsworth, who disliked the way this was going.

"Deal then," said Velvet, ignoring Farnsworth.

"Ride Sinbad once with me in the Park—with me beside you. Show me your skill at the bit and convince me you will not be in danger on my horse's back, and you shall have him for the week."

"Done!" laughed Velvet with a clap of her hands. "Famous good sport!"

"Ah, Comtesse," said Farnsworth, "I am persuaded *you* do not see this as famous good sport?"

Marie de Condé did indeed have her doubts as to the wisdom of all this nonsense, but she was herself only five and twenty and ready for little adventures here and there. Besides, she certainly would not be dictated to by this self-assured Englishman. She eyed him for a moment and replied, "As to that, my lord, I do not see the real harm. Mr. Martin will be in attendance, and should the horse be more than what my Velvet can handle . . . ? Well, then, she will dismount!"

Summarily, Marie had dismissed his objections. He met her eyes for a moment, and it came home forcefully that Talgarth had already poisoned the comtesse's mind against him. Farnsworth felt his blood surge with deep-rooted anger. He inclined his head toward her and suddenly got to his feet. "Comtesse, I am afraid I must be going. I am promised with my cousins to Napoleon this afternoon." With some satisfaction he noted that her eyes flickered ever so slightly. He turned toward Velvet and bowed low. "Well then, Lady Velvet, I leave you quite bent out of shape." He smiled. "I'm hurt to the quick, a veritable ruin of a man, for I have not found favor enough to win even the hope of your company in the near future."

Velvet quickly hastened to repair the damage, for she was a soft-hearted creature and did not like to think that she had slighted anyone. "Oh no! How can you say that?"

"Then you *will* take a drive with me in my phaeton tomorrow morning?"

"No, but if you like, I will take a drive with you tomorrow afternoon. I shall be managing Mr. Martin's horse tomorrow morning."

Once more he inclined his head, pleased enough. "Then I must be content, but on tenterhooks until I find you once more. Tomorrow, then, at one o'clock."

Velvet inclined her head and felt a twinge of something she could not name. She could see Marie's expression out of the corner of her eye and knew her cousin was quite disturbed. Over the past year, Marie had met many of her admirers and also dealt with many of Velvet's madcap predicaments, but this was so far removed from any of those reactions that it left Velvet in some discomfort.

After Farnsworth left, the banter in the comtesse's salon became quite lively and most entertaining. Velvet and Marie found Miss Martin to have a great deal of wit, and her brother, too, was never at a loss. Politics soon became the subject of conversation, and they were avidly discussing their varied opinions when Lord Talgarth and Sir Harold Gillingham were announced. Miss Leslie Martin snapped her head around in such a way that Velvet could not help but notice.

"What was that devil Farnsworth doing here?" demanded the marquis as he strode into the room. "I saw his card in the foyer."

"Ah, *cher,* here you are. Do you say good morning?" laughed Marie as she extended her hands.

The marquis gave her fingers a squeeze and put them to his lips. "There, I bid you good morning, sweetheart. Do but tell me what that blasted man was doing here? No, don't, for I already know." He turned toward Velvet and pulled her to her feet. "Eh, brat, we both know what he was doing here." He held her hand. "No, don't snap my head off. Here, give us a kiss—after all, I'm your guardian, ain't I? Have a right to know what's about."

Velvet was definitely not proof against his easy charm. She laughed and got to her toes to give his cheek a quick peck. "Good morning, guardian sir, my lord marquis, oh great one!"

He tweaked her nose and turned to the company at large. "Eh . . . hallo! Martin of the wild horse. Greetings, ol' boy. You must be Miss Martin?"

Edward Martin made haste to introduce the marquis while Gilly stood in silence staring at Leslie Martin as Marie introduced him.

Miss Martin smiled, "Ah, but, Comtesse, Sir Harold and I have already met. Do you remember, sir?"

"I? How could I forget?" breathed Gilly.

"Ah, *mais oui*, Gilly did say that you took a dance together. Is it not so?" She looked at the two and giggled, *"Oui, oui,* it is so."

"Do sit beside me and tell me how you happen to be here, Sir Harold. I had no notion that you were going abroad."

Gilly promptly sat beside her, thinking to himself that she was even more magnificent than his memory had allowed. "The thing is, had no notion I'd be doing anything but following hounds." He looked toward the marquis. "Talgarth forced me to it but don't mind half as much . . . now."

Leslie Martin lowered her lashes, a trick she greatly despised as coy. "Why, Sir Harold . . ."

Velvet had watched this exchange covertly as Mr. Martin and the marquis bandied the amenities. When Marie entered their discourse, Velvet yanked at the marquis's sleeve to whisper, "Do you see Gilly? Do you see?"

"Well, of course I see Gilly. Would have to be blind not to see him."

"My lord, my lord, I mean do you see him with Miss Martin?" hissed Velvet on a low note. " 'Tis famous. I think Gilly has been struck!"

"Struck? Struck? What the deuce do you mean? Struck by what? Looks well enough to me. You ain't known Gilly long enough . . . always has that glassy look in his eyes."

" 'Tis love, my lord," said Velvet with some exasperation. "Why, look at the way he is hanging on every word Miss Martin utters."

The marquis regarded the couple through narrowed eyes. "Love, eh? Got that wrong, child. Gilly in love? Daft notion. Only just met the chit once before. Gilly? Love?" The marquis shook his head. "He is not in the petticoat line. Probably hanging on every word because he doesn't understand what she is saying. Never understands the females," grinned the marquis.

Velvet gave him a doubtful look and then returned her gaze to the couple. She smiled to herself then and in a soft voice said to the marquis, "We'll see . . ."

Edward Martin had already bowed out of his friendly chat with the comtesse and had taken the few steps to his sister across the room to say, "Well, my dear, we don't want to overstay our welcome."

Leslie Martin briskly got to her feet as Sir Harold jumped to his. She gave him a half smile as she answered her brother, "Yes, of course, Edward." She moved off to take leave of her hostess and Velvet, but she heard Gilly stammer at her back, "Mr. Martin . . . er . . . a moment?"

Edward Martin turned his fair head toward Gilly. "Sir?"

"Well, the thing is, we are promised to Comte de Beaupré this evening. In fact, we shall all be making quite a party of it. Would you . . . do you think . . . I mean, I know 'tis short notice, but would you and your sister care to join us? I know that Armand would be happy to have you. He told Dusty and me to bring along any countrymen we could find—casual affair, you see, the more the merrier. I am persuaded Miss Martin might find it entertaining."

Marie de Condé had been listening to this and hurriedly added her entreaties, *"Mais oui.* Armand is my brother and throws the most wonderful parties. He is *fort amusant!* You and your sister must come."

Mr. Martin looked to his sister, and from the uncharacteristically demure expression on her face, he guessed that this plan had found great favor with her. He inclined his head. "Whither thou goest, madam, so must I."

Marie laughed softly. *"Voyons,* 'tis settled, *enfin!* I am very happy, and Condé will be very happy, for he will be with us tonight." She walked the Martins to the door and waved them off.

Gilly, suddenly remembering they didn't have Armand's direction, called out, "Wait!"

All eyes looked with some surprise at him, and

he blushed as he moved to the writing desk, scribbled something quickly on a card, and held it out as he rushed toward Edward Martin to explain, "Comte de Beaupré's direction. Need it, I think." He then bent a magnificent bow and said softly to Miss Martin, "I look forward to seeing you this evening and hearing all about your adventures in Italy, Miss Martin."

"Indeed, Sir Harold," returned the lady quietly, "I look forward to describing them to you."

The couple left, and Gilly turned to find his friends staring at him. "Fancy that," said Gilly, who then moved toward the sideboard and poured himself a generous amount of brandy.

Talgarth's blue eyes opened wide, for Gilly never drank until evening. "Fancy what, ol' boy?"

"The Martins here in Paris . . ." Gilly gave by way of explanation.

Velvet yanked the marquis's sleeve and saucily said, "Hmmm . . . not in the petticoat line? Not in love, eh?"

"Gammon!" snapped the marquis, regarding her with thoughtful eyes. His Gilly in love? Well, well.

Nine

As it turned out, the Tuileries Gardens Fair at which Velvet and the Beaupré brothers found themselves later that day was nothing like they had expected. It was a moderate exhibition with booths set up to display trinkets, china, flower arrangements, leathers, and various ordinary wares. They had been hoping for the unusual, such as performing bears, dancing girls, an exhibit of new and modern machinery. Instead, everywhere they looked they found cakes and strawberries!

"Bah!" Louis pulled a disgusted face. "We shall die of boredom."

"No, we shan't," laughed Velvet. "Come, there is an organ grinder with a monkey. We can go have a look."

The young vicomte had been restlessly attending his brother and Velvet, and had not been himself. Velvet had attributed this to moodiness. Surprisingly, she saw dismissal in his eyes as he laughed and said, "Children, go and play with the monkey. It is not for me. No, I have other amusements that draw me."

"Wait, *mon frère!*" Louis sounded almost desper-

ate, which Velvet found unsettling. "You must not
. . . I mean, you cannot desert us. *Non, non,* it is too
bad of you."

"There are times, young Louis, that a man must
be alone," said Jacques, still with a smile.

"You are not going to be alone!" accused Louis.

Jacques laughed good-naturedly. *"Non,* and there
are times a man must be with someone other than
his brother! I am off." He was kissing the air to
them and moving away quickly.

Louis took a hasty step after his brother only to
be recalled to his senses by Velvet. "What is wrong
with you? Let him go, Louis. After all, you cannot
stop him."

"Perhaps I could have . . ." Louis ran his hands
through his fair head of light brown hair. "I should
have milled him down and kept him from his purpose!"

"What are you talking about? What purpose?
What is wrong with you?"

"Not me, Velvet, not me. It is my brother. You saw
the other night. You recognized what it was. He has
gone back . . . and he goes back there now!"

"What? Gone back? Where?" Then dawning lit
in Velvet's eyes. "Oh no. He has gone to that hell?
That gaming hell? Oh, Louis, no!"

"Oui, oui . . . He went back there the very next
day. I stood and watched him, and, Velvet, there is
a woman there. She is older and has bewitched him.
It worries me. She stands with him when he gambles
and she urges him on." He shook his head. "You
see, he cannot stay away. He has gambled his money,

all but a few coins—an entire quarter's allowance! What will he tell Papa?"

"What of your allowance?"

"It is gone. . . . He took it from me. I did not realize at first how very bad it was with him," Louis groaned.

"Never mind." Velvet patted his shoulder soothingly. "There is nought we can do now."

Louis was gloomy. "My brother will be ruined."

"No, he cannot be ruined in one day." Velvet attempted to laugh off Louis's concern. "Tomorrow we will see what the two of us can do."

Farnsworth stood a moment and stared. There was Velvet, looking like a vision of loveliness. She wore a walking ensemble of twilled yellow muslin trimmed with white lace at the square collar and at the cuffs of its matching spencer. On her head of golden curls, she wore a straw chip bonnet delicately trimmed with the same lace.

Farnsworth turned to the tall older Frenchwoman at his side and whispered, "Do you see? That is Lady Velvet."

"Ah, yes, I have seen her often with the comtesse." Nicole Davenant inclined her head consideringly. "I quite approve, darling. She is something of an heiress . . . charming child. Indeed, you are quite right to want that one. How may I help you?"

"I should like to get her at a social function where her guardian, Lord Talgarth, will not be present."

She laughed. "How may we accomplish that?"

"You could invite her with the comtesse—chaperon enough, don't you think?—for a small dinner party. Would that not serve?"

Nicole Davenant was a forty-year-old beauty whose husband was very close to the First Consul, Napoleon. Her position in society was most enviable. She did what she wanted when she wanted, and she thought it might be amusing to play at intrigue with her cousin, Dale Farnsworth. She smiled. "Very well . . . Present me."

Velvet saw the couple coming and nudged Louis. "Louis . . . Louis . . . That is Nicole Davenant with Lord Farnsworth, and they are coming here. What shall we do?"

"Run like mad," said Louis at once. His father and his aunt Marie avoided Nicole Davenant and her husband whenever possible. She was an autocratic society despot who used her influence with the First Consul for and against her friends and enemies. The Beauprés and the Condé family attempted to stay neutral.

"We cannot. She sees us and is coming our way. Oh dear, dear . . . I do not like this. I have a dreadful feeling."

"*Moi,* I tremble. All things are going wrong. This means something, Velvet. It is—what do you English say? It is, it is *un mauvais augure!*"

"An ill omen? I think you're right, Louis. In fact—"

There was no time for more. They were upon them with Farnsworth bowing low. "Lady Velvet,

Monsieur de Beaupré, how nice. Allow me to present Madame Nicole Davenant, my cousin."

Louis gave Madame Davenant an impressive bow, and Velvet dropped a curtsy. Madame said approvingly, "Well, what lovely children, indeed." She turned to Farnsworth. "How nice for you to find one of your own amongst all of us." She scarcely took a breath before turning upon Velvet to take her hand and graciously say, "*Ma petite,* the comtesse must bring you to a little dinner party I am having for the First Consul this Friday night. It will be *très amusant.* Me, I am persuaded you will enjoy the affair greatly."

Velvet inclined her head. She had been on the town and under the skilled guidance of her cousin Marie long enough to know when her hand was being deftly manipulated. She did not like it. "Oh, Madame, it is a sorry thing, but I know that my cousin, la comtesse, has already promised us elsewhere." She sighed. " 'Tis such a shame."

"Indeed?" returned Madame at her haughtiest. "There is no elsewhere when Napoleon is involved." She managed a softer look. "Never mind, child. Do not trouble your head. I shall stop by tomorrow morning and speak with the comtesse. Rest easy on this."

She turned to Farnsworth, who had remained quiet during all of this exchange. "La, darling, but if we are to meet with Davenant, we must hurry . . ." She took his arm and waited only long enough for him to bow his farewell to Velvet. As they walked away, she whispered, "There, are you happy, beloved? You know, you must not wear your heart on your sleeve. Nothing repulses a woman more. Do not let her see your purpose. . . . Be mysterious."

Velvet waited only long enough for them to be out of earshot before groaning, "Louis, this is dreadful. We have to rush home to Marie and let her know about this at once. She will not be pleased! Why should that woman want us there . . . with Napoleon? Oh dear, oh dear, and she did not invite Talgarth and Gilly. I shall be in the suds this time for certain!"

"I do not like it. Me, I see terrible things ahead. Now there is this Davenant woman looking on us the eye of evil, for she is not to be trusted. They say she turns on those who do not do her bidding. What to do? And *mon frère*? We must save him from this madness. Velvet, what are we to do?"

"I don't know. I have to think, but first we must return home and speak to Marie!"

Ten

Comte Armand de Beaupré had not taken smaller lodgings when his dear wife had died. He maintained quite a large establishment on the Rue de Honoré. Within its walls were still all the furnishings he and his late wife had chosen together. He had changed nothing, for he was very much a sentimentalist. He had known many women before her and a great many after her death, but none like her. At times like these, when he would host an intimate dinner party, he would miss her the most. His younger son touched his father's shoulder, for he, too, missed his mother. "Papa, all goes very well. Tante Marie will be much impressed!"

Armand smiled ruefully and looked round. "What I don't understand is how your brother could have forgotten that we are entertaining tonight?"

Louis attempted sang-froid. "Oh well, Papa, no doubt he met with some old friends." He grinned. "We heard that two of our closest friends have been sent home from school only yesterday . . ."

"Indeed?" returned his fond parent grimly. "Nothing to grin about, my boy! Well, I suppose I must be thankful *you* are here."

They turned as their butler announced the arrival of his sister and her entourage. Marie and her husband entered bandying remarks with the marquis, Gilly, and Velvet. Armand smiled as he went forward to welcome them, but Louis hurriedly took Velvet aside to whisper, "Jacques never came home, Velvet. What can this mean? I know what it means! There will be trouble."

Velvet's well-defined brows drew together, and her cherry lips formed a pout. "That is very bad of Jacques. Really, I am very surprised at him."

"Mais non, Velvet, do you not see? 'Tis that woman at that gaming den. 'Tis, oh, I don't know . . ." Louis was beside himself.

"Well, we must put a stop to this Louis. Your father must be wondering where he is. What did you say?"

"I made up a story about some friends being sent down from school. I told Papa that Jacques must be with them."

"Did he believe you?"

"I think so, but he has not had time to consider—"

"Louis, don't worry. Perhaps Jacques is in his cups, foxed, you know, and does not want to make an appearance in an inebriated state."

Louis's face cleared for a moment. *"Oui,* maybe that is it."

The marquis had been watching Velvet and Louis with troubled blue eyes. The two were very cozy. Well, this wouldn't do. For one thing, Louis was still a schoolboy. For another, he was French. He looked at Velvet from head to toe. She was a taking little

thing in her pale blue gown with white embroidery.
Her golden ringlets framed her piquant face, and
her cherry lips certainly were enticing. Well, well,
he could understand an inexperienced cub like
Louis making calf-eyes at her, but she really shouldn't
take advantage of the lad. He walked to them and
said jovially, "Well, you two, what schemes are you
hatching?"

The two jumped apart to disclaim together,
"Nothing!"

"Why, we are only . . ." began Velvet, blushing
furiously.

"Chatting about mutual friends," stuck in Louis,
feeling she needed help and thinking that he was
getting to be very good in these matters.

The marquis was highly suspicious, but there was
nothing he could do about it at the moment. He
would have to keep his eyes on these two. Really,
Velvet, he thought, how can you lead the poor boy
on?

The butler reappeared to announce Monsieur
and Mademoiselle Martin. Gilly blushed and looked
to Armand to say simply, "Friends of ours. English,
you know. Met your sister. Thought you wouldn't
mind."

"Voyons! Gilly, it is of considerable pleasure for me
to meet your friends," Armand assured him as he
went forward, Gilly trailing at his back.

Introductions were quickly done, apologies made
for the missing vicomte, and everyone settled into
comfortable, lively conversation until Mr. Martin

smiled at Velvet and inquired, "Well, Lady Velvet, all set for your ride tomorrow morning on Sinbad?"

"Sinbad? Ride tomorrow?" interjected the marquis, suddenly on the alert. "What the devil are you talking about, Martin?"

Velvet pulled a face at Edward Martin and then turned to the marquis to bat her dark lashes. "My lord, you recall, don't you? You thought a woman could not handle a high-spirited prime blood. I thought a skilled woman could. We made a wager . . ."

"Wager? I don't remember making a wager," snapped the marquis, who remembered very well.

"Oh yes. In the park, my lord, after Mr. Martin's little incident with Sinbad. You said I was just a silly giggling female and that a female couldn't handle prime blood. I said that a skilled horsewoman, namely me, could certainly handle a horse like Sinbad."

"Blast it, child!" returned the marquis, flustered to have words spoken in haste flung back at him. "Didn't quite say it like that, and I didn't think Martin would actually lend you the blasted horse." He turned to Martin. "Thought he would know enough to put you off, but I ain't blaming him, for if ever there was an imp of a girl scampering around and barking up scrapes . . ."

Mr. Martin squirmed under the marquis's sharp blue eyes and offered in his defense, "I only made the offer to watch and see how she handled Sinbad on a quiet ride. I said that if she proved her skill with him, then she could have him for a week of schooling."

"Schooling? Are you daft, man? Do you know

what could happen?" retorted the marquis. "It isn't bad enough that she needs must ride him, but now you mean to let her try and school him as well? He has the devil's own will, and you know it! Damn, he'll try and kill her the first time she crosses him."

"No, no, I assure you," said Mr. Martin hastily, "Sinbad hasn't a mean fiber in his body. He is playful, young, but certainly not nasty."

"Well, and that is very easy for you to say and then dismiss. She ain't your responsibility!" returned the marquis caustically.

"My lord, I would not allow Lady Velvet to be in any danger. Rest assured that if I see him begin to act up, I shall be on hand to do whatever necessary."

Velvet had said nothing during this heated exchange. She had watched the marquis, who seemed genuinely concerned for her safety, and had felt warm inside and something else she could not name. Then all at once the word *responsibility* made the feeling explode into myriad pieces and lose itself. Of course, his concern for her was because she was his responsibility. How very degrading. She bolstered herself and managed to say, "My lord, why don't you join us tomorrow and see for yourself just how capable I may or may not be of handling Sinbad?"

"Deuce take it, girl, did you actually think I wouldn't be there? Invited or no, I would have been there." His glittering blue eyes raked her face. " 'Tis why I'm here in Paris . . . because of you."

"Yes, of course, because your grandfather could not make the journey, I know," said Velvet, looking away.

The marquis frowned over this, but Armand was already holding up his hands to take over the scene with great aplomb. "Perhaps we may suspend all this chatter of Sinbads and schooling and go into my humble dining room to enjoy my chef's—the best chef in all of Paris—he is—delectable repast." In a soft aside to the marquis, he bantered, "Well, *mon cher,* you make *très bien* nursemaid. *Moi,* I am very impressed."

"Go to the devil," grinned the marquis as he offered his arm to Velvet.

Velvet hesitated. In some surprise the marquis quizzed, "Ho, am I out of favor then? Perhaps you would rather go in on Mr. Martin's arm? Shall I bow myself off? No, too late. He already has Marie on his arm. What then, shall I give you to Louis?"

Velvet laughed at his antics. "Stop it, wretch, dear wretch." She put her hand on his arm. "There is no one in this room I would rather have take me to dinner, and you know it, Dusty!"

"Do I?" he shrugged, but he was smiling happily. "But, then, it has been such a long time since I have heard you say my name. I wonder why that is? When you were younger, you would say it all the time even though I carefully instructed you in the proper way to address a marquis."

She laughed. "Dusty, Dusty, Dusty . . . since I have become a responsibility instead of a friend, your name eluded me."

He looked at her sharply. "Brat!"

They laughed together and, once more in the comfortable regions of harmony, followed the others

into the dining room, where only Louis's meaning-
ful glances cast a shadow over Velvet's enjoyment.
Obviously Jacques had not returned, and poor
Louis was growing more concerned every minute.

After dinner when the women were once more
joined by the gentlemen, the marquis was finding his
interest piqued by his dear Gilly. He watched his old
friend attentively play the gallant and heard him uttering words he had been certain were not known to
the baronet. He watched Gilly make sheep's eyes and
other amazing gestures. All was for Miss Martin.

Gilly had never played the role of the aggressive
lover before. In fact, Gilly had never chased an eligible female as far back as the marquis could recall.
Gilly's liaisons over the years usually were with
women who knew the rules. The marquis frowned
as he attempted to remember how many of these
there had been. Ah yes, two or three lovely actresses
. . . and every one had singled Gilly out to offer
their favors. There had been many tavernmaids over
the years, easily forgotten, and there had been that
damned widow near Gilly's hunting box, who had
tried to trap him into marriage, but never had Gilly
courted a female! The marquis looked toward Velvet,
in deep conversation with Edward Martin. Well, well,
the chit had called it earlier, hadn't she?

Condé leaned in his direction, "You are very faraway, dear boy."

"Aye, got to thinking, you know."

"Ah, of course. Your friend is in dangerous waters, and you think to save him?" He shook his head

and gave the marquis a gentle smile. "Don't. He won't thank you for it."

"No, I don't suppose he would," said the marquis, who then watched Louis catch Velvet's eye and request her attention.

Again Condé smiled. "Now there bears something worth watching, for youth is forever in need of help they won't thank you for giving but need all the same!"

There was no time to respond to this, for Condé moved off immediately and touched his wife's arm. "Darling, your brother, I am certain, is ready to throw us all out. I believe he has a card game to attend and is now overdue."

Marie giggled. "Armand, could you?"

"As much as I adore you *ma petite, oui*, I think I could, for as your very brilliant husband has observed, I am promised elsewhere." He smiled at his much-surprised company, for the Martins were not used to such frankness. "However, you are most welcome to stay and continue to enjoy yourselves. My son Louis may play host . . ."

Marie slapped his arm, "Odious man, *voyons*, "she exclaimed as she got to her feet. "Moi, I am a sister most kind. I leave, and I take my people with me. Come, everyone, bid my brother adieu, for he must go lose his money at cards at once."

The Martins laughed and immediately got to their feet, for Armand had already gone to his bellpull, laughing over his shoulder, *"Non, non,* I am luckier than that. It is but a friendly game. No fortunes are handed over at our table, I do assure you."

The butler appeared and was requested to have their carriages brought round, and the footman arrived with their various cloaks and hats. As they prepared to leave, much jesting ensued, and Louis took the opportunity to draw Velvet aside, "Did you not see me motion to you earlier, my girl?"

"Indeed, I did. It is my belief that half the people in the room saw you motion to me, you silly boy," hissed Velvet. "What? Should I cut Mr. Martin off in mid-sentence and rush to you? No, I think not, Louis, and well you know it."

"Very well, but I am concerned for Jacques."

"As well you should be, but you don't want your father and aunt to find out, do you?" chastised Velvet.

He hung his head. "*Non*, but, Velvet, he is not home. What shall I do?"

"I don't know. I must think."

"I will go to the gaming hell and carry him off."

"He won't go with you if he is in a state." Velvet thought a moment. "However, he might if he saw me there. He might come with both of us." She touched his shoulder. "Louis, I will be changed and ready by midnight. Come for me. If you do not, I will know that Jacques is home safe. There!" She finished quickly, for she could see the marquis bearing down upon them.

Louis whispered before he thought the marquis could overhear, "Done!"

Eleven

Since it was early in the evening, the marquis casually suggested to Gilly that they pay a visit to Mason's, a gentleman's club. Gilly sighed an answer. That notion put aside, they walked in silence the short distance to their exclusive hotel, for both were lost in thought. Somehow they made it to their suite of rooms, though had you asked either one, they would have been hard-put to tell you how they got there. They had not brought their valets with them on this trip, thinking they would be returning to England within a short space of time, and had been allowing hotel staff to attend to their clothing. Gilly remarked about this as he entered the sitting room, "Running out of smallclothes, Dusty. We had better go shopping in the morning if we mean to stay here for another week."

"Hmmm," agreed the marquis as he absently watched his friend pour out a glass of wine. "Do me one, ol' boy. Aye, that's it," he said, taking the proffered brew with yet another sigh. He sipped at it, looked at it, and said shortly, "Good stuff, this!"

Gilly agreed, "Damn good," and moved to their terraced window. He opened the long lead-paned glass door and stepped out to stare at the sky and remark, "Well, and she is right. There is a face up there. Come and have a look, Dustin."

"What? Oh, the face." He shook his head. "Now don't go telling me you have never seen the face before? Don't be daft, man."

"Well, and I haven't. Miss Martin told me to look at it tonight before I turned in. Never really noticed it before . . ."

"What I want to know is what that dratted boy could have meant?"

"About the face in the moon?"

"Will you stop babbling about faces and moons! Armand's boy, Louis, making sheep's eyes at Velvet and then whispering that something was 'done.' I have a bad feeling about this, Gilly, and so I tell you."

Gilly frowned. "You're right about keeping Farnsworth away from her, but, blister it, man, Louis is Armand's son. Good blood there, and he seems a decent sort of boy—no harm in him."

"Zounds, Gilly! The boy is eighteen. Too young, and besides he is French."

"Well, got a point there," acceded Gilly reasonably. "What's more, don't feel comfortable in Paris. Got a funny notion people stop talking when we enter clubs." He rubbed his nose. "Got a notion we have no more than a month or so and that the Frogs mean to go after us again. What say you?"

"I say you are very right, Gilly. Napoleon wants war . . . needs it. The sooner little Velvet has her ball and we're off for home, the better!"

***

Once again the night found Velvet clothed in Louis's old riding garments with the hood of his dark cloak pulled low over her eyes. She was just a touch frightened lest they get caught, for the full weight of what they were doing had really sunk into her brain. If anyone found out, it would bring shame to Marie, whom she loved and wouldn't hurt for the world.

She held the material of Louis's coat as they raced through the streets and made their way to Picard's. Velvet eyed the dirty building with repugnance. "Louis, you cannot really believe Jacques has spent his entire day and night in this . . . this dreadful den?"

"Oui, ma petite, it is what I believe. It is where I found him the last time."

Velvet steeled herself as they made their way within. Once inside, a large burly man grinned stupidly at Velvet and then sank to the floor directly in her path. She wanted to scream but controlled herself as they stepped over him and managed to squeeze through to the gaming table. Jacques was not there.

"Come, Velvet, we must look in all the booths." Louis pulled aside the curtains to one of the chambers and there found a man and woman smoking opium.

"What are they doing?" Velvet was amazed and somewhat curious.

"Velvet, Velvet, my heart cries. It is opium. Those

that smoke it go into dreams, and then they must do it over and over. I have heard much . . . much. It is bad, so bad." He ran his hand through his hair. "I am mad to bring you here—we must leave. You should never had seen such as this!"

"No, Louis, it is good that I have seen. One is better able to fight what one can see for oneself. Come now, we must find Jacques."

They found him in the very next booth. He was slumped on a bench with his head in the lap of an attractive woman whose charms had seen better days. She was scantily dressed, and upon seeing Louis, she laughed and invited him to join their party. Jacques laughed, too, and reached up to fondle her.

Louis was enraged and took his brother by his coat lapels and hauled him to a sitting position. "Up you. Hear me, *mon frère!*"

"What? What?" screeched the woman. "Leave him! Leave him!"

Louis pushed her off his brother. "Jacques, we must go home. Look who is here to help."

Jacques was in a drunken cloud. He had not eaten and he had lost his money. Attempting to focus, he patted his brother's arm. "Louis . . . Louis . . . Do you want a pretty? Let me get you one."

"Get up, Jacques!" Velvet said gruffly. "Your father is waiting at home, and there will be the devil to pay." She spoke in French without a hint of her being female or English. She turned to the Frenchwoman. "If you do not wish any trouble, you will not encourage this boy to stay. It would not go well with you. This, I promise."

The wench eyed the youth doubtfully, but knowing that Jacques came from an influential family, she backed away. Jacques allowed his brother to help him up. He leaned heavily on his cousin and his brother as they took him out of the gaming hell.

Just before they cleared the doorway, Jacques looked into Velvet's face and grinned. "Ah, *ma petite* plays a boy again, eh? Velvet, Velvet . . . you will be in trouble."

Jacques was giddy and laughed loudly over this as he leaned into Louis and Velvet. He allowed them to walk him outdoors. The fresh night air hit his nostrils with a force that intensified his dizziness, and Jacques complained bitterly, *"Mon Dieu.* I was fine, then you come, and now I am sick."

They ignored him and managed to pull him along until Louis saw a hackney and called out, *"Venez ici. . . . Ici!"*

Some moments later they were dropping Velvet off, watching as she scrambled out of the cab. Louis called to her softly, "You will manage the climb?"

"Yes," she laughed. "In fact, 'tis easier going up and in than it is getting out and down." She threw a kiss toward Jacques. "You will not remember in the morning what you have done, but *I* plan to remind you, *mon ami!"* She said sweetly, "I do so hope you have a terrible head in the morning, dear Jacques." She then hurried off for the Condé courtyard and her window trellis, and Louis motioned for the cab to proceed.

None of them suspected that while at Picard's a well-dressed Englishman had been watching their progress with avid interest. Farnsworth had been fondling the piece of muslin lounging on his lap when the Beaupré lads caught his attention. He frowned, forgetting the girl nibbling at his neck, as he watched the brothers with their smaller friend. Well, well, schoolboys on a lark. Nothing to be gained there. Or perhaps there was . . .

Twelve

The Comte de Condé pursed his thin lips and turned away from his young wife to gaze out onto the sunny street. These were difficult times in France. All familiar things were vanishing right before his eyes. Napoleon? A dangerous man who would not be satisfied with the title First Consul and would not be satisfied with peace! The Davenants were in favor at the moment with the quixotic Napoleon, and it would not do to do anything untoward at this particular time. "What exactly did she say to you, my love?"

Marie's hand waved about distractedly. "She is a terrible woman, darling, but I was very polite. I explained that we were already engaged to dine with our English friends and then we were going to the theater." Marie shook her head. "It was then she said, 'Ah, well, English friends and the theater do, of course, take precedence over a few moments with the First Consul at my humble soirée.' "

"I see," the comte said quietly.

"I suppose we must go. I just so detest being dictated to in this manner, Condé. It is wicked of her, and I cannot like it."

"No, my love, and we should not go. Nicole Davenant oversteps herself, and in truth Napoleon would not like his name bandied about in such a manner. However, we are being served a ticklish problem, are we not?"

"I fear Dustin will be greatly displeased, and it is most irregular. How can we cancel our plans with him when he is Velvet's guardian and take Velvet elsewhere? 'Tis absurd," she said.

"Precisely. One wonders why she goes to such lengths? I wonder if our First Consul would be amused?"

"Well, as to that, perhaps he would be, for he would like to serve the English so, would he not?"

"Not just now. It is my belief he is readying himself for war with England and is his most charming at such times. No, he would not like it to appear that he has asked for our English guests to be excluded. Do not accept her invitation just yet, Marie."

"Condé, what are you going to do?" Marie looked worried.

He came over to her and took her chin. "Do you doubt me to see us through this?"

She rubbed his hand with her cheek. "Oh no, how could I doubt you in anything?"

The door opened wide, and Velvet peeked in. "Oh, do I intrude?" She started to back out of the room, but both Marie and her husband laughed as they waved her in to join them.

Velvet pulled a face. "That Davenant woman was here, wasn't she? Do we have to go to her dreadful soirée? I think she is a horrible woman."

Condé laughed and Marie shrugged, saying, "We shall see. 'Tis an odd thing for her to expect us to take you from your guardian in such a manner."

"Indeed, I don't think that Dusty will like it at all," mused Velvet.

"What won't I like?" asked Dustin, standing in the doorway. He had waved aside the butler and advised that poor worthy that he and Gilly would show themselves.

Gilly leaned over to him. "Any number of things. Stands to reason, we are in France. Don't like much myself, ol' boy."

Marie heard this and giggled. "Dearest Gilly, that is most insulting."

He blushed and began to stammer about rich foods, a weak stomach, ignorance of the language until she kissed his cheek and ordered him to be quiet.

The marquis made a second attempt. "Well, brat, what won't I like?"

Condé put up his hand and took his attention. "My dear Dusty, it appears we have something of a problem staring us down. It involves you and our little Velvet."

"Eh, how is this?"

" 'Tis that Davenant woman," said Velvet, who then received a look from Condé and promptly apologized.

"Indeed, as Velvet says, it is the Davenant woman," said Condé.

The marquis frowned. "Sorry . . . ?"

"She is one of Napoleon's . . . shall we say satellites? Yes, we shall say that. She is also cousin to Lord Farnsworth, whom you dislike so intensely."

"This grows very interesting," said the marquis, suddenly grim.

"Indeed, I agree, for what must Madame Davenant do, but extend an invitation to us and insist that we attend, even though we have indicated that we are promised elsewhere Friday night."

"Friday? Tomorrow? But we are dining together and then going to the theater with the Martins," said Gilly.

"We explained that to her. She then said that her guest of honor would be the First Consul himself and that he would be surprised to find that the Condé family chose to enjoy themselves instead with their English friends."

The marquis released a long low whistle. "So . . . he means to play hard and dirty, eh? Damn his eyes!"

"No doubt you are speaking of Farnsworth," said Condé.

"Yes, but what does this mean?" asked Gilly, unused to such sly dealings.

"It means that the Davenant woman has invited Velvet and the Condé family to her affair, but not Velvet's guardian," said the marquis absently, for he was thinking. He turned back to the comte. "Of course, you will understand that I cannot allow Velvet to be manipulated in this manner?"

"I would be most shocked if you did," replied Condé. "However, it does leave things . . . shall we say sticky?"

"I would be deuced surprised if you didn't say it. Can't allow Velvet to be used so, but can't allow you to land in the suds either. Only one thing to do," said the marquis with some determination.

"And what is that?" asked Condé curiously.

"You go to this Davenant affair; I take Velvet and return to London." The marquis snapped his fingers. "Can't expect you to produce Velvet if she ain't here." He looked toward Marie, who stood up to object in some distress. "Sorry, m'dear. I know you have that ball planned for next week, but under the circumstances, nothing for it."

Velvet wanted to object for Marie's sake, for principle's sake, for pride's sake, which balked at running from a problem, but in truth she did not like to be manipulated either, and she applauded the marquis's determination to take her out of such a situation. She did not have the opportunity to speak, however, as Condé, who understood the marquis's position, was still looking for a solution that would satisfy his wife. He put up his hand. "You could, of course, do that. It is your right, but I would hope you would first allow me to take a stab at this."

"What are you planning?" The marquis did not like agreeing to anything without knowing the facts.

"Trust me in this, my Dustin," said the comte. "If I do not arrange everything to your satisfaction, you will take Velvet and be off. It is agreed."

"Right then," said the marquis. He looked at Velvet in her riding ensemble of blue linen. "Well then, brat, wipe that frown off your face. However am I to marry you off if you are forever frowning?"

Appalled, Velvet's hands went to her hips as she sputtered for a reply. Instead, Marie waved her off. "He is quite right, you know, and it will make wrinkles. Go, go, be off for your ride."

"Zounds! Listen to that woman, my girl," said Talgarth, grinning as he made a low mocking bow to Velvet. "That's right: no frowns and off we go, for today is the day you mean to make me eat my words." He was more than happy to change the subject to something more lighthearted.

Velvet eyed him with arms folded across her chest before she leapt forward and ruffled his hair. Her green eyes glittered playfully, and she was conscious of the fact that he had really been concerned for her welfare and was now trying to change the mood. "Devil," she whispered.

"What? Don't you think you will make me eat my words?"

"Ha! *You* don't think so; I know that."

"Oh, but I do, I do," laughed the marquis as he flicked her pert nose.

"Can we go now?" asked Gilly anxiously. "I think the Martins will already be at the stable."

Velvet moved to the mirrored wall table where she laid her hat earlier. Pulling the brim low over her forehead, she adjusted the cascading curls at her ears, smoothed the white feather that twirled round the blue linen, and then set it all with a hat pin. She turned and announced that she was ready.

"I should say so," breathed the marquis, taking a moment to look her over. She was an exquisite little thing and would do his grandfather proud once he had her safely in England.

She waved herself off, throwing a kiss to Marie and the comte, and saying with a wiggle of her shoulders that was most fetching, "Well, my lord, the time is now."

"So it is," he answered glibly. "Sinbad beware! My girl means to have at you." He laughed and then said to her softly, "I think you *will* conquer Sinbad, and I know you will conquer all other . . . er . . . studs."

"Flattery, my lord? I don't think so. You are teasing me once more, but no matter. In a very short while, we shall see what we shall see." She dismissed the marquis with a flash of her eyes and turned to Gilly. "There, Gilly, don't fidget. We are leaving right now, and the stables are only a very short walk, I promise you."

So saying, she took Gilly's arm and threw a saucy look over her shoulder at the marquis as they left. He threw back his head with a bark of laughter. She was like no other girl he had ever known. All woman, and yet a wild hoyden of a creature as well, a most enchanting combination. Indeed, he felt himself quite happy to be playing nursemaid.

It was soon afterward that Velvet found herself sidesaddle on Sinbad with her hands quite full. Leslie rode her mare quietly beside Gilly at the rear, and Velvet found herself flanked by Edward Martin and the marquis. Sinbad was feeling his oats. This was a strange park in a strange city, and he was accompanied by strange horses. He pulled at his reins in an attempt to get to know his new companions, sniffing and then snorting at them. He also pulled at his reins in order to test his rider, who he knew very well was *not* his very familiar master.

Velvet felt her arms tugged out of her sockets by the strong gelding's constant yanking, and she shortened rein. "There now, 'tis very impolite of you to treat a lady like that," she said softly, giving him gentle instructions with leg and fingers. He objected, though, to the short reins and threw his head up. "No, you don't, my boy!" said Velvet firmly. She spread out her short reins on either side of his head and held him steady. "There, no games."

As she schooled him to her will, she forgot the presence of Mr. Martin and the marquis. There was only her and this wonderful, spirited animal. She had no intention of breaking his spirit, only of channeling it, and Sinbad seemed instinctively to respond to her gentle, yet firm wielding. He pranced; she held him in place, checking and releasing his bit, bringing him under her leg, wishing she were riding astride to better school him. Sinbad was a quick study. He understood after only a few moments that when he did not tug at her, she released, and when he misbehaved, she brought him back on the bit.

Within fifteen minutes Sinbad settled beneath Velvet, snorted, and decided to relax with his companion horses. Velvet laughed, patted his neck, and said lightly to him, "Ah, what a good Sinbad. There, you see? There is nought of which to be frightened here.''

"Well done!'' approved Mr. Martin admiringly. ''I am astounded. It usually takes me a full canter to calm the fidgets out of him.''

Well-pleased with this, Velvet looked at the marquis expectantly. ''Well, my lord, what say you?''

"I shall withhold my opinion until I have seen you ride off alone. After all, Sinbad is flanked by our two calm geldings to keep him secure. How would he do by himself?''

Vexed, Velvet's impulsive nature took over and got the better of her usually sound judgment. She turned a cold shoulder to the marquis and gave Sinbad leg. They were off immediately!

The marquis could have cursed himself, but instead he shouted after Velvet to hold up. She did not listen, for Sinbad's canter was swift and ever so comfortable. She moved him on, urging him forward, loving his stride, forgetting they were in a park, forgetting not to allow him to gallop. They were moving as one, and it felt as though they were flying over the earth, not touching ground. It was heaven!

"Devil a bit!'' hissed the marquis, not wanting to give chase and perhaps to spur Sinbad out of control.

"Blister it!'' snapped Mr. Martin. ''If Lady Velvet is in danger now, 'tis laid at your feet, my lord. What made you needle her like that?''

The marquis nearly withered Mr. Martin with a look, but he managed to control himself and not give the man a scalding set-down. It was, however, at this moment that the entire company was left speechless with horror. A small boy broke away from his nanny and went after a butterfly. Unaware, the child, hands in the air, chased the pretty thing onto the bridle path. Sinbad saw an unknown creature, hands and arms up threateningly, or so it seemed to him, and he knew not what to do. He zigged and zagged as he felt his rider take in reins and request him to stop. Sinbad did not want to stop with this little creature so very close. Better, he thought, to bolt and outrun it.

'Tis what he tried to do, but Velvet brought his head round, bending his neck nearly in half as she attempted to make him circle wide without unseating herself at such a speed. She clung to her saddle and circled him, calming him all the while until he came to a stop and pranced himself into a lather. By that time the boy's nanny had scooped up her startled charge and had hurried off, and the marquis was first upon Velvet. "Damnation! How dare you! Of all the inconsiderate, ill-thought, immature things to do. You could have caused harm to others as well as yourself!"

Velvet hung her pretty head. "I . . . I am sorry."

Edward Martin arrived with Gilly and his sister. He moved his horse close to Sinbad and reached out to touch Velvet's arm. "I applaud you!" he said. "You managed him with quick thinking and skill, Lady Velvet. Tell me, were you born in the saddle?"

She looked at him gratefully and blushed. "Very nearly, sir. My grandfather put me in the saddle when I was three, and I have spent a great deal of my time there ever since. 'Tis a passion of mine."

"Sinbad is yours this week . . . if I may ride yours in exchange."

"Oh, thank you! I do enjoy him. What do you think of my gelding Rollo?"

He patted the neck of the chestnut under him. "He is a splendid animal."

Velvet smiled but felt more than a little subdued. She knew she had been unwise, even thoughtless. She had put both the little boy and Sinbad in harm's way by opening the horse like that. "You are very kind, Mr. Martin, and I am so terribly sorry for losing control like that. It was dreadful of me. I think we had better walk back to the stables now, he is so terribly lathered."

Mr. Martin felt no more should be said on the matter, for he could see that Velvet was feeling ashamed of herself. He instead maintained an easy flow of idle chatter all the way back to the stables. In this he was joined by his sister and Gilly. Velvet, however, was not able to do more than offer half smiles and monosyllables to the conversation. The Marquis of Talgarth kept a stony silence until they reached the stables, at which time he graciously thanked the Martins for their company and the use of their very fine horse.

The short walk back to the Condé residence seemed an eternity to Velvet, all too painfully aware of the marquis's displeasure. She felt that his silence was worse than his ranting and raving. Gilly was vaguely aware of her discomfort, but was too wrapped up in faraway dreams to offer any help. Thus, silence reigned.

Once within the central hallway of the Condé town house, Velvet turned to bid her escorts good day, but the marquis said abruptly, "In the salon, miss, if you please!"

"I do not please," said Velvet quietly, "but I suppose I do not have a choice." She attempted to peep at him flirtatiously and hopefully change the mood.

He was cold stone, answering her grimly, "No, you do not have a choice." He turned to Gilly. "I shall only be a moment, ol' boy."

Gilly was thrilled to be dismissed and well out of what he was sure was going to be an ugly scene. He knew Talgarth well enough to know that he was in a white rage quite out of character. He had only seen the marquis in this state once before, and he had been the very devil to deal with at that time. The odd thing was that Gilly could not understand why his usually jovial friend was so out-of-reason cross. Velvet had done no more or less than any of them had done in their heyday. Of course, she was a girl, and that made it a bit sticky, but no harm done in the end. After all, the marquis had already given her a scold and that having done so in front of all of them was punishment enough. Gilly was a soft-hearted fellow and felt a wave of pity as he left poor young Velvet to the marquis's wrath.

Thus, he stood a moment and frowned, finally calling after his friend, "Dusty, ol' man?"

The marquis turned. "Well?" His mood showed on his face and would brook no argument.

"Well, the thing is, she shouldn't have done it, but, well, it's over with, done . . . finished . . ."

"I shan't be long," said the marquis stiffly. His dearest friend was taking sides with Velvet. Well, he wouldn't have it. Gilly was far too soft.

Gilly shrugged and moved off to take a seat in the hallway and await the marquis, who then turned a cold look upon Velvet. She was bolstered by the fact that Gilly seemed to be in sympathy with her. However, the look that the marquis gave her withered all hope, and with drooping shoulders she entered the salon and turned to hear the marquis's lecture.

Talgarth closed the doors, then turned to seethe at her, "How dare you? How could you behave as you did? Where were you raised, in Bedlam?"

"How dare *you!*" snapped Velvet. She felt sick at heart, but this last had triggered her own hot temper. "I am sorry. I have said that I was sorry. I behaved poorly. There. What more do you want, my blood?"

"Your blood could have been spilled all over Paris today. Yours, that young boy's, and Sinbad's as well," he snapped back.

She hung her head. "I know."

In the face of her utter dejection, he could say no more without appearing a tyrant even to himself. He stared at her a moment and then allowed, "Very well. We shall say no more." He started for the door.

A small voice halted him. "My lord . . . ?"

He turned and still appeared a man of stone. "Yes?"

Velvet eyed him, sighed, and said, "Nought . . . nought."

"Good day then, Velvet."

He was gone, and Velvet watched hopefully, thinking perhaps he just might come back, but he did not. All at once the sun lost its glow, and the sky, though a wondrous shade of blue, seemed black. There seemed to be absolutely nothing that was good about anything, and Velvet sank into the folds of the large winged chair and felt as though her heart was about to burst. All she could think was now he must loathe and despise her as a fool. Her heart's desire, her beloved Dusty, her knight of knights would never, ever love her. On this conclusion, Velvet began crying into the sleeve of her riding ensemble.

Thirteen

Velvet was sniffing some twenty minutes later when her cousin Marie entered the salon. The young comtesse came in chattering about something when all at once she realized that Velvet, now attempting to hide her tears, had been crying. She dropped her gloves and reticule, going to Velvet and exclaiming, "What is this? La! *Mais non, ma petite,* tears? *Vraiment,* they are tears!"

She plopped onto the footstool at Velvet's feet and took Velvet's hands. "Who has done this to you? What man makes *ma belle* cry? It is a man. It is always a man. Men! Bah! They do not have hearts. How could he do this to you?"

Velvet listened to this diatribe and giggled. Marie clapped her hands. *"Ma petite* laughs? *Bien,* it is *moi.* I come and I make you laugh. *I,* you see, am a woman!"

Velvet bent over with mirth and found it a great release. She laughed and laughed and hugged her cousin to her. "Marie, Marie, I love you."

"Oui, it is so, and I love you. Now you will tell Marie why there were tears, *oui?"*

"Marie, I have been very bad today. I am so

ashamed, and you will be ashamed of me when you hear."

"*Non,* of this be certain. I cannot be ashamed of you. *Moi,* I did many, oh, many naughty things when I was your age. I know the feeling."

"But, Marie, I broke the rules in a thoughtless and dangerous way. Oh Marie, you would never have been so bad."

"*Tiens!* Tell me and we shall compare badness, eh?"

Velvet related the story to her and then hung her head. "I galloped, Marie, and what is worse, I knew it was wrong to do so in the park, and I just took off without even being polite enough to tell my company that I was going to do so. Then that little child . . . Marie, I could have killed him."

"And you did this just to be bad?" Marie asked glibly.

"No, no, Talgarth was being very provoking."

"Ah, so you lost your temper and cantered off. Have you never seen me do that in the park with my own beloved Condé?"

"Well, er, I suppose, but not like this . . ."

"No, well, you were on Sinbad. He wants schooling—but you then stopped him, did you not?"

"Yes, but—"

"And you see why the rule of galloping applies in the park. Bien. 'Tis well."

Velvet laughed. "It was dreadful of me, whatever you say."

"*Mais oui,* very dreadful. You are bad, very bad."

Marie shrugged. "But tomorrow you will be better, for such is life. . . . You had a lesson."

"Such a horrible one, and now Talgarth thinks I am detestable."

"*Non, non,* silly girl," laughed Marie, "Talgarth? No doubt you gave him a scare. Men do not like to be frightened. It makes them cross."

"Well, Talgarth was very cross with me," sighed Velvet sadly.

Marie looked at her with thoughtful hazel eyes before she said, "Do you know, when Condé and I were on our honeymoon, and I was not much older than you are now, we had a terrible argument. We were out riding in the most beautiful Italian countryside, and I rode off ahead of him and out of sight. I wanted him to be sorry. Oh, I remember it still so much like it was yesterday. I was very angry and not thinking anything except that I wanted him to feel bad.

"I was out of his sight, and he was coming along slowly, for he was angry with me, you see, and when Condé is angry, he is quiet, reserved." Marie shrugged. "So, I did it. I took a jump into the woods, dismounted my horse, and lay on the ground as though I had fallen and been unconscious, you see. My horse moved off not too far to graze, so that when poor Condé came around the bend, he saw my horse first and then he saw me on the ground.

"Well! He jumped off his animal and over the fence, crying my name and dropping to take me into his arms. I couldn't let him suffer any longer, so I opened my eyes. He was so happy, laughing my name, kissing my face, touching me to see where I was hurt, and then I told him the truth, teasing him with it as well."

Marie shook her head. "Well, he was angry . . . very, very angry, and it took a great deal of time before he would even look at me, and my Condé is not quick to anger."

"Marie, that was wicked of you," breathed Velvet, much shocked.

"*Oui*, very wicked, but it was over, done. We moved on, and *moi*, I learned a valuable lesson. You see."

"Yes, I suppose, but, Marie, now Lord Farnsworth is coming here to take me for a drive in his phaeton, and, oh, Dusty, the marquis, I mean—well, he will think I am driving out with Farnsworth for spite. Oh, this is terrible."

"Why should he think such a thing?" Marie eyed her and then said with some exasperation, "*Ma petite, non*. You said you would tell him this morning of the problem of Farnsworth. Did you not? Why, he would have understood the delicacy of the situation you found yourself in yesterday. Oh, this is too bad."

"Marie, it isn't what you think. I meant to tell him, just as I promised you that I would, but . . . but . . . well, then we . . . the incident with Sinbad happened and . . . In all the commotion, I just forgot."

"You forgot." Marie rattled off a few choice words in French before saying, "Upstairs. Wash, change your clothing, and be ready for that dreadful man.

I, too, I promise you, shall be ready, and you will
not be out long. That, you may believe!"

Velvet squeezed Marie's hand and got to her feet.
"That, I do believe."

"Chèrie, there is something in this Farnsworth that
I cannot like. I think your Dustin speaks truly about
him."

"He is not *my* Dustin, and we really haven't given
the man a chance," said Velvet as she left the room.
She stopped at the doorway and turned back to say,
"He is eligible, and he is quite good English *Ton.*"

"You are playing now with me, so, *moi,* I do not
answer you. I tell you there is something lacking in
Lord Farnsworth's heart, and this shows in his eyes.
It has nought to do with *Ton* and everything to do
with the soul."

"Faith, Marie, but you give me chills when you
speak like that. My grandfather taught me that
things are never just black and white, but full of
delicate shades. I would think souls are not so read-
ily seen and not so easily judged."

Marie waved her hands in exasperation. "Go now,
before I lose patience."

Velvet laughed. *"Oui,* Marie, I am going, but,
Marie, I fear it won't be long before I am in the suds
again with Dustin before I am even dried from my
last soaking!"

Louis de Beaupré was at his wit's end. His father
had called him to his room, and Louis stood before
his parent with downcast eyes while he was raked

over the coals. He attempted a defense of his brother: "Yes, Papa, but it was not Jacques's fault. There were several of us—"

His father stopped him cold. "I tell you, Louis, and I would tell that brother of yours if he were here to listen that the road you have chosen will end in disaster. It is time you returned to school and begged the dean to allow you to attend classes again."

"Yes, Papa, but it is recess now, so we must wait for two weeks."

"Very well, but in the meantime, you will compose a letter of apology."

"Yes, but, forgive me, Papa," said Louis doubtfully, "you made us do that when we first were sent down, and the dean wrote back saying that we were not fit for studies."

"I remember that very well, Louis," snapped his father. "However, you will write once more and tell him that you have learned a valuable lesson and would like the privilege of returning to your studies. Louis, you and Jacques will one day own vast estates. Ours is a fortune in lands, and although you are a second son, the will provides for you as well. In order to run such complicated estates as ours, you must have a good education. In order to do well in the society of which you are a privileged member, you must understand social, political, and economic history. You must have an understanding of the arts. It is all very important."

Louis hung his head. "I know, Papa. I am sorry we have disappointed you."

Armand touched his son's shoulder. "You are good boys." He frowned. "But I don't understand what is happening to your brother. Where is he?"

"Jacques?" Louis was trying to think fast.

"Do you have another brother?" Armand was growing impatient of such nonsense. His sons had been sent down in disgrace from school nearly a month ago, and until this morning, he had not seen any remorse in either of them.

Louis stammered, "I . . . I did not see him when he went out this morning, Papa. I am sorry, but no doubt he went to visit Delacorte."

"Delacorte? At this hour? What then, is there a cockfight he needs must attend?" Armand grimaced. "I am sadly disappointed in your brother. He is the titled son and must bear the weight of example."

"He is only a year older than I, Papa, and, well, Jacques was always more restless than I." Louis attempted to defend Jacques, whom he adored.

"Yes, yes, it is well that you love one another," Armand frowned, "which also is another thing. Why does he leave you these days? You used to be inseparable."

Quick-thinking Louis looked at his shoes. "Perhaps there is a girl, Papa?"

"A girl?" Armand suddenly laughed. "Well, well. I see." He moved to his writing desk. "Ah, son, did you or Jacques borrow my diamond pocket watch?"

Louis blanched. "Pocket watch?"

"Yes, yes, you know it well," Armand snapped. "The one your mother gave me . . . I seem to recall putting it down on my desk yesterday where I usually leave it, and it was not there this morning." He shrugged. "No doubt I left it upstairs on my night table. No matter, it is somewhere in the house."

"I am sure of it, Papa," said Louis as he left the room and closed the door at his back. In the corridor he stood for a full moment. *Mon Dieu!* Not Papa's pocket watch!" No, it was impossible. Jacques would not, could not, have taken it. They both knew that it had been the last gift to their father just before their mother had died . . . Jacques wouldn't have—would he?

Farnsworth glanced at the beauty beside him and smiled to himself. She was enchanting in her pale pink ensemble. He silently applauded her taste in clothing, in colors, in the manner in which she conducted herself, but he wondered at her withdrawn nature this afternoon. He had found her far more vivacious in the past. Attempting to bring her out, he said, "Well, Lady Velvet, something other than the lovely spring day is on your pretty mind?"

"Now, my lord, how would you know that?"

"It shows in your fine green eyes."

"In my eyes? Well, there. You, too, seem to put a great deal of store in the content of one's eyes."

"Ah, someone else has been talking to you of your eyes?"

She smiled at him. "No, my lord, not of my eyes, but . . . never mind that. It is indeed a glorious day, and I was enjoying it. I compliment you on your matched bays. Did you make the journey with them or are they French blood?"

"They are, in fact, my cousin's team and phaeton. I traveled to Paris in my barouche."

"Madame Davenant's team, I see," said Velvet almost curtly.

"Ah, something *is* wrong. You do not like Madame Davenant?"

She smiled an apology. "Were that true, I certainly would not insult you by telling you so. We do not know each other well enough to trade blows yet, my lord."

"Your smile bewitches me, so by all means, have at me," he answered glibly.

Velvet shook her head. "I suppose you are looking forward to entertaining Napoleon tomorrow night?"

They were playing cat and mouse; he felt it, and the notion excited him. "Are not you?" Farnsworth smiled.

Velvet eyed him then quite seriously. "No, my lord, I am not. In fact, it quite worries me."

"Does it? It should not. Under the auspices of my cousin, an Englishman need have no fear, if that is what is on your mind. Besides, I doubt that Napoleon is ready to strike just yet, though I do agree with you. I think before the year is out our two countries will be at war."

"How dreadful . . . how absolutely dreadful! To be separated by war from my dearest relatives?"

"No, do not think of it," said Farnsworth, who managed to hold the driving reins with one hand

and take Velvet's hand with his other. He put her gloved fingers to his lips.

Velvet sighed. "No, I won't. Perhaps it is all a hum."

"Indeed, it is to be hoped." Farnsworth felt her remove her hand and said idly, "How was your ride this morning on Mr. Martin's horse?"

Velvet looked ruefully at him and answered, "Spirited, my lord, very spirited."

"Enjoyable, I take it."

"If you like," said Velvet evasively. She then spied Louis crossing the avenue and waved to him. He did not see her as he rushed across and then down the street into the crowd.

"One of the Beaupré lads?"

"Hmmm . . . cousins of mine, the Beauprés," said Velvet, wishing now their drive was over. Why was Louis rushing madly down the street? Why was he without Jacques? Was everything all right?

Was she warning him off, advising him that they were relatives? Well, well, there were depths to this girl. He eyed her and said after a moment, "They seem young to be on the town?"

She smiled indulgently. "Scamps! They were sent down, my lord, and in some disgrace."

"Ah, but their father coddles them." Farnsworth meant to be disapproving, meant to make her speak in their defense, wanted her to slip.

"No . . . What makes you say so?"

"Well, he allows them to go about."

"What? Should he shackle them?"

"No, as to that, of course not, but I would not

allow my sons to frequent the sort of places—well, I have said too much." He looked away from her and applauded himself on his acting.

Velvet turned white and then flushed, stammering, "Wh-what can you mean, my lord?"

"Nought, nought. Please forget . . ." He eyed her then, and as though confidingly, as though concerned, he said, "Though as their cousin, you might wish to advise them that their father, if he does not know, would not like to know that their nighttime games take them to forbidden parts of the city."

"My lord, I am greatly shocked. You should not be having this discussion with me," said Velvet.

" 'Tis only because I am convinced that it would distress you, Lady Velvet, to find the Beaupré boys had fallen into . . . bad company. I only mention it to you, because perhaps they would not like their father to know . . . under the circumstances, that is."

Instinct struggled with reason and won out. Velvet felt suddenly that to fall into this man's clutches would be like falling into the hands of the devil himself. She was being ridiculous, she told herself. This sudden feeling was absurd. Yet, just what was Farnsworth doing? Was there a veiled threat in what he had been saying? If so, why? To what purpose? What did he hope to gain?

Farnsworth had made his point. He drove it home by taking up her gloved hand once more and managing this time to find the skin beneath the lace at her wrist. His mouth gently touched her as he glanced up at her face and quietly said, "I know that I must return you now to your cousin, the comtesse, for I have kept you already too long. However, I can't tell you how eagerly I await tomorrow night when I hope to have the pleasure of waltzing with you at Madame Davenant's soirée."

Velvet said nothing to this. He was very certain that she and the Condés would attend the Davenant soirée. She wanted to snatch her hand away, but something that smelled of danger, danger to her loved ones, kept her hand in place and froze a smile on her face!

The marquis, his mouth agape, stood across the street and watched the perfidy in shocked silence. He couldn't believe his eyes. What was more, he knew and sensed that Velvet was not herself. She appeared to him like a trapped animal. Why? What was that blasted devil saying to her? What was going on here? Damn the man's lips! Damn the man's eyes! Damn his hands and his black heart! Talgarth would have his blood for this. He would tear out Farnsworth's insides and feed them to the dogs. He would, but at that moment Farnsworth managed to wend his way through the traffic that had momentarily stalled him on the street, and they were moving out of sight.

Talgarth turned to Gilly, who was beginning to pull at his neatly tied cravat in something of a fidget, and demanded, "Gilly, did you see that?"

Unhappily Gilly admitted that he had, but said, "There may be a perfectly good explanation, I am sure, Dustin. No need to have an apoplexy over the thing."

"Good explanation? Damnation, Gilly, you are forever defending the chit, but I tell you there is no defending her in this. She flouts my will at every turn. It's time I washed my hands of her. March her right back to England and into m'grandfather's care!"

"Dash it, no!" returned Gilly. "Not the time to leave Paris. Besides, you are making too much of it. Good little thing, Velvet—you are making her out to be some kind of she-devil."

"Blister it! There you go again. Gilly, she nearly got herself killed this morning. I thought my heart stopped, damn, I was *sure* my heart stopped when I saw her maneuver that horse of Martin. Thought she was going to fly over its head, thought . . . well, never mind. That's done with, but here she is allowing that blackguard to make love to her in public for all the world to see! I won't have it!"

"No, Farnsworth is a bad sort—not at all the man for little Velvet," agreed Gilly with a sigh. "What's to do? Can't leave Paris now, must see that."

"Don't see that at all."

"There is the ball the comtesse is having in Velvet's honor next week. Can't run out on it. Dastardly thing to do."

"Fire and brimstone, what care I for balls when Velvet is in danger?"

"Well as to that, can't say she is in danger." Gilly shook his head. "I mean, Farnsworth won't dare anything clandestine with Velvet. After all, she's a Colbury, you know . . . family and all."

"Wouldn't he, though? Gilly, I tell you the man would do anything to achieve his ends . . . anything."

"Then warn her of him. Tell her what he is," suggested Gilly.

"What sort of rum touch would I be then? I am not a bleater, Gilly."

Gilly shrugged. "Seems to me, if he oversteps the line, it wouldn't be blabbering; it would be speaking the truth."

"Not yet, Gilly, but mark me on this: I will put a stop to that fellow going after Velvet, and I mean to march right over to the Condé establishment and lay down the law."

"You know what, Dusty?" Gilly objected gently.

"Ay, I know what. I know that my grandfather has a veritable saucebox for a ward and I shall have my hands full until I can give her over to him!"

Fourteen

The marquis sprinted up the stone steps to the Condé town house and turned to frown at his lagging friend. "Are you coming, Gilly?"

"Well, yes," said Gilly blandly, "but I don't find it necessary to charge the comte's front door!"

The marquis gave him a withering look but refrained from answering him as he used the knocker and found himself admitted by the Condé butler. They had only taken a few steps into the large central hall when they were met by the Condé, hat in hand and obviously on his way out.

"Ah, Dustin, Sir Harold," said the comte with a smile. "I am sorry. My wife is out and not expected I think for at least an hour. Velvet, too, is out, though I must suppose she will be back shortly if you care to wait."

Talgarth went for the meat. "Are you aware, Condé, that Velvet is out driving with Farnsworth?"

Gilly reached over and pinched the marquis's arm through his sleeve. The marquis released a short howl and turned on his friend to gravely threaten him. Gilly glared back defiantly.

"Indeed, Dustin," said Condé. "My wife made me

aware of this circumstance before she left for the afternoon. I know it is not what you like. It is not what Marie or I like either, for we are in accord with you on the subject of Farnsworth. However, he drives with her in an open phaeton with a groom at their backs. It is most respectable and even fashionable. We could hardly forbid it to her." He put out his hand and invited, "Come, let us discuss this in my study. I have a moment before I must leave."

Gilly followed the two men into the study, a room decorated in brown velvet and gold braiding. Walls were lined with shelves of books and precious artwork. He looked about and took a backseat to the proceedings, for he had every confidence that Condé, who he greatly admired, would be quite able to handle the marquis. In this belief, he was able to relax. The comte was nearly as old and as wise as his own father had been when he had died three years ago. He could see that, although Dustin stood stiffly, he did lend an ear to the comte's reasoning.

"So, are you here to lecture my wife on the evils of allowing Velvet out with Farnsworth?" asked the comte, smiling.

"Well, er, not exactly, but I take leave to tell you that there are evils attached to everything Farnsworth does; in fact, when I saw them on the open street, the blackguard was attempting to make love to Velvet heedless of the public."

The comte's brows rose. "Quite a feat if he also had to manage his horses."

Gilly coughed. "Quite true about that. He was

kissing her wrist, looking into her eyes . . . stalled in traffic. Not the thing."

"I see. You are quite right to disapprove, but, again, my dear Dustin, only the veriest sticklers would find fault with such mild flirting, after all."

"Then I must be counted a stickler!" snapped the marquis, "And I don't mean to allow Velvet to attend that damn soirée tomorrow night."

"Ah, I am afraid you do not have a choice. Apparently we must make something of an appearance even if it is only for a short while. Napoleon mentioned the soirée to me himself. It would not do to insult Napoleon, my boy."

"Damn Napoleon. He insults me! Expects my ward to be present without her guardian."

"True, but he does not recognize you as her guardian. He hinted as much to me today. Said she is of French blood, my wife's family. He felt we should keep her as he doesn't trust English law."

"Well, I say," Gilly sputtered.

"I don't like this," said the marquis, frowning darkly. "I have a notion to whisk Velvet out of France before this gets dangerous."

"It is already dangerous. I have the feeling that Napoleon doesn't think First Consul is an elevated enough title. He is looking to war to achieve greater success. Next week Velvet will have her ball, and directly afterwards you may slip out of the country—quietly."

Gilly stood up. "Are you saying that war is imminent?"

"I am afraid so, *mon ami*. I think we have but a

month of peace left between our two countries."
The comte sighed. "Come, join me. We will walk to
my club together and play a set of cards, perhaps?"

Thus it was in a somber mood that the three men
left the house and made their way toward the
comte's club, unaware that their departure had been
observed by Velvet.

As Farnsworth had managed his team round the
bend, Velvet had caught sight of the comte linking
arms with both the marquis and Gilly as they left
the house. It was all she could do to refrain from
calling out to them, so great was her agitation. They
did not see her, and she prayed that Farnsworth
would not wish to enter the house with her when
he walked her to the door. She was heartily sick of
his pawing, insistent flirtation. He had followed her
line of vision but failed to see what it was that had
caught her attention as he handed the reins to his
groom and helped her out of the phaeton. "Something catch your pretty eye?"

"Hmmm," Velvet responded idly. "A new style of
walking dress."

"Shall I take you immediately to your favorite
modiste and buy it for you?"

She looked directly at Farnsworth and did not
smile. "How very improper of you to suggest such
a thing." She offered her hand but withdrew it before he could put it to his lips. "Thank you for the
drive, my lord." It was all she could bring herself
to say.

"Until tomorrow evening then," he answered
softly as he bowed himself off.

Velvet entered the house with a feeling of relief that nearly overcame her. She wanted to scream, but when she asked herself why, she wasn't able to answer. Farnsworth had frightened her, but it was nothing he had said, nothing he had done. There had just been something about the man, about the way he looked at her, talked to her, that had been chilling.

She went to the salon and discarded her hat, gloves, and spencer, then moved to the fire, now quite low as the room had been unoccupied for awhile. She picked up a small log and placed it on the burning embers, took up a poker, and fiddled for a moment. The door opened, and she looked up and round just as the butler announced, "Mr. Edward Martin."

Velvet went forward, hand outstretched in a warm welcome. "Mr. Martin, how very nice."

He bowed over her fingers, but made no attempt to kiss them, and Velvet felt relief. He sensed it at once, and as she invited him to sit, he asked, "What is it? What is wrong, and don't try and bamboozle me into thinking that there isn't anything amiss."

She smiled warmly at him and sat with him on the yellow damask sofa. "Now, Mr. Martin, what could possibly be wrong? I have only made a great fool of myself this morning and endangered that wonderful horse of yours. I wouldn't be surprised if you were here to tell me that I may not ride Sinbad anymore." Velvet's green eyes twinkled as she pulled a rueful face.

"I am here to tell you quite the opposite, Lady

Velvet,'' said Mr. Martin on a short laugh. ''I think you were magnificent this morning! Sinbad is very much the better for your no-nonsense handling, let me tell you.''

''Oh do, do tell me, sir, for I have been feeling so very low,'' said Velvet, leaning toward him eagerly.

Mr. Martin did not think his eyes had viewed such a vivacious beauty before. Her green eyes glistened with feeling, her cherry lips pursed so that he had to exert great restraint and refrain from kissing her. He could not resist, however, from taking her small hands and holding them tightly. ''Dear Lady Velvet, I could not bear it if I thought you were brought low because of Sinbad or because of me.''

''Sinbad? You? Oh never, never. 'Twas because of me and my foolishness,'' Velvet assured him, giving the hands that held hers a soft squeeze. ''I must appear a complete hoyden in your eyes.''

''In my eyes? Dearest girl, you appear a goddess in my eyes,'' said Mr. Martin gallantly. He took her precious hands and pressed an almost feverish kiss upon her knuckles for emphasis.

The marquis halted in mid-stride and advised his companions, ''Going back!''

''Going back? But where, dear boy?'' inquired the Comte de Condé in some surprise.

''He means he is going back to your establishment, Comte,'' said Gilly on a resigned note. ''No doubt he'll drag me along . . . always drags me along. Forced me to leave my hounds and come here to Paris with him—though I don't mind as much now—but there you are . . . never telling where Dusty will end."

This speech so bewildered the comte that he brought up his quizzing glass and eyed Gilly doubtfully. Gilly was quick to assure him, "Don't fret, Comte. You can go along to your club. Don't think Dusty wants you. Just me. Don't know why, but there it is."

"Don't want you either," snapped the marquis. "You run along with the comte and enjoy yourself, ol' fellow. Mean to have a word or two with Velvet, and then I'll follow."

The comte accepted this gracefully, though he cautioned, "Of course, though, it has been my experience with women that one does better for oneself when the temper has cooled. Time has a wondrous way of putting matters in proper order, you know."

"Don't have time!" announced the marquis, who waved himself off and strode purposefully back to the Condé house. This he reached in less than seven minutes. The butler wished to announce him, but the marquis put the fellow off, saying he knew very well where the salon was located. Thus the marquis walked in to find Velvet's hands being feverishly kissed by Mr. Edward Martin.

Talgarth further witnessed the two on the sofa hurriedly, guiltily almost, jump apart. "So!" he boomed.

"My lord," greeted Velvet at once, "where is Gilly?" She attempted to create some light conversation. " 'Tis so unusual to find you without Gilly in tow."

"Mr. Martin," the marquis managed to nod politely, "I see your sister is not here with you."

Mr. Martin shook his head and attempted a smile as he got to his feet and inched toward the door. "No, she had some shopping this afternoon. I begged off . . ."

"And were lucky enough to find my ward home alone," said the marquis, regally acting the part. "Well, we look forward to seeing you tonight. Gilly tells me you and your lovely sister will be attending the Champagne fete."

"That's right, my lord. Monsieur Champagne and his sister were such good friends of my mother's, you see. I am quite looking forward to it."

Martin made his farewell bow to Velvet. Obviously the marquis had dismissed him. He was a fair-minded man, though, and felt that Talgarth was certainly in the right of it. He had no business dallying with Velvet when he found her alone. It was just that he could not resist.

Edward Martin had been gone just about a second when the marquis turned on Velvet. He was angry, but not in the white rage he had experienced during the morning. "Tell me, minx. . . . Do you allow every man to plant fevered kisses on your fingers and wrists?"

Velvet put up her chin. "Not every man, no."

"Ah, but Farnsworth? He is allowed your wrist?"

Velvet faltered. "Well—"

"And Martin?" interrupted the marquis, his blue

eyes gleaming as he moved closer to her and took her shoulders. "Is he a favorite?"

"Oh, as to that, I like Edward Martin very much," answered the lady.

"As much as Farnsworth?" Talgarth needed to know the depth of her feelings for Farnsworth.

"I don't think I even like Lord Farnsworth," said Velvet, looking away from the intensity of his blue eyes.

"You don't even like him, yet you defy me and drive out with the man?"

The marquis was angry now, and he shook her shoulders, then found himself bending to kiss her mouth. He was very near those cherry lips when all at once he recalled who he was, who she was, what they were to each other. He was acting as her guardian. What in thunder was he doing? He was behaving no better than Farnsworth. Damn his soul, he had almost stolen a kiss from her!

The marquis fairly threw her from himself. "Do you see? That is how easily a man can take advantage of you. You are nought but a green girl . . . a child." He was backing away from her, running his hand through his hair.

Velvet stared at him. He had nearly kissed her, and, oh faith, how much she had wanted that kiss! She had thought finally he wanted her, finally he cared, but no, no, all it had been was a lesson. He only wanted to show her up as a fool. How could he be so heartless? She managed to look away from his burning blue eyes and say, "My lord, I am so very tired. It has not been a good day. I think I will retire to my room."

He took a step forward. He had made her miserable. What kind of a cad was he? What was wrong with him? He had never treated a woman so shabbily. Why was he forever ranting and raving? He was a brute. He found himself taking her hand, amazed that she allowed him to do so.

"No, not yet. Not like this. Velvet . . ."

The door opened, and Marie stood in its threshold, feeling sparks of electricity in the air. Her fine brows rose expressively, and because no one realized she was there, she said merrily, *"Voyons!* I am here."

The marquis turned around and managed a smile. "Ah, so you are, Marie. I am glad of it." He sighed wearily. "I have made poor sport of my little one, all because you were not here and she was alone with Edward Martin."

"Ah, you are very right. The proprieties . . . Tedious, but they must always be observed. Did he make desperate love to you, my dear?" Marie touched Velvet's cheek.

All at once, Velvet could stand no more. She looked from the marquis to Marie and, with a sob, fled the room. Marie's eyes rounded as she turned on the marquis with a wagging finger. "What have you done, you dreadful man?"

"Nothing, everything. I have scolded her to death. First the horse, then Farnsworth, then Martin here kissing her fingers as though he were at her lips! Don't tell me. I know I am the very devil," said the marquis in the throes of unhappiness.

"*Non, non* . . . You are but a man after all. Go now and let her rest. I will see her later."

"Yes, but, Marie, this Farnsworth. . . . I won't have it, you know. He must not be allowed near her."

"Tell me, dearest, why is this so?"

"Suffice it to say that he is evil to the heart."

"It is not enough. Tell me, what he has done to you?"

"To me, to another . . . It was beyond repair and without remorse." He shook his head. "Trust me, Marie, he does not want Velvet; he wants at me!"

Fifteen

Farnsworth sipped at his brandy as Madame Davenant flipped through some invitations at her writing desk. She glanced at him to say idly, "I think you should prepare yourself to return to England by the end of the month. I tell you, *mon cher*, that it will be dangerous for Englishmen in Paris before long."

"Indeed, I stay only long enough to attend Lady Velvet's ball."

"What can it hope to get you chasing that one, eh? You have said yourself her guardian, Talgarth's *grand-père*, will never give his consent to the match. What will you do?"

"I mean to have Velvet Colbury one way or another."

"Bah! It is obsession with you, Dale. You should be wise and forget her."

"Trust me in this, darling cousin of mine. I will have Velvet Colbury."

"Yes, yes, but how?"

"I am working on it. Perhaps her cousins may help."

"You speak in riddles. I think you are mad."

"Perhaps, just perhaps, but I do not leave France until she is my bride." He stared at the brew in the elegant snifter. "Indeed, and it will not be long coming!" Obsession? Perhaps. He had not started his courtship feeling this way, but he had not known that Talgarth was actually her guardian. Damn his soul! Farnsworth felt a welling of hatred both unreasonable as it was deep and sure. Talgarth's grandfather would never allow him to court Velvet; on this his cousin was correct.

There, too, Lady Velvet had not been receptive today to his flirtation. Could it be that Talgarth had actually broke from his code of honor and told her of his sin? No. Velvet would not have driven out with him had she known. What then? Why had he seen a look of fear when he had tried to bring matters to a point, to let her know where his flirtation was headed? Why had she not invited him further? Well, well, no matter. Lady Velvet was his for the taking, and that taking was going to happen. Velvet was going to be his, as much now to spite Talgarth as to enjoy having her in his own bed!

His face contorted as he thought of Talgarth, who held himself up as superior! So very superior that he would not stoop to spread the tale of what Farnsworth had done all those years ago. Talgarth would not talk about it because to do so would be to dishonor the girl's family. To do so would not be honorable. Honor? Such an intangible thing. How did honor ever benefit anyone? It did not. Honor sent a hero to his death! Honor demanded by gentlemen of gentlemen. Well, he had managed to fool

them all, and honor had never a thing to do with
his dealings! Honor, indeed!

Marie knocked on Velvet's door but did not wait
for the invitation as she opened it and peeped round
the edge. *"Voilà!* Look at me! What think you?"

Velvet eyed her cousin admiringly, for Marie was
clothed in pink and silver. She sparkled from the
top of her short curls to her dainty toes. She held
a pink spangled mask on a stick and teased Velvet
by putting it to her eyes saying, *"Voyons!* With this I
am *très mystérieux,* am I not?"

Velvet clapped her hands. "Beautiful. You are
bang up to the mark!"

"Bang up? What is this?" Marie wrinkled her
nose.

Velvet got to her feet and went to hug her cousin.
"It is a man's vulgar expression, but it means you
are very much the thing, very much in style."

"Ah, *oui,* this is true," laughed Marie happily. She
took Velvet's bare shoulders and spun her around.
"Tiens! You are not only beautiful, *ma petite,* but
there is something more . . . perhaps too naughty
for one your age. This gold silk, it hugs your figure,
oui? Oui! It is cut lower than I remember. How is
that?" She waved the objection off. "Never mind. It
passes in Paris, though not, I think, in London. You
wear this tonight, eh? *Moi,* I think you mean to break
a man's heart tonight. Who is this man you wish to
break?"

Velvet's smile vanished all at once. "No, oh Marie, I do not."

"La, *ma petite*, so much fuss you make? Why?" Marie clucked her tongue and snapped her finger across the air before Velvet's frowning face. "This I do not understand. It is not a bad thing to break a man's heart. *Non*, it is a thing wonderful, for it teaches them how to love. This is something they must be taught, you know. If a man's heart has never been touched, bent, he walks about like a bull in a pasture, surveying all, taking all. If some lovely woman touches him here," Marie's hands went to her chest, "and here," then to her forehead, "ah, well, then perhaps that woman or another woman can make of him a man instead of a bull. Understand?"

Velvet laughed. "Marie, that is dreadful."

"*Non, non*, 'tis true. Men are very full of themselves, you know. They need women to show them the way. In such a gown, *ma chèrie*, you shall show them the way. Ah, one must pity the bulls tonight."

They laughed, then Velvet took up her shawl and started forward, only to hesitate. "The thing is, I cannot be certain that Dus—the marquis will think this gown respectable enough. His notions seem far stricter than I remember them to be in the past."

"This is strangely true. Dustin was a merrymaker when I knew him in Italy. Tsk, tsk, never mind. Your gown is provocative, daring, Parisian at its finest, but it is respectable, *enfin!*" Marie eyed her thoughtfully. "Your dragon marquis will not be displeased; this I promise you."

Velvet smiled softly. "He is a dragon of a man, is he not?"

"*Oui*, an oddity. An idiosyncrasy, as you English would say. *Moi*, I say he is a rogue who does what suits him, and it suits him now to . . . well, watch over you." Marie shook her head. "Never mind. Soon your dragon rogue will see you, and we shall know what he thinks, is this not so?"

"*Oui, oui*, Marie, this is so!" laughed Velvet as she followed her cousin out of the room.

The Champagne family was a wondrous mixture of old and new regime, full of playfulness and old-world traditions. Outside, their garden was lit with gaslights and had been decorated with flowers. Music and revelry filled the air. Many of the guests had even worn costumes, delighting in one another's imagination.

Indoors, a buffet dinner had been set, a huge floor had been cleared for dancing, and another orchestra played. Everywhere there was wine, laughter, and young people in high spirits. Velvet created no little sensation when she entered the ballroom and was immediately accosted by several young bucks demanding to dance with her. However, she put them all off, except for Edward Martin, to whom she promptly gave her hand, allowing to lead her off. Thus, the marquis, when he walked in only a moment later, was able to see his exquisite ward at her most elegant doing the steps of the cotillion.

Marie was quick to greet him. "It is *très bien,* is it not?"

"The fete? Indeed, first rate." The marquis smiled, then bent gallantly over her proffered hand. "As you are."

"And your ward? She is not really your ward, but I suppose I must call her that in the absence of your grandfather." She sighed mockingly. "A terrible responsibility, for I can see it weighs heavily on you and destroys your peace and your, shall we say, good humor. . . . *Oui,* we should say that."

He acknowledged the hit amiably. "Yes, we should say that. I'll be deuced glad to hand her over to m'grandfather and have done. Playing nursemaid to a wild minx of a girl is not what I have been bred to do." He watched Velvet move and noted the way the gown moved with her. "Did you choose that piece of gold material? I must say there is not very much to it."

"It activates the imagination, but reveals nought. *Oui,* I chose it. Velvet was concerned that you would not approve."

"Yet she wore it anyway," he said quietly.

"Only at my insistence. I did not think you would disapprove. Do you?"

He grinned. "No, Marie, I don't. She is a beauty, a completely natural beauty." He frowned. "Martin seems taken with her."

"*Oui,* but, me, I don't think he will do for Velvet, though she shows a decided preference for him. In fact, I have not seen her care for any man quite as much as she likes this Edward Martin." She nodded toward Leslie Martin huddled in a corner with Gilly. "His sister intrigues our Gilly, does she not?"

"Confound it, there is a sure truth in that," laughed the marquis. "Have my hands full with these Martins in town."

"You do not like the Martin girl for your friend?"

"Well as to that . . ." The marquis shrugged. "Don't know her. . . . Don't want Gilly hurt, for he just might be in earnest, and she . . . well, mayhap she is just passing the time."

"Ah, you do not give your friend enough credit, my rogue. Clearly you have not thought this out." Marie drifted off on that remark, and the marquis moved toward Velvet, for the music had stopped and Martin was walking her off the dance floor.

"Mr. Martin." The marquis inclined his head, but his blue eyes were on Velvet.

Edward Martin smiled a return greeting, but his attention also was on Velvet. He turned and excused himself. "I see my hostess motioning to me, Lady Velvet, but I hope to have the pleasure of your company again before the night is over."

"I look forward to it," said Velvet sincerely before she turned to the marquis, an inquiry in her green eyes. "Hallo, my lord. Am I still out of favor?"

"Do you want to be?" Again the twinkle had returned to his deep blue eyes.

"How could you think so?" she twinkled back. "Have I somehow given you the impression that I am a surly, brazen, defiant schoolgirl? How can that be?"

"Indeed, what a sad character I must be to ever

have thought such a thing of such an enchanting creature. Velvet, you do quite take a man's breath away."

"Do I? Every man's breath?" she teased. "Faith, are all the men in this room gasping for air? I must leave at once."

He threw back his head and laughed from the heart, and then put an arm about her shoulders. "Have I told you what a delightful trial you are to me?"

"Not quite in those words," she answered saucily.

He chuckled. "Well, I am sorry if I have behaved like an old twiddle-poop. 'Tis all so new to me, this job of guardian."

"Oh no, Dusty, you have not once behaved like a twiddle-poop," returned Velvet anxiously. "It was I. I have been so dreadful—with the horse, and then Farnsworth. But he invited me out for a drive, and I was not able to decline gracefully. Please believe me, Dusty."

He gave her shoulders a squeeze. "I do, love, I do. Do you not like Farnsworth, then?"

"No, I do not. There is something about him that almost frightens me."

"There is no need to be frightened of him, though, truth be told, he is the very devil, without a heart, without pity or compassion, but he shan't hurt you while I am about," said the marquis grimly.

"What did he do to you, Dusty? What could he have done?"

He touched her cheek with his free hand, and all at once he realized he was holding her far too tightly. He let her go. "Never mind that. So then, minx, you do not like Farnsworth, but you do like Edward Martin?"

"Oh yes, very much. He is witty, he is amusing, and ever so ready to understand . . ." Her voice trailed off as she noted the fanfare given to Madame Davenant and Lord Farnsworth's entrance. "Dusty, they are here."

Velvet's whispered words, her stiffening beside him, made him realize just how much she dreaded meeting both Davenant and Farnsworth. He looked at Velvet, and his blue eyes were intense as his tone was grave. "Velvet child, shall we leave tomorrow? We can be packed and on the road to Le Havre where I have my yacht and crew awaiting us."

Velvet was momentarily diverted. "In Le Havre? I thought Gilly said you came from Dover to Calais?"

"We did," Talgarth pinched her chin, "and I had my crew sail down to Le Havre. I thought the return trip would be nicer for you overland to Le Havre."

She touched Talgarth's fingers. "Oh, Dusty, how thoughtful. Then we shall sail into Portsmouth?"

"Aye, do you like Portsmouth?"

"Yes, oh yes. 'Tis near the New Forest, where my grandfather had one of his estates, you know."

"Well then, girl. Shall we take to the road?" The marquis was ready to go. He was uneasy now in France, and he would not be comfortable again until he had Velvet back in England.

"Oh, would that we could," sighed Velvet. "But Marie has been planning this ball for me for months. We cannot run out on her, and, too, it would not be right to leave in such haste. It would not look good for Marie and the comte with the First Consul, you know."

The marquis frowned. "There is that! Damn, I don't like it—ho, what's this?" He looked up to find Madame Davenant coming toward them. "Does she really think she can come over here and take you away from me and give you to her blasted cousin?"

"Can she do that?" Velvet asked, wide-eyed. "I hope not."

He laughed, "No, pet, she cannot." He was already leading her toward one of the musicians. A moment later a coin was exchanged, and one of the new waltzes was struck up with a wink and an inclination of the head. The marquis drew his ward to him by her waist and took strong hold. One hand was held high, near his shoulder, as he led her through the steps of the new dance.

Velvet's green eyes sparkled, because in England the waltz was not yet accepted. "Well, my lord, I must say you dance the waltz ever so beautifully." She felt him gently lead her about, and they moved as one unit, flowing about the room as though they scarcely touched the floor.

"Ah, practice, my girl." He grinned scampishly down at her pixie countenance.

"How is that? I did not think the waltz had the approval of the Jersey?"

"No, no . . . you are out there. She withholds approval at Almack's for the new debutantes only." He shrugged. "There are many households which still do not allow the waltz in their ballrooms. Sticklers."

"And, of course, you approve?" she teased, her green eyes lighting.

" 'Tis the best of all dances. You see how close a man gets to hold a woman, steer her about. Oh yes, I learned it very quickly," he bantered.

He saw Edward Martin hanging about in the wings. "No doubt," he continued after a moment, "Martin will lead you out next if he can?"

Velvet could not miss the sudden darkling look that came into his eyes and inquired doubtfully, "Don't you like Edward Martin?"

"Aye, I suppose I do," admitted the marquis.

"Then why should I not dance with him?"

"No reason," sighed Talgarth reluctantly, and then added, "I suppose 'tis only that I don't find him quite good enough for you, Velvet."

She laughed. "Now *that* is a piece of nonsense, and besides, we are not talking of marriage, but of dancing, friendship, and such. Oh, Dusty, how funny you are."

The marquis clamped his lips together, for he did not want to injure the pleasant mood of the moment. The truth was that he could find nothing wrong with Edward Martin, but he wasn't for his Velvet. That was the long and the short of it. "As to that," he said at last, "you need a Season amongst the beau monde in London—choose a fellow from our own set. Shouldn't make up your mind till you have a look over at home."

"Well, how very calculating," said Velvet, suddenly very depressed. So he wasn't jealous. He just

wanted her to choose a man after a London Season
and make a distinguished match.

"Not calculating. But, well, Velvet, you are a beautiful woman with a large competence. Need to be
sure the man who wins you, deserves you."

She touched Talgarth's cheek. "How sweet."

As he twirled her and she held his face, they came
closer, and he knew a sudden urge to kiss her cherry
lips. Damnation! This was absurd. She was his
ward . . . in a manner of speaking. He shouldn't be
feeling such things. He would have to keep her at a
distance. Setting her farther from his chest, they
continued to waltz about the room, and far too soon
the waltz was over. With something of an effort, he
released her, but she held his hand and looked up
at him, troubled. "My lord, have you seen Jacques
or Louis this evening?"

"No, why? Shall I look for them? I see their father
talking with that Davenant woman right now, in fact.
Devil a bit! No doubt she is inviting Armand as well
to her little soirée tomorrow night. Deucedly provoking . . . her neglecting to invite Gilly and me,
you know."

"Yes, I certainly do think it was on purpose, but
then you make no secret of your dislike of Lord
Farnsworth."

All at once Edward Martin was there bowing over
Velvet's hand. "It's my good fortune that the orchestra is striking up another waltz," he said as he pulled
her onto the floor.

The marquis watched as Velvet gave a small smile
and went easily into his hold. Damn the man's eyes!

He frowned over the problem. He rather liked Edward Martin, and after all, there was no harm in his dancing with Velvet, was there? No harm, he held her too tightly! He held her too close! Deuce take the fellow, he was looking down into her eyes with something far too close to passion!

Talgarth sighed over this minor irritation, but he was momentarily distracted by the sight of Farnsworth staring at the couple on the dance floor. Talgarth started forward, for he wanted to go and have a word with Lord Farnsworth once and for all! However, Farnsworth saw him coming and disappeared into the crush of people at his back.

Sixteen

Louis sat at the writing desk in his father's library, a quill in hand. There were letters from friends that needed to be answered, but his mind wandered with deep thoughts. The morning was filled with sunshine, and the sweet scent of spring flowers was brought to him from the courtyard through the open window. Jacques had not returned home last night, and his younger brother was sick over the problem.

The library door opened, and there, looking fresh as a newly opened spring bud, was Jacques. "Louis! There you are. What! Never say you are at work on such a glorious morning?"

Louis stared at his older brother as anger welled up inside him. There he stood as though he had done nothing wrong. It was almost unforgivable. But though Jacques was groomed and well-dressed, Louis could see the darkness under his eyes. "Close the door, Jacques," Louis said on a low, hard note.

Jacques was surprised but did as his brother commanded, laughing it off as he entered the room and approached the table laden with a tray of coffee, hot chocolate, and freshly baked buns. "Ah, coffee . . . Shall I pour you a cup?"

"No, I have had my coffee, thank you." Louis watched his brother sip at the dark brew and finally could contain himself no longer. "It grieves me to say this to you, Jacques, but you are like a stranger to me. I don't know what has happened to my brother."

Jacques was startled. He stared at his younger brother. "What the devil is all this? I go off a few days without you and suddenly I am a stranger? What, must we be forever together?"

"No, and you know that is not the problem. Jacques, you stole Father's watch!"

Jacques turned white, and he lost his composure for a moment. "Never say Papa knows . . . ?"

Louis couldn't believe it. He knew that Jacques had taken it, but even so, his brother's easy admission was very hard to accept. "No, he doesn't know it was taken. He thinks it was misplaced."

"Bon, bon. Well, I have put it back this morning in his top drawer."

"But, Jacques, you took it. How could you?"

"Never mind that. I borrowed it, and I was very lucky last night. I was able to retrieve it and quite a sum on top of that." Jacques patted his side where he had a wad of bills in the inner pocket of his coat.

"Jacques, have you lost your mind? You could have lost Papa's watch. It was given to him by our mother, and you could have lost it."

"But I did not," Jacques said complacently. "So, 'tis done. Forget it. No one was hurt."

"You were!"

"What ails you, little brother?"

"What ails me? You, you ail me. You gamble without caution, without sense for more than a moment's pleasure, and in the worst possible dives. You sleep with a whore in an opium den, and the last time I looked upon you, you were not drunk with brandy but with opium! My brother, who I have ever looked up to, is taking opium! How can this be? Why?"

"What? Am I so different from Papa?" Jacques struck back angrily. "Does he not gamble? Does he not drink? Does he not whore around? And as to the opium . . . I tried it only once just to know what it was. I shall not touch it again."

"You are nothing like Papa; sorry to say, Jacques! Do not compare yourself with him. Papa is a gentleman. If he gambles, he does it with friends and not among the dregs of our countrymen! If Papa gambles, he does so in moderation, and he does not steal another's property in order to do so! If Papa whores around . . . Well, he has lost our mother and must have a female, but he does not choose them from the gutter! No, you are not doing what Papa does!"

"Louis?"

"There is nought you can say. I have lied for you. I have taken care that Papa does not know what is toward, but if you persist, I shall not protect you any longer."

"Louis?" Jacques repeated his brother's name once more.

"What?"

"Go to the devil!" Jacques started for the door. " 'Tis where I am headed, so perhaps we shall meet there."

"Jacques! Jacques!" Louis called after him, but his brother had already left.

At home, Velvet was still in her soft lavender riding ensemble, though her top hat had been discarded, leaving her golden curls in a beguiling disarray round her pretty countenance. Sinbad had attempted a playful trick or two during his schooling session, and Velvet had managed him wonderfully.

Edward Martin was duly impressed and excitedly found Velvet's hands as he warmly thanked her. "How have I put up with the brute and his cavalier manners? 'Tis no wonder he was not welcome in the hunting field, but there is no doubt I shall be able to hunt Sinbad next season after you are finished with him. What he needed was a woman's instinct to catch him up!"

Velvet wagged a finger at him. "A woman's instinct, is it? Why not a woman's skill?"

He bent low. "I beg your pardon, Lady Velvet, and bow to your superior skill."

She slapped the top of his head lightly. "Stop! You know very well 'tis not superior skill but different purposes. He will go on being a bad boy if you encourage him as you have done in the past, and this week will mean nought. You must reinforce his lessons always. He will still give you speed when you ask for it, and he has heart, he will never lose that, but manners, Mr. Martin, are a must. You house him, feed him, groom him, and in return he must do his job."

Edward Martin laughed out loud. "True, absolutely. I have just been too lazy to give him the leg-work. I have just slipped into the saddle and held on for dear life—so much fun, you see. I suppose I am a devil."

"Not a devil, Mr. Martin, but a man," teased Velvet.

Leslie Martin, followed by Gilly and the marquis, entered the room at this precise moment, and Mr. Martin's sister immediately dove into the conversation with great enthusiasm. "Silly creatures, all of them!" However, she then chanced to find Gilly's eyes on her and happily amended, "Well, perhaps not all . . ."

Gilly blushed and played with his hat. Mr. Martin grinned and said amiably, "Well, and thank you, dear sister. Where have you been at all morning?"

"Breakfasting with these two gentlemen and the Comte de Beaupré at the hotel." She released a mock sigh. "What else could I do when you and Velvet deserted me for the lures of Sinbad?" She moved toward the open window overlooking a court-yard filled with spring blooms. " 'Tis a lovely morning. Faith, we have been blessed. I don't think it has rained in a week!"

During this time the marquis had been strangely silent. He had not missed the fact that Edward Martin was in high spirits and that he and Velvet were apparently getting along very well. In truth, he liked

Martin, if he were honest about it, Edward Martin was a fine match for Velvet. However, truths were annoying things, and at the moment he pushed them off. After all, his grandfather wanted Velvet safely delivered to England for her Season. That was his job, and that was what he intended to accomplish. Besides, Velvet was too young to settle on Martin. What did she know of such things?

He noted at that moment that Martin leaned over to hear something Velvet was saying and that he managed to touch her arm as she spoke to him. Damn the fellow's impudence!

Velvet had smiled a greeting at the marquis when the three had walked into the morning room. She had an urge to go straight to him, but she couldn't very well leave Edward Martin in mid-sentence. She did, however, manage to introduce a subject on which Gilly immediately became animated, and that was on Sinbad's suitability as a hunting steed. She left Martin to Gilly's description of a perfect hunter and went straight up to the marquis to say in a bantering manner, "Well, are you not going to ask how I did?"

"How you did what?" Talgarth grinned, for he knew full well what she was talking about.

Velvet's hand went to her hip. "I shall tell you, my lord, that I taught Sinbad a thing or two, and I shall do so again tomorrow and tomorrow and tomorrow!"

"Ah, Sinbad, is it? From my vantage point, seems to me that it is Edward Martin that is getting the lessons."

"What can you mean?" Velvet blinked in surprise.

"Say you do not know," he demanded impatiently.

"I do not know."

"Idiot," said the marquis.

This was not something that Velvet could take with equanimity, and her green eyes sparkled with fire as she attempted to control her temper and give him a cool set-down. The marquis was too fast for her, though.

He realized the error of his ways almost immediately and clasped her shoulders. For a moment it was as though no one else was there, and he had to shake this feeling off. He smiled at her and said, "Beautiful idiot. What I mean to say in my clumsy manner is that he learns of bewitching charm in your company, Velvet. You are most certainly the most ravishing woman in all of Paris, and poor Martin is falling fast."

"Do you think so?" Velvet felt as though she was dreaming. He thought her ravishing. He thought her a woman, not a child, but a woman. She was not referring to Martin's infatuation but to Dustin's opinions.

Talgarth frowned. "Don't you? Are you so blind that you don't see what is happening, or are you a tease, Velvet?"

She awoke from the dream with a snap. "A what? Oooh! You are forever rude, my lord. No, I am not a tease, but you—well, there is no saying what you are!"

She turned away from him and moved off to sit with Leslie Martin, who was mesmerized by Gilly's oration on hunting, hounds, and prime bloods. "He loves the chase," said Leslie simply.

"Does he?" Velvet asked, and then with dawning, "Oh, you mean Gilly and the hunt. Yes, I believe 'tis his greatest passion."

"Hmmm. Must see if I can make it his second greatest passion."

Velvet eyed her with sure understanding, and then touched her hand. "Oh, Leslie, I am so glad. I have thought Gilly in love from the moment he discovered you were in Paris. Such a look came into his eyes."

"What do you mean?"

"The day in the park, Leslie, when your brother came upon us and we exchanged names. Why, you should have seen Gilly's face." Velvet giggled.

"But we had only met briefly . . ." Leslie blushed. "Oh, and I thought it was only me. I came away from the dance with Gilly wishing that we would meet again soon." She shook her head. "You must know what an oddity that is, for I am not a romantic, yet here I am feeling as though I fell in love at first sight." Leslie vanished into her thoughts, which was just as well as Velvet sighed over this and turned to find the marquis contemplating her gravely. She had to restrain herself, for she had the sudden infantile urge to stick her tongue out at him. Instead she mustered up some genuine sang-froid and gave him a frigid shoulder.

The Marquis of Talgarth was not used to such behavior from a woman. He was considered quite a prize on the marriage market and had discovered that women, whether enamored of his charms or not, usually fawned and swooned for his attentions. He was baffled by his feelings for Velvet. He was baffled by Velvet's behavior. He was baffled by his own clumsiness in handling her. This was not like him. He had always known what to do in every given situation. This new sense of total confusion was most disconcerting.

He went toward Velvet with the sudden resolve to sit her down and talk it out. However, this admirable decision was stopped by the comtesse, who burst into the room in an explosion of excitement to say, "La, darlings. You are all here. This is an excellent thing, for I have the choicest piece of gossip to give to you. *Mon Dieu,* you will scarcely credit it. Only think what I have discovered about our First Consul's dearest Josephine!"

Jacques sulked as he made his way to his new favorite gaming hell. He made excuses for himself as his mind grumbled about his brother, his father. He rationalized his motives for his destination, and within a short period after his arrival, he had managed to consume a quantity of some very poorly made brandy.

He was on his fourth glass of this awful brew and blowing a cloud with his new set of friends when the fancy piece of his choice strutted by. He reached out, grabbed her by the waist, and pulled her onto his lap. His new set of friends laughed loudly over his antics. He liked these fellows. They were different from any of the boys he had ever known. They were full of wit, untold mysteries, experiences he had never dreamed of, and they seemed to have formed a deep affection for his company. He was enjoying the attention.

He was also enjoying his manhood, discovered in the skills of the girl on his lap. He was thrilled to be able to touch a woman at will. Until recently women were things that evoked desire, but one could only gaze and long for their touch. Well, no more. Catalina was his for the taking whenever he wanted, and when she was close like this, he wanted her all the time. "Eh, Catalina, shall we go upstairs?"

"Non, it is early yet. We will play first," she teased as she nibbled on his ear and deftly worked her fingers over his shoulders.

"Now. I want to go up now," he insisted.

"First you will buy for us a dream?" she whispered. She was an opium addict. She was seventeen but looked thirty. She was a prostitute and had been for five years, and there was nothing more in life that she wanted except for the dreams that opium could bring.

Jacques did not like taking opium. It frightened him. He had tried it with her the other night, and he had been badly shaken by its strong effects. He knew from talk at school how addicting opium could be, and he did not want to be caught up in that kind of web. The gentleman in him did not want her to have it either. *"Non.* Those dreams will only lead us away from each other. Come, we will make our own dreams," Jacques cajoled sweetly.

"*Mais oui,* oh Jacques. A dream for me at least . . ." she coaxed. "I will show you such things . . . teach you new tricks. Come . . . buy for me a dream. Please, Jacques, do not deny me this pleasure."

He frowned. To his way of thinking opium was a danger. "*Non,* Catalina, *non.*"

She jumped off his lap in a fit of impatience. She needed the opium to get her through the afternoon, through the evening. "You want me, Jacques? You meet my price!" She turned her back and started off.

He reached out for her wrist, and she shrugged his hold off with disgust. "Moonling! You are a boy, not a man."

Jacques started after her when a voice called his attention. "Let her go, Beaupré. Men such as we do not chase after whores like that. There are better, healthier than she to be had by such as yourself."

The man spoke in French, but Jacques felt he was English. He looked at him. The man knew him, and Jacques had a vague notion that he had seen him before somewhere . . . met him somewhere. Jacques was embarrassed, for he had not liked to be spoken to in such a manner, but politely he inclined his head. "As you say. Do I know you, sir?"

"Indeed. We met at your aunt's some days ago when I was paying a morning call to Lady Velvet. And I am well acquainted with your father."

"*Mon Dieu,*" breathed Jacques. His knees suddenly felt weak. This was the end. He was so ashamed. To be caught—here—by one of his father's cronies? *Mon Dieu, mon Dieu, mon Dieu!*

"Non, non, Jacques. Do not think I mean to take you to task. Do not think I will go running to your father. I am a firm believer in a lad's coming of age, exploring life unhampered by parental ties. Armand shall not know of your little hideaway from me," Lord Farnsworth said lazily. He looked round and casually invited, "Here, sit with me, Jacques. Let us enjoy an afternoon drink together?"

"Eh bien," said Jacques, much relieved. He pulled up a chair at the nearby corner table and stared at Farnsworth. "Pardon, your name, it escapes me."

"Ah, of course. Lord Farnsworth. English, like your so charming cousin, Lady Velvet. In fact, it is my great hope that we may all be related soon."

Jacques eyed him dubiously and then comprehension dawned. "Oh, you are a suitor of Velvet's? Oh, well as to that, there is never any saying what Velvet wants." He chuckled, now very much at ease.

"Is there not? Well, yes, of course, she must have many suitors?"

"Oh, *oui, oui.* My tante Marie is forever turning them off." He leaned toward Farnsworth confidentially. "It is my personal belief that she is holding out for an Englishman." He shrugged. "Me, this I cannot understand. The English are so cold-blooded; how can they make good lovers?" He then realized that the man opposite was English, and he blushed deep red.

Farnsworth felt himself stiffen, but this was no time to take umbrage with a puppy. Better to have the puppy in his hands, deep in his hands. "Yes, it is as you say. However, Lady Velvet is an English-woman. No doubt she will in the end be more comfortable living with an English husband."

"Yes, yes, of course." Jacques hurried to repair his error and drank down his bumper of ale quickly.

"Look, I have a few hours with nought to occupy me. Would you care to play at cards? A gentleman's game—gentleman's wagers, of course."

"*Oui*, with great pleasure I will play with you."

"Good. Very good," said Lord Farnsworth, calling for a deck of cards with the snap of his fingers. Indeed, he meant to have Jacques very much in his hands, and so the afternoon passed into evening!

Seventeen

Velvet was dressed in satin the color of bronze. Her hair glittered with topaz ribbon, which had been threaded throughout the carefully styled disorder of blond curls. The comtesse beside her was wreathed in silver satin, and it hugged her tall slender figure most provocatively. Together, they made quite a startling entrance at the Davenant soirée.

Condé came up behind them and managed each very well at his side as they entered the fray. The room was buzzing with the latest gossip. There were politics to be argued. There were Josephine's discreet and indiscreet activities. There was the threat of war with Great Britain looming over their French heads, and there was Napoleon behind it all.

Madame Davenant was upon them at once, detaching Velvet from the Condés and hugging her to herself as she moved toward Farnsworth, who was already on the scene. Velvet wanted to cry with vexation. She didn't want to be here. She wanted Talgarth. Everything was always so much brighter when the marquis was about.

She didn't want to meet Napoleon. She didn't want to listen to gossip about Josephine or hear how wonderful Napoleon's Legion of Honor was for its official program of honoring the soldiers. She wanted to leave this soirée, and she could have stamped her foot at Madame Davenant for not inviting the marquis and Gilly! The evening could only be dull sport without Talgarth there to tease her, infuriate her, make her feel alive. Even the prospect of Napoleon hovering over them could not excite her spirits, and, oh no, here was Farnsworth practically leering as he bent low over her hand. Velvet wanted to scream.

Farnsworth managed easily to detach Velvet from Madame and lure her to a quiet corner. Velvet knew what he was doing and did nothing to prevent it from happening. What could she do? After all, they were surrounded by people, so he could not ravish her, but his eyes told her that was exactly what he wanted to do, and she felt herself tremble.

"Are you cold, my sweet?" he asked solicitously. "Shall I fetch a shawl for you?"

"Oh no, I am fine . . . really." She smiled and looked round the room.

"Indeed, it would be a sin to cover your lovely shoulders." His hazel eyes raked her as he spoke, and his hand managed to grasp her elbow and draw her near on the pretext of moving her out of a passerby's way.

Velvet wanted to shout at him, but she restrained the impulse and, though they had been speaking in English, said on nearly a whisper, "Do you feel it, my lord?"

"Feel it? I'm famished from it," he said, making it very clear what he meant.

She pulled a face at him. "Be serious now. I'm talking about the tension in the room."

"Yes, now that you mention it, I do." Farnsworth looked round and then shrugged. "I suppose it is because of Napoleon."

"No. There is something in the air—oh dear, I fear it so. Here we are with May in all its beauty, and war threatens at every turn. It hovers, leaving the future to uncertainty. If France and England engage once more, Paris will be closed to us, travel will be restricted. I dread it. You must, too, for you have relatives and friends here."

"Indeed, it troubles me greatly." He put a comforting arm about her. "Our ambassador has been here negotiating with Napoleon. Perhaps he may yet preserve peace. At any rate, you must not worry your pretty little head over such matters."

Faith, she detested this man's condescending attitude, his unconcern, his insincere mannerisms. The marquis was right—he was always so right. Farnsworth was an odious person. She wondered what he could have done to Talgarth. She contemplated her satin toes and casually remarked, "There is a matter that does concern me, pretty head or no . . . and that is why my guardian was not invited to your cousin's soirée. It is something I find most odd, even insulting, but I suppose it has something to do with the feud you and he have been at for years?"

"Perhaps it does. Perhaps it is because I wanted

some moments alone with you and our 'feud,' as
you put it, encourages the marquis in keeping us
apart."

"You wanted to be private with me?" Velvet's brow
rose.

"Indeed, you see, there is a matter which I think
concerns you to some degree."

"Really?"

"It is about your cousin, Jacques de Beaupré,"
said Farnsworth confidingly. He saw sudden interest
light her green eyes and continued, "Ah, I rather
thought you would be curious."

"Of course, but what can it be that you would
bring to me and not to his father?"

"I rather thought you and he were friends. Perhaps I am mistaken?"

"No, no, of course we are friends, but . . ."

"Well then, as his friend perhaps you will understand that Jacques would not wish his father or his
aunt and uncle to discover the trouble in which he
now finds himself embroiled."

"Faith! What is it? Does Louis know?"

"Alas, Louis and his brother have not been getting
along very well these days." Farnsworth shook his
head in mock despair.

"My lord, please, what is it?"

"Tomorrow, my dear, I shall come for you with
my phaeton at noon. We will be more private that
way. Here there are so many curious ears."

"Yes, but we are speaking in English. Please, just
tell me: is Jacques all right?"

"No. I fear that things are in a sad state of affairs with your young cousin."

"How may I help?"

"Tomorrow, for I do believe the First Consul has arrived, and we must give him our full attention."

Indeed, Napoleon had stepped into the room. Velvet looked round and discovered him at the entrance of the ballroom. She had seen him before from a distance and was surprised that he was even smaller than she had thought him. His dark slick hair was thin and closely framed his uncovered head. One curl seemed pasted to his forehead. His eyes darted quickly about as he scanned and assessed the room. His smile was almost shy and his manner oddly peculiar as he moved about the room chatting with his intimates. He was everything that Velvet had thought he would be, awe-inspiring in spite of his diminutive size and his eccentric behavior.

Madame Davenant was at his side, whispering into his ear, and suddenly they began strolling toward the Condé couple, quietly chatting some distance from Velvet.

Velvet had not been aware that she had been holding her breath until she suddenly released it. Farnsworth noted this and smiled at her, taking her bare arm in his hands and saying confidingly, "There, there, you will do fine."

Velvet knew what was coming, for it was all so very obvious. A moment later, the Comte de Condé was standing over her with Napoleon at his side and saying, "My cousin, Lady Velvet Colbury, First Consul."

"Enchanting," said Napoleon, touching her cheek

as Velvet came up from a deep curtsy. "So you are related to the comtesse on your mother's side? A Beaupré, in fact."

"*Oui*, First Consul. How very kind of you to notice," answered Velvet prettily.

Napoleon turned to Condé. "She is most certainly a treasure. Quickly, Comte, marry her to a Frenchman and keep her here in Paris." So saying, he quietly moved off.

"Well done, Velvet," said the comte, who tickled her chin and moved off toward his lady.

Velvet watched him go and nearly stamped her foot in some vexation. Would no one save her from Farnsworth? She turned to his lordship and smiled politely. "Ah, I see Aunt Louise is motioning to me." She dropped a quick curtsy and was off to her tante Louise, who was pleased but very surprised to find Velvet come up from behind and hug her thankfully.

At the other end of the room, the comtesse leaned into her husband and said, "I think I shall develop the headache . . . and we go, yes?"

"Yes, I think so, but quietly, my dear. I shall go and pay my respects for us. Catch Velvet's eye. She should be at your side attending you."

"Yes, of course, we do not want them to try and keep her." Marie's eyes opened wide and her hand went grandly to her forehead. "What a perfectly dreadful evening!"

As though by mutual consent, the coach ride back to the Condé residence was completed in silence.

The comte and comtesse were lost in thought, and Velvet was glad to have a moment to think. Things were suddenly moving along so fast, too fast, and she just didn't know where matters were heading.

They entered their home to the information that the marquis and Gilly awaited them in the library. All three anxiously entered that room to be greeted by the marquis with, "Well, finally! Zounds, I thought the devils were going to keep you all night!"

Gilly cleared his throat and apologetically offered, "Tried to take him to our hotel, but, well, here we are. That's Dustin, you see."

"Oui, oui, mon cher," said Marie, touching Gilly's hand and leaning toward the marquis simultaneously to receive his tribute to her cheek. "Just as you should be, for there is much to discuss."

"What? I knew it. That damned Farnsworth! Only tell me he has already approached you about Velvet? I'll have his blood!"

"Non, non, you mistake. The problem, momentarily, is not Farnsworth," offered the comte quietly. "There are larger dilemmas before us."

"Such as?" the marquis said, on the alert.

"Apparently war between our two countries is closer than you think."

A groan went round the room, and Marie went to her husband to take his hands. *"Non . . . non . . .* He would not. What is to be gained?"

"Everything, my dear," said the comte softly. "If Napoleon wins against England, well, he will rule the world, or so he envisions."

"What makes you think he means to provoke war now?" asked the marquis.

"He sold Louisiana to the United States. . . . Why such a valuable land? Why, but for money to wage war!"

"He sold Louisiana months ago," Gilly stuck in doubtfully.

"Aye," said the marquis, "to raise his army. Just so, why would the Frenchmen in power allow this war?"

"They are as greedy as he, and you must remember that Napoleon has ruled France with much wisdom and vigor."

"It is not wise to wage war against the English," said Gilly patriotically.

The marquis smiled. "No doubt Napoleon feels his gains will never be secure with England opposing him, and there is the problem of Malta."

"Just so, Dustin. Your ambassador and Napoleon have been arguing all week about Malta, and I fear your man runs out of patience. There is not much time."

"Is my little one in danger if she remains for her ball?" asked Marie anxiously.

"No, things are not so dire as that. There is time to get Velvet and the boys out of France before war is declared and word reaches the small towns they must travel through."

"Why must we have war?" Marie cried in great distress.

"Without war, Napoleon cannot be named Emperor," said the marquis. "Is that not right, Comte?"

"Indeed, it would help for him to win a battle or two against the English, for he does see himself in such a light."

A lively discussion ensued then, enabling the marquis to take Velvet aside and softly say, "I am sorry, little one. I know you were looking forward to your ball, and if things continue along these lines, we may have to leave Paris before then."

Velvet waved this off impatiently. "What is that? Nought. Oh but, my lord, to be at war with France and not be able to see Marie and my cousins . . . ?"

He patted her shoulder and found himself putting his arm about her to draw her near. "There, there, child, we'll find a way through."

She smiled tremulously at him. "Oh, Dustin, I was so uncomfortable at Madame Davenant's, and I think I very nearly detest Lord Farnsworth. I don't know why that is, but it is. Though he is charming and very attentive—"

"Damn his soul," cut in the marquis. "Attentive, is he? May he rot in hell before he has a chance to be any more attentive to you!"

"What is it? Why do you hate him?"

"He is an evil man who had the opportunity, because I gave it to him, to tear out my heart and feed it to the dogs!"

Velvet wondered if he was speaking about a woman and felt a pang of jealousy as she pursued. "Ah . . . your fight was over a woman?"

"Not precisely. 'Tis not what you think. 'Tis worse, so much worse, but now is not the time."

"Will you ever tell me?" she asked hopefully.

He looked at her long and hard. "Probably not, sweetheart."

"Why not?"

"Well, you are a female, and females tend to prattle," he said simply.

Velvet stamped her foot. "Well, and I wouldn't. I don't at all understand you, my lord." Then she shook her head. "You don't like the man, yet you won't tell me the horrible thing he did."

" 'Tis a matter of honor. There is another name involved in this tale. To give away part would be to lose all." He put a finger to her lips. "There, that is enough." He turned to Gilly. "Come on then, lad. We have kept these people far too long." He nodded to Marie and blew her a kiss as he moved to the door. Turning to the comte, he said, "You will, I am certain, keep me posted?"

"As best as I can."

All was understood, and Velvet watched as the marquis took his friend, then waved and departed. She had chased him off with all her questions, she thought sourly. What was wrong with her? She always said the wrong thing to Talgarth. She always provoked him. He always provoked her; yet he had been the best part of her evening! She sighed sadly to herself. He would never want her. She didn't stand a chance with the Marquis of Talgarth.

Eighteen

Velvet was concentrating on Sinbad and unaware of her surroundings as she put him through the motions. Mr. Martin was not far behind, admiring her progress, but Velvet had forgotten even his presence as she worked Sinbad through his lesson.

The horse was alert and his ears were moving as she applied pressure to his flank with her spur. She had disregarded the horn of her sidesaddle and was momentarily riding astride without the benefit of stirrups. Her calves were pressed hard at his sides, and gently, softly she worked the reins, insistently reminding him what he was expected to do.

"Look there . . . gently, gently . . . to the left, lad," she said assuagingly, encouraging the animal by cooing when he performed well. She used reins and leg in gentle unison of motion nearly imperceptible to the onlooker, but infinitely meaningful to the horse. Her stick remained unused in her boot, for she only took out the crop when he misbehaved.

"Good boy. You see, there is no need to fight me. You know what I want." Velvet patted his neck as he successfully completed the movements, displaying that he understood the new language of leg yielding. Velvet looked round and smiled. "Well, Mr. Martin. He *is* coming along, is he not?"

Edward Martin laughed. "I am astounded. I know that you are riding Sinbad. I see that it is Sinbad, but you're on a horse I just do not recognize."

Velvet laughed happily. " 'Tis Sinbad, and he deserves a nice quiet walk back to his stable now." She sighed and then noted that the sun appeared to be directly overhead. "Oh dear! Never say 'tis past noon?"

Edward Martin consulted his pocket watch and was amazed to find that it was indeed ten minutes past noon. He smiled softly at Velvet. "I can't believe the morning has just swept past us. I lost track of time watching you handle Sinbad. I must admit I could watch you at anything all day."

He was surprised to see the look of distress flutter into Velvet's green eyes and immediately reached out to stroke her arm. "What is it, Lady Velvet?" He saw her urge Sinbad forward and realized that she was pressed for time. "Dash it! What a dunce I am. I did not realize I was keeping you so long. Did the comtesse need you back by noon? I am sorry. Do forgive me? I will see you to your door and walk the horses back to the stable myself. There is no need to go out of your way today. 'Tis no difficult thing."

"Oh no, 'tis not your fault. How could it be when you had no idea? And, by the bye, please call me Velvet. I think the time is past for 'Lady Velvet' and 'Mr. Martin,' don't you?" said Velvet sweetly.

Edward Martin could have stood in his stirrups and started to sing. He had been thinking for some days now that he might be more than just a little infatuated with the beautiful Lady Velvet. To be sure, she was a bit more outgoing than he was used to in the females he ordinarily fell in love with (for he definitely liked the ladies), and she was certainly more spirited. Nevertheless, the prospect of calling her by her first name made him lighthearted. "Thank you. I have been hoping to hear my name on your lips and to say your name familiarly."

She looked archly at him. "Really? Then why did you not try it . . . ?"

"If you had refused me the honor, I think that I would have died," he said dramatically.

Velvet laughed out loud at this piece of flummery. "No, you would not have died, for you are, I am persuaded, not so silly. La, but I have met so many silly fellows in Paris. They are forever dying for my eyes, my lips, and my hair. Still, even though I have denied them all three, they go on living!"

Daunted, Mr. Martin hung his head in mock dismay. "Run through."

Velvet laughed. "Not at all, but now we must rush, for I think I shall take you up on your offer and allow you to walk both horses back to their stables. I hope Sinbad will not be a bad boy and prance. Perhaps the prospect of returning to his stall and his feed will keep him in form."

"Indeed, I think the ol' boy will be relieved to be heading home. Besides, the distance from the Condé residence is no great thing." He eyed Velvet thoughtfully. "Again, I am sorry for keeping you. I hope the comtesse will not be out of temper with us."

"Not the comtesse." Velvet shook her head. "I am desperately late for an appointment that although I dread with all my heart, I am afraid I must keep."

"Really? And would I be too bold to ask who it is you dread?"

"Well, Lord Farnsworth convinced me to take a drive with him in his phaeton. He was to take me up at noon, but there you are. I forgot." Velvet shrugged her shoulders.

Mr. Martin pursued, "And you dread Lord Farnsworth's company?"

"Oh . . . how unkind of me to say so." Velvet frowned. "I have no reason. Please disregard it."

Mr. Martin inclined his fair head. "If you wish." Once more he leaned over, and this time he took up Velvet's blue-kid-gloved hand. "I hope you know I would stand your friend if ever you needed one?"

"Indeed, it is how I feel about you and Leslie. I was sorry that she had to leave us so early this morning." Her countenance turned quizzical. "In fact, she looked a bit rattled when she left."

"Rattled? Aye, I have never seen her act so eccentrically. Says she must have a new gown for your ball. It was very kind of the comtesse to include us, you know."

"Hmmm. I think Gilly had something to do with that," Velvet said teasingly.

Mr. Martin laughed but felt a moment's irritation, for he had hoped that Velvet had been at the bottom of the invitation. He didn't know what to make of

Velvet's "step forward, step back" playfulness. Was she a coquette? Did she only think of him as a friend? Was she waiting to see how he felt? Had he not shown her?

These thoughts were interrupted suddenly as a phaeton pulled up short and an English voice called out, "Well, and there you are!" Politeness veiled the annoyance the speaker felt.

Velvet looked round to find Lord Farnsworth jumping nimbly from his phaeton, handing the reins to his small groom, and walking toward her. She looked toward Martin, but, of course, she was being silly, for her first reaction was to ask for help. Instead, she turned to his lordship and offered in the way of greeting, "My lord, please forgive me. I lost track of time and was just now returning to meet you."

Farnsworth looked from Martin to Velvet, nodding only very slightly to Martin. "Really? Well, no harm." He reached up for her and said, "Allow me."

She did not want him to put his hands on her waist as she turned in the saddle to hop down, but there was nothing for it. His fingers lingered on her trim waist, and she felt a moment's revulsion. Mr. Martin looked on in some consternation, for he could see that Velvet was unhappy, and he did not care for Farnsworth's proprietary manner over Velvet. He looked at Velvet and said softly, "Shall I stop by and advise the comtesse that his lordship found you with me?"

"Oh yes," breathed Velvet finding some relief in this.

Farnsworth was most displeased and raised a brow at Martin, saying, "Really, sir, do you think she is in danger of being abducted? I take offense at the suggestion."

"No such thing. However, when I see a lady out, I also see her home. Any alteration of that procedure requires me to inform her people."

"Thank you," said Velvet hastily as she turned to Lord Farnsworth and gave him her hand in order to distract him and avoid any further words on the subject. "There, my lord, we have a perfectly lovely spring afternoon for our ride. Where shall you take me?"

Edward Martin watched as his lordship spoke softly to Velvet and noted how close he kept her to himself, but Martin had to keep his horses walking as Sinbad began to prance impatiently at his rear. Velvet was in no danger. Of course, she was in no danger. How could she be? Yet, he had an uneasy feeling. The feeling had begun with her admission and then had grown when Farnsworth arrived. Martin did not like it. He would return the horses and go at once to the comtesse, though for the life of him, he did not know just what this uneasy feeling could mean.

Velvet had a terrible sensation that Farnsworth was hatching some scheme in which she was the prize. He had a way of looking at her, the way a man looks at a piece of new art he has added to his collection. There was nought she could point out, nought she could say to prove this feeling. He was everything that was polite. He was solicitous and gallant. He never took too great a liberty, yet she wanted to quit his company as soon as he hovered over her. There was a burning in his eyes that made her uneasy. There was a possessiveness in his touch that made her feel as though he were about to undress her. She knew this was absurd, but could not banish the sensation. Oh, she wanted him to leave her alone. Why was she here? Jacques. What could he have to do with Jacques?

Farnsworth was irritated with Velvet. She was a beauty in her blue riding ensemble with the matching sky blue top hat sitting rakishly on her blond curls, but she was far too aloof. He had tried everything to warm her to his courting. Charm, finesse, gentle urging had not rewarded him. He and Madame Davenant had been unable to impress her the other night with even Napoleon's attendance at their little soirée. Why did she keep him at bay? Was it Martin? Damn the fellow's impudence! What was he? Nought. Well then, if his courting would not win Lady Velvet, he would have to resort to force. One day she would learn to appreciate him, appreciate his love, the love they could have together. He had made up his mind to it. Velvet Colbury would be his wife.

They drove on in silence around the outskirts of the park, each lost to thoughts they were unwilling to share, when all at once Farnsworth pulled up his phaeton and ordered his young groom to the curbing. "I'll come back for you in thirty minutes time, so don't stray."

The youthful tiger was English and was not about to wander off on French turf. He nodded and advised his employer that he would be just where his lordship left him.

Velvet's hand went to Farnsworth's wrist involuntarily. "No, no, my lord. I am sure my cousin, the comtesse, would object. She would not think we were observing the proprieties driving about together unattended."

"How is that," he smiled benignly as he clicked his horses forward, "when she allows you to ride unattended with Mr. Martin?"

" 'Tis quite a different thing," said Velvet, her chin going up. "We may be in an open phaeton, but we are sitting very close together. No, I am certain—"

"Velvet," said Farnsworth, cutting her off and using her given name without her leave, "we need to be alone because I don't want any man to hear what I have to tell you about your cousin, Jacques de Beaupré."

That was right, thought Velvet, that was why she was here. Oh dear, she fretted to herself, what had Jacques done? "You are, of course, quite right." She frowned to herself, for she did not like to be obligated to Farnsworth.

"Indeed, I did not think you would want anyone to know your cousin's very private business."

"How is it, my lord, that *you* know his business?"

Velvet asked directly. Her green eyes raked his face, but Dale Farnsworth gave nothing away.

"I was present at the time and could do nought to prevent what occurred. For that I am sorry. For *you,* I wish to do everything in my power to help the lad out of his dilemma."

"What dilemma is that?"

"Apparently he has fallen in with a bad set of fellows at a place which is quite frankly worse than any English hell I have ever frequented, even as a lad."

Wouldn't Farnsworth be shocked to know that Velvet knew exactly what he was speaking of and had been there herself on two unfortunate occasions. She eyed him gravely. "I believe that his brother Louis is doing what he can to keep Jacques away from this place you speak of."

"Poor lad, unfortunately a younger brother does not have that power. Jacques continues his predilection for this lowly establishment and has fallen into a very awkward state of affairs."

"What do you mean?" Velvet was startled.

"Apparently his gaming has run into amounts I can scarcely credit. A debt of honor, you see, is a serious business, and a gaming debt is such a thing. It must be paid before any other debt, and I am afraid Jacques will be unable to do so. One fears for a lad in such a situation."

These things were matters on which men put great importance. Velvet knew this from tales her grandfather had imparted to her many times when he was raising her. She did not doubt for a minute that Farnsworth was telling her the truth. "Oh no! He owes this to the gaming establishment?"

"No. He owes it to just one man."

"Who is this man?" Velvet asked as she watched Farnsworth's eyes.

"Ah, yet another matter of honor. One does not spread such things about. It would not be honorable for me to give you this man's name. It is, in fact, questionable for me to even speak about this incident with you. Suffice to say that the sum is quite vast and that it was won fair and square as the saying goes." He did not think he should mention that he was the gentleman involved and that poor young Jacques had been sadly inebriated at the time.

Velvet's brow was up. "I cannot think it dishonorable to give me the name of a man who calls himself a gentleman in error! How can he be an honorable man and play fast and loose with a boy who is underage?"

Farnsworth pulled on his reins and brought his phaeton to nearly a screeching halt. He eased it to the curbing, applied and set his brake, all while Velvet watched in something close to fear. He turned to her and took up her hands, though she allowed this most reluctantly. "My dear, I quite see how a delicately nurtured female would view this situation. It pains me to bring it to your attention. Perhaps I was wrong and should have gone straight to Armand—"

"No, no, not to his father," Velvet hurriedly objected. "You could not be so cruel."

"No, I could not, though perhaps it would be

kinder than to allow the boy to go on worrying about his debt?"

Velvet did not for a moment think that Lord Farnsworth was extending his hand to her and her cousin out of kindness. Her instincts told her that his lordship was only interested in furthering his cause with her. What to do? She could not allow Jacques to be trapped in his predicament, even though it was of his own making. She could not have Armand hurt in such a way. Jacques had not been himself, and she could not allow his youth to be ruined by his error in judgment.

She attempted a cool exterior. "If you think so, then I must bend to your decision. After all, perhaps I am wrong and his father should be told everything."

She had played her cards quite well. Farnsworth was momentarily taken aback. He had not expected this. They were now at a complete stop at the curbing nearest the park. He eyed her a moment and then shook his head. "In truth, I feel a dastard going to his father with such a tale. Jacques should be allowed to extricate himself from his problem first. How else will he ever grow up if he must look to his father to forever whisk him out of trouble?"

Exactly as she thought! Farnsworth was attempting blackmail. Well, she had called his bluff, but still she could not risk taking it all the way.

"Oh, that would be unfair. So then, you will allow me to go to Louis and not tell Armand anything about this muddle?"

He put his arm around Velvet and ignored the

fact that she attempted to escape his hold. She belonged to him, and so he would show her. "Indeed, my darling. I shall not tell Armand anything at all . . . unless *you* deem otherwise."

"Thank you," Velvet managed to say as she pulled out of his embrace. This man frightened her in every conceivable way. How she was going to keep him at arm's length for the rest of her stay in Paris, she could not guess. Oh, but now she wished the marquis would come along and save her. She sat stiffly, and as he reached for her fingers to press yet another caress on her, she said, "You have been most kind, but I think I have stayed out too long. The comtesse will be looking for me."

"Your gratitude is not what I want, Velvet. However, I will settle for it this afternoon."

She said nothing to this, for he took up the slack in the driving reins and clicked his horses forward. What was she going to do about Jacques? How could he have fallen into such a dreadful scrape? This was no longer larking. This was very nearly wicked, and so she would tell him as soon as she could get her hands on him! Oh faith, she thought, she was in the devil of a fix. She wanted to leave Paris and go home with the marquis and Gilly, but she couldn't leave Jacques until she knew he was out of rough seas! What to do? What to do?

Gilly's hands were clasped behind him. Beside him was the lady that had stolen his heart and, he told himself, his good senses. He had left the marquis at breakfast to rush off to meet Leslie Martin at her dressmaker's, and then they had gone off to the park for a quiet stroll. Why they must meet in this clandestine fashion he could not understand, and so he was saying, "Why are you keeping this a secret from your brother? Doesn't he approve of me?"

"Oh my dear," said Leslie, taking his arm in her strong clasp, " 'Tis that he *does* approve and has been teasing me incessantly ever since he realized how things were with us." She found herself blushing and put a gloved hand to her cheek. "Oh, look at me. How perfectly dreadful."

"How perfectly charming," said Gilly, amazed to find himself being gallant, feeling so romantic, uttering words he had never heard himself say before.

She preened beneath his approval and continued, "I just could not tell him that I wanted you to see the gown I was having made. Oh, what he would have said!"

"What could he say?" laughed Gilly.

"He . . . Well, you see, Gilly, I have never been . . . in love before."

Gilly's eyes clouded over with strong feeling, and he took up her gloved fingers. "Leslie!"

"Gilly . . . Oh dearest Gilly!" she uttered with deep meaning. However, a profound distraction then caught her attention, and it was with some concern and consternation that she said, "Gilly! Look! Oh dear, but Velvet looks to be in trouble."

Gilly turned round in time to view Farnsworth taking an unwilling Velvet into his arms in his phaeton. Velvet appeared to be terribly distressed as she resisted his lordship's relentless efforts.

"Dash it! Damn, if Dusty isn't in the right of it and that fellow *is* the devil! Fact is . . . must be! Look at him manhandle the child. How dare he!" He took a step forward, his hand going out toward the phaeton as he called out Farnsworth's name, but his lordship was already in the midst of traffic. "Confound the blackguard!" he spat.

"Gilly, I don't like this. Something is wrong." She lowered her voice. "You don't think he is abducting her?"

"No, even he would not dare it. Dustin would have his blood, and so he knows!"

"Yes, my brother told me he had overheard something that led him to believe that the marquis and Farnsworth were . . . well, not quite friends."

"That, my love, does not even begin to describe their relationship. They hate one another, though Dustin has cause and Farnsworth does not."

"Yes, well, as you say, he would not dare to; yet he dared to behave inappropriately in public toward her, and, Gilly, he had no groom in attendance."

"Did he not, by Jove?" Gilly shook his head. "Don't like that, Leslie. Don't like that one bit."

"Perhaps we should repair to the Condé house at once and advise the comtesse?"

"As to that, 'tis a sticky matter. Can't very well walk up to Marie and tell her Velvet was being—well, can't, you know. No doubt it would distress her unnecessarily."

"Then you don't think we should go and . . . ?"

"Yes, must go. If Velvet doesn't return within a short space, then we'll tell! That's the ticket!"

"Oh Gilly, you are so wise," said Leslie Martin adoringly

No one had ever told Gilly he was wise. He puffed up with pride and joy, and taking his dearest's hand, he tugged her along in something of a run as he made tracks for the Condé residence.

Edward Martin returned to the stables. He handed over Rollo, Velvet's horse, to one of the livery boys and quickly attended Sinbad himself. Satisfied that both horses were sufficiently cooled down to water, he allowed them to be taken to their stalls where water and hay awaited them. He saw that their saddles were handed to a groom for cleaning, and with a quick look-in at his sister's horse, he left them to make his way to the Condé house. This he did with his thoughts in a jumble of irrational avenues.

What was he going to do about Velvet Colbury? He was taken with her, so much so that he rather pictured her as his wife. Something about this picture jiggled his nerves, but he brushed it away. His sister liked her very well, though she had teased him and said that the pretty Velvet would never do as a wife for him. "Why is that?" he had asked in earnest.

Leslie had looked at her brother indulgently and shrugged. "Well, there is never any telling, for Velvet may settle down when she is married and has a brood of children, but she is not in your usual style, is she?"

"And what do you imagine is my usual style?" he had been irritated into asking.

"Why, some pretty silly widgeon of a girl, who will no doubt annoy me to tears." She sighed. " 'Tis what you like, though, have noticed it. You want some frail creature with no interest in politics save your own. Some biddable child, and Velvet will never be that."

He had smiled ruefully, for indeed, Velvet's lively spirits were not precisely what he wanted in a wife. He was fond of his sister and knew her to be an estimable female, but she was a practical creature, an "I'll do it myself" woman very much like Velvet. That was not what he wanted in the woman he meant to devote himself to in the future.

He sighed over the problem, for he wanted an answer. What then did he want from Velvet? Zounds, she was so beautiful. That was all he really knew at the moment. She was a charming beauty whose company he was enjoying immensely and he cared for her a great deal. Hang all the rest!

More than this question troubled his mind. Velvet had wanted him to go to her family and advise them that she was with Lord Farnsworth. He moved purposely in that direction rather more hurriedly than the errand required, for he was greatly disturbed by this afternoon's encounter with Lord Farnsworth. Velvet had said she dreaded her appointment to drive about the park with his lordship. Well, he had a sister and from her learned that women often "dread" this or that without it meaning anything terrible. Yet he had witnessed the manner in which

Farnsworth had collected Velvet and rushed off—as though she were his property! Most odd. Worse, Velvet seemed genuinely frightened. Her face told quite a story, and it wasn't the typical histrionics he had often observed in other women. Velvet's dread was quite real.

Formerly he had excused Farnsworth's proprietary behavior as the action of a man in love. He put it down as misguided and deplorable, but nevertheless understandable. Now he was not so sure. His mind went over the scene over and over, and an uneasiness took over his senses. All at once he couldn't get to the Condé residence fast enough!

Nineteen

The comtesse entered her home at half-past noon to the intelligence that Lord Farnsworth had called to take Lady Velvet out for a drive. He had been advised that she was out riding in the park with Mr. Martin, and his lordship had been vexed enough to leave in something of a temper. Marie's servants were loyal beings interested in all the doings of their household.

She thanked the butler and went to collect her flower basket, garden gloves, and straw shade bonnet. Some minutes later found her in the small garden where she enjoyed growing a variety of spring flowers. She had been only a little distracted by the news she had received. However, as the time progressed and Velvet did not return home, she found herself on edge.

Gilly and Leslie Martin arrived, advised the butler they would announce themselves, and hurried through the library and the lead-paned glass doors that led to the courtyard garden. There they found Marie cutting flowers for her various vases.

"Comtesse," said Miss Martin breathlessly.

"Marie, we are so glad to find you at home," said Gilly on a high note.

Marie put down the basket of flowers on a nearby glass table and said, "I knew it. One knows these things. Tell me; it is my Velvet! What has happened to my Velvet?"

"Did you know that she is with Lord Farnsworth?" asked Leslie, getting directly to the point in a manner that was very much her own.

"Know? How could I know this? How did this happen when he was not able to find her here and I am told left in something of a huff? This is most odd. How do you know this?"

"Marie, Velvet was beside him in his phaeton, and I must say she did not look pleased," offered Gilly haltingly, for he did not wish to make too much out of the situation and perhaps frighten the French-woman.

"Oh, but I detest him. Dustin is very right to feud with him. Moi, I should like to cut him!"

Leslie Martin opened her eyes wide at this blood-thirsty remark, but Gilly nodded in agreement. "Dustin has been wanting to, er, cut him these many years past. Wish he had."

The butler caught their attention with the reso-nant announcement that Mr. Edward Martin had arrived. All eyes turned his way as he strode hard across the library and met them in the garden to say, "You here, sis? Gilly, too . . . Good." He turned to the comtesse and inclined his head. "How are you today, Comtesse?"

"Moi? What has that to say to anything, sir? You

rode with my Velvet. Did you lose her? If so, how and where is she now?"

"Yes, we rode together. It seems, however, that Lady Velvet had an arrangement with Lord Farnsworth. The way I understand it, they were to meet here and go for a bit of a drive together. From what she said to me, I gathered she was not looking forward to the protracted excursion in the least."

"Wonderful, the way your brother puts his words together," said Gilly in an undervoice to Leslie Martin.

"She does not like this Farnsworth person, this I know," said Marie waving her hand in the air. "She does not like him at all."

"With good reason apparently," stuck in Miss Martin with a grimace.

"Ah, what are you hiding from me? What has he done with my Velvet? I will send a note to my Condé. He is at the club and will come to me immediately. I will ask him to pink this Farnsworth person!"

"Hold a moment. What is going on?" asked Mr. Martin in some surprise. "Leslie, do you know something about all this?"

"Gilly and I saw Farnsworth near the park, and, oh Edward, the dreadful man was making advances that Velvet was loath to accept, and he had no groom in attendance. I can only assume that he dismissed his groom to be alone with Velvet. Edward, he was behaving the cad!"

Mr. Martin looked at Gilly, for he felt that women tended to exaggerate. "Is this true, sir?"

"Zounds, your sister just told you, didn't she?"

Gilly frowned at him. "Don't you believe your own sister?"

Edward Martin became momentarily flustered. "Well, as to that, of course I do. I just thought I could get a different point of view on the subject."

"Subject? Subject? We speak of my Velvet!" Marie stuck in caustically. "English! Forever you are a cold-blooded lot. *Moi*, I have not the patience. *You!*" She pointed at Gilly, who took a step backward, for he knew to be wary of excitable Frenchwomen. "Why did you not stop this horrid man from taking a liberty with my poor child?"

"Well—" Gilly started.

"He did try!" retorted his beloved, cutting him off. "He went after the phaeton, but they were already lost in traffic."

"Where is she now? Abducted? Do you think she has been abducted by this Farnsworth? Would he dare?" Marie asked as she clutched her hands together. "Why has he not brought her home?"

"Please, Comtesse, do not distress yourself. 'Tis scarcely past one o'clock. Lord Farnsworth has not had time to bring Velvet home."

"Yes, well, that may be, but, *moi*, I think it is all very dastardly!" Marie wailed and moved past them to enter the library, wringing her hands. "One tells me this Farnsworth runs them to earth and takes poor Velvet away with him. The other tells me this Farnsworth takes a liberty with my Velvet. She is a Colbury, protected by the house of Condé, by the Duke of Salsburn, by his grandson, the Marquis of

Talgarth! What? Are we to be intimidated? *Non,* and *non* again!"

"What the deuce has you in the boughs?" chuckled the Marquis of Talgarth from the library threshold.

"Ah, it is you!" cried Marie, rushing to take up his hands. "I am so glad. Talgarth, you must go and find my Velvet and bring her home safely to me and take a pistol and shoot him through the heart!"

"What? Where is Velvet? Shoot who through the heart? My dear Marie, calm yourself. What scrape has Velvet fallen into now?" Clearly the marquis did not seem alarmed, for he, too, seemed to be of the opinion that Frenchwomen in general were an emotional lot.

"Perhaps you had better sit down, ol' boy," said Gilly, attempting an exterior of calm good sense.

The marquis raised a brow and felt himself tense. There was something about his friend's demeanor that made him uneasy. "Eh . . . don't want to sit. What is all this about? Where is Velvet?"

"That is just it," said Mr. Martin. "We believe she must still be with Lord Farnsworth."

"What?" ejaculated the marquis. He couldn't believe what he was hearing. He maintained control over his sudden irritation of nerves and attempted logic. "It doesn't make sense. Why would Velvet be with Farnsworth? Rather thought she didn't like him. Damnation and brimstone! Know she doesn't like him. How could he have managed this?"

"You are right there," said Mr. Martin.

The marquis eyed him grievously. For some unknown reason he did not appreciate Martin's opinions in this matter. "Thank you, but I don't need anyone to tell me that."

Martin pulled a face. "What I meant was, Velvet told me that she dreaded her appointment with Farnsworth; yet she seemed obliged to meet him all the same. Thought you should know that."

"There is more to this than meets the eye, and I'll be damned if I'll stand here and play a guessing game. Martin, why don't you explain—from the beginning, if you please."

Edward Martin did just that in his slow meticulous style. However, he was often interrupted by his sister or Gilly, who felt they had to add whatever facts they had at hand. There, too, the comtesse interjected now and then with her fervent desire to draw Farnsworth's blood. Eventually Martin's tale was complete, and the marquis withdrew to a corner to rub his nose as he was lost to deep thought.

This seemed to worry Gilly, who stepped toward his friend to ask, "Dustin, what say you?"

"As to that, ol' boy, this time there is nothing left to be said. When Velvet returns, we will discuss our departure." He turned to Marie. "We will leave the morning after your ball. I trust that will be convenient?"

Marie went to him and touched his fingers. "*Non,* it will never be convenient. There will be a war, and I will never see my little Velvet again."

"Nonsense. This time next year, perhaps we may all meet in Italy, in Venice. You will like that," said the marquis kindly, kissing her fingertips.

"*Oui, oui*, oh so very much, and Condé will arrange it, you will see." She brightened at once. "That is what we shall do, and Velvet, if she is wed by then, she will make her husband bring her, *oui?*"

"I am certain of it," said Dustin on an odd note.

"Oh! I am sad once more. Velvet goes to England and I shall not see her wed!"

"I was not aware that I was in danger of being married," said Velvet from the doorway.

All eyes turned to find Lady Velvet standing at the library threshold, looking quite in dishabille. Her blue top hat was nearly falling off; her blond curls were disordered; her blue riding ensemble was wrinkled; and the white lace beneath the jacket of her ensemble was slightly torn. Marie uttered a cry and rushed to take her young cousin in her arms. "La, what has that villain done to you?"

"Oh, he is a perfectly dreadful man! He, oh Marie! He kept trying to . . . to hold me, and when I couldn't bear it any longer, I pushed him off, and what must he do but lose the driving reins in the midst of traffic! He nearly turned us over only blocks from here."

She gave Marie a hug and found the marquis's blue eyes scanning her. Without even realizing what she was doing, she went to him.

He took up her hands to his lips and pressed them with a kiss. He was experiencing an odd assortment of sensations, uppermost being relief. She was home, she was with him, she was safe! It seemed to be all that mattered, that and never allowing her to be alone with Dale Farnsworth again. All others in the room were momentarily forgotten as he whispered, "No hurts, little one?"

She shook her head and checked the tears that started in her green eyes. "No hurts save one, Dustin. He means to use me to get at you. I am sure of it."

"Well, we won't let him do that, will we?" Talgarth frowned. "And in this perhaps you are not altogether correct. I rather think he fancies you, Velvet. Nought to do with me, except that I stand in his way."

"Ugh!" Velvet was revulsed and her shoulders shook. "He means to keep calling on me."

"He will not be admitted to this house, and you will never be in a position where you will be allowed to be alone with him." Talgarth looked round at the assembled group. "You have endeared yourself, my girl, to all of us, and we mean to take watch."

Edward Martin moved forward and said staunchly, "Depend upon it, my lord. Farnsworth shall not catch me off guard again. I have cursed myself time over for allowing him to take Velvet from my protection this morning. I knew it wasn't right. Should have sent her home first. Bad *ton* to take her off like that." He shook his head.

In truth, Martin was having a great adventure. He had traveled all over Europe. He had been on the London scene for a great many seasons, but this was making him feel like a knight in shining armor protecting a damsel in distress!

"We shall all be on the watch. Deuce take the fellow," agreed Gilly. "Wish we were all well out of

Paris." He looked at Marie and stammered, "Well, what I mean is . . . you see . . . with all this and . . ."

"Never mind, Gilly." Velvet's irrepressible smile peeped. "Marie knows what you mean."

The marquis took Velvet's fingers back to his lips and lightly kissed their tips. "Go on, little one. Go up and take a nice soothing bath. You'll feel better for it."

"Will you be here when I have changed?" Clearly she did not wish to quit his company.

"No, child. I have something that must be done." Talgarth's tone was grim.

Velvet held him to her with a pull at his hands. "No, no . . . You won't see Farnsworth alone?"

He laughed. "Don't you think I can handle him?"

"Yes, but he can be ever so sly. Oh, Dusty, don't, please."

"I shall be with Dustin, don't you worry, Velvet," announced Gilly.

Velvet turned to Gilly. "Don't go, Gilly. Don't let him go. There is no saying what someone like that could do. He doesn't think like you do. He doesn't feel like you do, and he is capable of a great deal of harm."

"How do you know all that?" Dustin asked, staring into her green eyes. Had Farnsworth done more than try to steal a kiss? There was a glint of steel in his blue orbs that spoke of danger.

"I don't *know* it. . . . I *feel* it," cried Velvet in some distress.

The marquis gave her a half smile and led her to the library doors. "Go on upstairs, sweetheart, and forget Farnsworth. Perhaps I will give it a rest, and Gilly and I shall not visit with him just yet. There, does that make you feel better?''

"Oh yes, much.'' She squeezed his hands.

A moment later Velvet was gone, and the marquis turned to find Leslie Martin looking at him. "You fibbed to her, didn't you? You are going to see Farnsworth, aren't you?''

The marquis was almost curt in his response. "I did not fib to Velvet. I simply said that perhaps I would not visit Farnsworth just yet.''

"But you go? *Non? Oui, oui,* say you go! Run him through, Dusty. I should like that very much. *Moi,* I think he is a cad, a scoundrel. He must be punished for taking a liberty with a Colbury!" Marie said.

"Indeed, he must be punished for taking a liberty with Velvet," said the marquis grimly.

Leslie Martin watched as the marquis and Gilly took their leave. She had been silent during the exchange between the marquis and Velvet, and she had found herself greatly disturbed by it all. She knew her brother to be infatuated with Velvet Colbury and very near to being in love. She did not want to see him hurt. She liked Velvet, but from the start she had not thought that Velvet suited him. Now she was sure of it. If she was not mistaken, Velvet Colbury was in love with the grandson of her legal guardian. There was no mistaking the light in her eyes when she looked at the marquis. She would have no room in her heart for another if this were true.

Leslie glanced at her brother. He seemed in a

high fettle of excitement, bent on protecting Velvet and oblivious to the fact that Velvet Colbury looked to be very much in love with the Marquis of Talgarth. What to do? Leave it alone. Perhaps things might work out. And at any rate, she couldn't bear to burst his bubble when she herself was floating on air. It wouldn't be sporting!

Twenty

Velvet made her way downstairs toward the library, where she had last seen her cousin, Marie. She was very much better for her bath and her change of clothing. Her blond curls were caught at the nape of her neck with a pretty red velvet ribbon. She wore a high-necked gown of white muslin dotted throughout with red velvet. The high waist of the gown was cinched with a wide red velvet sash, and white soft leather half boots covered Velvet's dainty feet.

She donned the matching spencer jacket she had in her hands and went toward the library door, where she encountered the butler. Inquiring after Marie, she was told that the comtesse was in the kitchen with the cook, who was not pleased with the shrimp that had been delivered and was having something of a fit. Velvet laughed and hurried into the library to scribble a quick note to the comtesse.

Dearest,
    Do not fret. I am feeling much more the thing and have run over to visit with Louis and Jac-

ques. I shall be home in time to have the English
tea you so detest.

Love,
Velvet

This note she folded and propped up on the desk
before she hurriedly left the house and walked the
short distance to the Place Vendôme and the Beaupré town house. She was taken to the study, where
she tapped her foot impatiently until the door
opened to reveal Louis de Beaupré. He went forward, hands extended, and in a strained voice said
thankfully, "Velvet."

"Louis, I am frantic. Where is Jacques?" demanded Velvet anxiously as they hugged one another and dropped kisses on both cheeks.

"Ah, Jacques," said Louis disgustedly. "He told
me some rapper and left early this morning. He lies
to me. He keeps secrets from me. Jacques? I do not
know this person anymore. We never had secrets."
Clearly Louis was hurt.

"He is in trouble," said Velvet. "That is why he
is not confiding in you. I am sure he doesn't want
you to know."

"*Oui,* he does not want me to know. What? Am I
some . . . what you English call a 'Jack-Pudding'? I
am his brother. He should come to me."

"Louis, his trouble is much worse than we had
imagined," said Velvet breathlessly.

"*Mon Dieu!*" cried Louis, ruining his finely combed
waves with his frantic hands. "I knew it would come
to this. What has he done?"

"It seems that Jacques has gambled with someone of importance, but I don't know who this person is. However, he has apparently lost an enormous amount of money. Since a gaming debt is a debt of honor, I know that Jacques will not rest until his debt is paid, and I understand that he must take care of this almost immediately."

"*Sacrebleu!*" breathed Louis. He took Velvet's shoulders. "How do you know this?"

"Someone saw him and felt I should be informed. I suppose he thought I could help Jacques."

"Impossible! You . . . well, Velvet . . . you are a woman! You should be protected from these things. A Frenchman would never burden such as you with this outrage!"

"Well, he did . . . only, well, he isn't French," said Velvet.

"Who then?"

"Lord Farnsworth told me the whole. He said he thought I should be told before he went to your father."

"*Non, non* . . . my father? Why not come to me? It is not at all good *ton* to go to you when there is me!" said Louis, thinking out loud.

Velvet had never thought of this before. Her brows knit. "Well, I don't know the answer to that, though you are quite right."

"I don't like this Farnsworth of yours. He struts through Paris as though he were the Grand Turk! *Non* . . . what to do? *Mon frère . . . mon frère,*" he said sadly, "Velvet, Father will be so very hurt. How could Jacques do this?"

"What will Jacques do? Do you think he will go to a tens-in-the-hundred?"

"What is that?"

"My grandfather told me about them. That is a terrible person who gives a loan at exorbitant interest rate."

Louis shrugged. "We must stop him from further ruining his life . . . and my father's. I will not have it. Papa is a good man. He does not deserve to be so ill-treated. I don't know what has happened to Jacques. He has gone mad, I think."

"No, Louis. He was just spreading his wings and flew into the wrong territory. He needs help out, and we'll help him. First, you must confront him and demand to know how much he owes. Do not allow him to steal anything of your father's and do not allow him to go to a moneylender. Threaten him with exposure if you must, but keep him in tow!"

"Oui, oui, I will do this."

"I must go home now to help Marie with the flower arrangements for the ball, but, Louis, keep me informed!"

"Oui, sweet girl, my own sister, for you are more than cousin or friend." Louis kissed her fingertips and then each of her cheeks before she rushed out. He stood for a long moment staring after her and wishing that Jacques were home. He meant to confront him, imprison him by force if need be, but stop him from any further calamity!

* * *

Farnsworth had no idea that Velvet thought he had taken a liberty with her. He had no notion that she would return to the comtesse or, for that matter, to the marquis and complain about his behavior. He had of course, in spite of his conceit, realized that she was not receiving his advances with the enthusiasm he had expected, but this was a circumstance he blamed on Talgarth's influence. He was certain the marquis had managed to whisper some disparagement about his character in Velvet's innocent ears. Why else would she keep him at a distance? With this troubling his mind, he made his way to his cousin Nicole's.

Since Salsburn would not allow him to court Velvet once they had all returned to England, the only course open to him was a clandestine wedding. Such a thing would be possible with his cousin's assistance. She had displayed herself willing to do so, for she loved nothing better than an adventure. He had convinced Nicole that Velvet returned his feelings and that it was her family that kept them apart. Madame felt she was aiding a wondrous love match.

Well, he would need her services now, for she would have to procure a Special License. This was no easy task in France, for it just was not done. He would need a minister to perform the ceremony and he would need a safe haven where the ceremony could be performed. And there was the matter of Velvet. How would she react to such a scheme? She would have no choice, of course, but she was a spirited creature unlike most of her kind.

This was going to take great cunning and, of

course, Jacques de Beaupré. Stumbling upon Jacques had been the best of all good fortune, for that was his ticket to Velvet. How Jacques could be best used was something he had not completely worked out yet, but he would soon come up with a solution. Indeed, Jacques would be the tool.

He wondered if Velvet was even now rushing off to see her cousin. There was no chance that Jacques would tell her that he owed his gaming debt to him, thought Farnsworth confidently. He had extracted a promise of secrecy in exchange for allowing the boy twenty-four hours in which to come up with the money. Farnsworth laughed to himself as he remembered the boy's face. There was nothing Jacques de Beaupré could do, short of stealing the family heirlooms, to pay him what was owed.

He reached the Davenant steps and smiled to himself. In a short few days, Velvet would be standing at his side and carrying his name!

Gilly and the marquis walked the considerable distance to Lord Farnsworth's hotel in silence, both deep in thought. Gilly was trying to come up with some way in which to stall the marquis until his dander had cooled, and the marquis was actually trying to control his temper himself. At any rate, they were met with the intelligence that his lordship had left early that morning and had not yet returned. Talgarth managed to thank the desk clerk civilly in French and turned to his friend to utter in great frustration, "Damn the man's soul!"

"And his eyes, his heart, his damnably wicked mind—anything you like, Dustin, only let us leave it be for now," said Gilly amiably.

"Can't leave it be," said Talgarth caustically. "Must know that, Gilly."

"Sadly, do know it," said Gilly on a long sigh. "Still, can't be anything but pleased to find the blackguard absent, you know."

"What?" demanded the marquis irritably.

"Stands to reason," said Gilly. "You want his blood, I want you to have his blood, no doubt the comtesse wants you to have his blood, should have his blood . . ."

"Gilly," cried the marquis acrimoniously, "what is your point?"

"Wait to have his blood," finished Gilly, not at all put out by his friend's impatience.

"Wait? Wait until when?" asked the marquis incredulously.

"Until we are all back in England." Gilly patted his friend on the shoulder. "Have his blood then anyway you like."

"Don't be daft."

"Problem then," said Gilly laconically.

"What problem?"

"Well, in England you could have at him with your fives if you like. Plant him a facer . . . wham, it's over. Paris? Not so. Noticed these frogs take to the queerest sorts, you know. Don't want them throwing you into gaol. Being a marquis won't count over here."

The marquis's blue eyes lit with sudden dawning.

"Devil take his soul. You are speaking of his connection to Madame Davenant and her connection to Napoleon."

"Afraid so," sighed Gilly.

"And I should allow such things to weigh with me?" demanded the marquis, incensed.

"Oh well, then have at him," said Gilly blandly.

The marquis stopped in his tracks and stared at his friend. "You are the best of good fellows, but you don't believe I will let this pass, do you?"

"Yes, I do. Know you. Clever—always been more clever than I. Good heart, too. You won't want Velvet's name bandied about," said Gilly gently.

"Devil is in it that you are right. Have been telling myself just that all the way over to his hotel. However, I mean to find him all the same." Talgarth grinned. "No, don't look like that. As you say, I can always pick a fight with him in England, leaving Velvet out of it, but now I mean to put a stop to his visits to the Condé house. What say you?"

"Agreed!" cried Gilly thankfully.

Velvet turned the corner and nearly ran into Edward Martin. He stood back as he steadied her and thought she was the prettiest thing he had seen all afternoon. She was certainly a stunning creature in her white muslin with its red velvet trimming and the white lacy bonnet with its red ribbon.

They laughed a quick greeting and Velvet looked past him to inquire idly, "And where is Leslie? Strolling in the park with my dear Gilly, no doubt?"

He chuckled. "They do seem to be a twosome these days, don't they? However, I left Leslie in our hotel suite curled up with a box of bonbons and her favorite gothic romance."

"Oh my, lucky Leslie," Velvet smiled.

"Ah, you like those silly romances, too?"

"Well, yes, but I meant lucky Leslie curled up with bonbons. I haven't had a thing to eat since this morning's coffee, and I am half-starved. Faith, what I wouldn't do for a fresh hot bun!"

A passing hawker called out in guttural French that he had Paris's best hot buns. Velvet and Edward Martin exchanged glances and laughed out loud. Martin put up his hand and called to the urchin in articulate French. A moment later both were strolling towards the Condé house munching happily on sweet rolls.

"So then, where are you off to?" Velvet inquired between bites.

He swallowed the last of his bun, grinned, pointed to this fact as an excuse for not immediately answering and then managed, "Jeweler's. My timepiece has been acting oddly. Needs repair. I was told there is an exceptional jeweler near here, a M. Brionne?"

"Oh yes, Marie often goes to him," agreed Velvet, nodding. She smiled at him amiably. "I have managed to spend a coin or two there myself."

He laughed and inclined his head. "Care to accompany me on my errand? I should love the company."

"Indeed, that would be a treat for me, but I don't dare." She peeped sideways at him. "Besides, I am expected home and must admit that right now I want nothing more than to fall onto the sofa and sip a hot cup of tea." She giggled. "Marie pulls a face when I take tea in the late afternoon. She thinks I am ruining my insides with what she calls mulish water—whatever that is!"

He laughed, and as they had reached the steps of the Condé house, he bent low over Velvet's extended white-gloved hand. "Until tomorrow morning, my dear."

"Oh yes, for you must know 'tis very nearly the best part of my day, our ride." Velvet referred to her training session with Sinbad and had no notion that she had made Edward Martin's hope soar, but she did.

He took both her hands in his. "Every moment I spend in your company, Velvet dearest, is the best part of my day," he said feverishly.

Velvet's green eyes opened wide with sudden dawning and certain dismay. She liked Edward Martin very much. In fact, she liked him almost as much as any male friend she had ever known, but she had never really thought of him in a romantic light. Her dark lashes brushed her cheeks as she gently withdrew her hands and bid him a quiet, withdrawn farewell. She was very distressed that she might have mislead him and quickly vanished into the house.

Edward Martin was all too aware of her withdrawal, but was not disheartened in the least. He realized his timing was wrong. Velvet had experienced an extreme form of dalliance this morning by an unwanted suitor. He suddenly felt like a cad.

How could he have been so stupid? How obtuse he had been, thinking only of furthering himself with her. How could he have lost control and been no better than a schoolboy? He shook his head over his poor behavior and slowly continued down the avenue.

All this had been conducted under the very interested gaze of the Marquis of Talgarth. The marquis had parted from Gilly with the promise to meet him for dinner at their hotel within the next hour. He then purposely made his way toward the Condé town house in time to witness Edward Martin handing Velvet a sweet roll only yards away from the house. Talgarth pulled up short and could not help but stare as the two laughed, gestured, talked, and laughed some more.

Talgarth's brows drew together, and he felt a sudden despondency that nearly overtook the irritation he was feeling while he observed the two at play. Then he saw Edward Martin take Velvet's hands and draw her near. He nearly pounced on them at that moment, but he held himself in check and continued to watch. He noted Velvet's downcast expression and the quiet manner in which she left Edward Martin. Well, damn, just what was this? The girl led the man on and then cast him off! This was quite improper. She had been living with the French far too long!

* * *

Velvet was feeling very poorly. She entered the house and asked for her cousin only to be told that the comtesse was out and was not expected for another twenty minutes. She sighed and asked for tea to be brought to her in the library. She had only just discarded her bonnet, gloves, and spencer, throwing them aside on a chair, when the library door opened at her back to admit the marquis. Velvet's green eyes opened wide with surprise and a sense of great pleasure. "My lord, you have come. I am so—"

"Aye, I have come, and just in time, my girl, let me tell you!" snapped Talgarth, cutting her off as he went forward to take up her shoulders in his strong hold. "I don't know what you are at behaving in public as you do, but I tell you frankly, it must stop."

Velvet's eyes opened wider, and she found herself begin to feel a flush with the rise of her temper. "If you will pardon my ignorance, my lord, I don't have a notion of what you are speaking!"

"Don't you? No, of course you would not. Well, in truth, it ain't all your fault. Your grandfather always let you run about like a little hoyden," he put up his finger, "and that was fine. Just a child then, but I tell you, girl, you ain't a child any longer, and it won't do. Here is Marie leading you about, but she is French, and the frogs have a very different notion of dallying about than we English do."

"Dallying about? And with whom have I been dallying?"

"Don't play Jack-Pudding with me, Velvet. I just

witnessed your little game outside!" he retorted caustically.

"Have you been spying on me?" countered the lady, incensed beyond measure.

"No, but no doubt I should have been."

"How dare you!"

"How dare *you,* Velvet. Don't you know that Edward Martin is a decent enough chap and you shouldn't be playing fast and loose with his feelings?"

Velvet lost her color as her gaze discovered the carpet. "Oh no. Do not say so. I would never—"

"Wouldn't you? What then? Laughing, teasing, looking up at him as you do. What the devil did you think you were doing to the poor fellow?"

"I . . . we are friends, nothing more. I did not think—"

"No, you certainly did not think!" Talgarth gave Velvet's shoulder a shake and, then he released her. "Every instinct tells me to pack you up and take you home."

This time she moved to take Talgarth's lapels in her hands, and her green eyes held a plea as she looked up at his handsome face. "Oh no, my lord. Please do not. I will try and behave as you like, I do sincerely promise."

She was a beauty. Her green eyes melted him in a way he could not explain to himself. Her touch thrilled him in a way he would not acknowledge. "Do you, little one?"

"Oh yes, yes, I shall not flirt with anyone you cannot like, and I shall be very circumspect with

Edward Martin, though you cannot object to his courtship."

"Object to his . . . Velvet, do you want Edward Martin to court you?" He waited breathlessly for her answer, not understanding why it was so important to know.

"I . . . no . . . not really."

He took hold of her all at once. He didn't understand what he was doing, how he could allow his body to move in direct contradiction to his mind, but he was bending her to him, and all at once he was discovering the sweetness of her lips!

Velvet felt him take her into his embrace and relaxed welcomingly into his arms. She had waited all her life, it seemed, for this moment, and it was everything she had dreamed it would be. She felt the gentle pressure of his mouth on hers and then his exploring tongue. All thoughts vanished. There was only this kiss, his kiss. She reached up and touched his face, his neck, his shoulders as his kiss lost itself into another. Dreams became reality, and she gave herself to him in that moment.

The marquis wasn't thinking. He was only feeling, and it was a light and glorious sensation. Velvet fit in his arms as though she had been designed for him. Her lips sweetly parted into a kiss that sent him reeling into desire. As his body began to take over, his mind snapped to attention. Hell and brimstone, what are you doing? he asked himself. Cad, scoundrel, villain! How could he do this to the young girl he had been entrusted to protect? He set her away from himself as though she were on fire.

"Velvet, I . . . Forgive me?" he said.

Velvet felt as though someone had thrown her into a tub of cold water. Confusion set in. What was he saying? Was her dream over? No, no, this could not be happening! "What?" she asked hazily.

"Forgive me. I am nought but an errant rake!" He backed away from her.

"No . . . No . . ." She hastened to relieve him of such a notion. "Dustin, please don't say that, Dustin." What was wrong with her? Why couldn't she speak coherently? What drivel was coming out of her mouth?

"Not say that I am a cad to behave like this with *you*? What then must I say? What must you think?"

"It was me; I led you to it," she cried, reaching for his hand.

He yanked it away from her as though she had scratched him. "You led me to it? What, then, am I the child and you the guardian? No." He turned away from her. "I must go, Velvet. Forgive me. Mine is the fault, not yours!" He nearly ran in his haste to quit her. His mind was roaring so wildly, his heart could barely be heard.

Velvet watched him leave, and the sudden pressures of the day overwhelmed her staunchly brave heart. Tears welled up in her fine green eyes and spilled over. Marie walked in at that moment, complaining about Talgarth's very odd behavior as he had passed her in the hall. She cut herself short and went to Velvet exclaiming, "La, it is too bad of him! Has he been scolding *ma petite* again?"

"No, no, it isn't that. Oh, Marie, I feel like crawl-

ing into a dark corner and covering myself up!"
wailed Velvet, suddenly feeling lost.

"La, *non, ma chérie,* you do not. That is not my
Velvet Colbury, forever fighting, cajoling, laughing. . . . *Non,* there is not a corner for such as that.
Come, *ma petite,* we will sit and talk." She led Velvet
to the sofa and there held her a long moment before
asking, "Beloved, *chérie,* what now is it that is so
terrible?"

"He does not love me," cried Velvet on a hearty
sob.

"There are others," said Marie calculatingly.

"No, there is only Dustin. For me . . . only
Dustin."

"Ah, why do you think your Dustin does not love
you?"

"He kissed me," wailed Velvet. Unable to continue, she covered her face in her hands.

Marie pried Velvet's hands away from her face and
looked at her for a meaningful moment. "This I
understand not at all!"

"Marie, he kissed me and then ran off. He says
he is a cad because he kissed me!"

"Ah," Marie said softly and more to herself. "Now
it becomes clearer."

The marquis nearly ran the distance between the
Condé house and the club where he was to meet
Gilly for their evening drink and subsequent meal.
He was in a state of zealous rationale. There was
only one reason why he had succumbed to Velvet's

obvious charms, and that was the natural desire a
man feels when he has not been with a woman in-
timately for a great length of time. Well, he had not
had a woman since that opera singer in London last
month. No excuse, perhaps, but at least a reason of
sorts!

However, his heart rang a peal over this conclusion, and a voice told him things he did not want to
hear. He beat the voice down and made a decision.
He would seek out female companionship tonight,
and he would check his desire for Velvet's lovely ripe
lips. And, damnation, he had no business thinking
of Velvet's lips or anything else. This would have to
stop!

He reached the club, immediately found Gilly
chatting with Armand, and drew him aside. "After
dinner, Gilly, what say you we go to Vassaud's for
some feminine entertainment?"

Gilly's light eyes flashed confusion. "Vassaud's?
Well, upon my soul!"

The marquis grinned boyishly. "Famous good notion, eh? Been some weeks since we've sampled the
lovelies, and I understand that Vassaud's houses the
finest bits of fancy to be seen in all of Paris."

Gilly blushed to the roots of his fair hair. He was
in love with Leslie Martin, and he was a man whose
character was by nature very faithful. His mind had
planned a future with Leslie, and even the thought
of diverting from that plan made him feel a villain.
Still, he was a man and did not wish to appear foolish on the subject. "Er . . . well . . . er . . ." he
hedged.

"So then, directly after dinner, ol' boy, it's off to Vassaud's for us, eh?"

"No," said Gilly simply.

"No?" returned the marquis, his blue eyes opening wide with curious surprise.

"Can't tonight," said Gilly. The more he thought about being with another woman, the more distressed he felt. He started to fidget in a manner peculiar to himself that made his longtime friend eye him with some concern and inquire, "Gilly, what is it? What is wrong?"

"Thing is, thinking of getting married. Must provide the name with an heir," answered Gilly, thinking this to be perfect reasoning.

"Gilly, ol' boy, you are only nine and twenty. Time enough for that," retorted the marquis, chuckling.

"No. Want to get married . . . soon," answered Gilly, pulling at his cravat.

"Well, what has that to say to anything? Not married yet, so it's off to Vassaud's." The marquis laughed and slapped his friend on the back, not quite understanding what this kick-up was really all about.

"Can't," said Gilly, finally able to look directly at his friend's face. "Mean to pop the question soon. Have reason to believe I shall be accepted," he finished proudly.

"Devil you say!" The marquis was genuinely excited for his friend. " 'Tis Miss Martin, isn't it?"

"Love her," said Gilly by way of explanation.

"Yes, of course you do, ol' boy. Velvet called it a week ago." The marquis mused for a minute. "Well, it looks like I shall soon be wishing you happy, and, Gilly, you know I always do."

Gilly inclined his head. "Have a notion, Dustin."

"Aye then, what is it, ol' boy?"

"Don't go to Vassaud's."

"Well, I like that!" laughed the marquis. "You don't mean to—well, fine, I understand that, but *I'm* not getting married. I'm free, ol' boy, free!"

"Aye, so you are," said Gilly, looking at him thoughtfully. "Well then, Dustin, perhaps Vassaud's is just what you need."

Jacques de Beaupré leaned over M. Brionne's desk and whispered, "I would not be here if I were not desperate, but I trust that you will be fair with me. My family has dealt with you for many years."

"Indeed, Vicomte, but I am sorry. There is nothing I can do for you here."

"Why? Are not the gems worth a great fortune? I offer them to you, and you need only pay me half their worth."

"Your mother's diamonds, her collection handed down from your father's mother, are heirloom pieces and they are priceless. I would consider myself nothing more than the worst kind of detestable creature if I were to make you an offer without first consulting your father."

Jacques stared at him. "I shall go elsewhere, monsieur, and this is not a matter you should mention to anyone—not even my father."

M. Brionne inclined his head. "If you will permit an old man to speak?"

"Of course," said Jacques on a frown. "What is it?"

"Speak to your father about your problem. I know the Comte de Beaupré, oh, I think very well. He is worthy of your confidence."

"You do not understand, but I do thank you for your concern. I shall manage without worrying my father. He is, as you say, too worthy a parent to hurt with this business of mine."

Jacques took up his large leather satchel and walked out of M. Brionne's inner office into the elegant shop where he encountered Edward Martin.

"Vicomte," said Mr. Martin amiably, though he had only met the Beaupré lad on one occasion, when he had been dining with Armand. "What a pleasant surprise." Idly Martin's eyes strayed to the satchel the boy clutched to himself.

Jacques felt himself go white. He wasn't feeling well. The life he had been living had finally caught up to him mentally, physically, and emotionally. He was ashamed of himself and heartsick, knowing only that he did not want his father to know what depths he had reached in his wickedness. He wasn't able to smile as he exchanged a quick greeting. "Ah, M. Martin, isn't it? Are you enjoying your stay in Paris?"

"Immensely, thanks to your lovely aunt Marie and your amiable father."

"I am glad. Please, monsieur, excuse me. I must go," said Jacques as he hurried past the Englishman.

"Of course. Please do give my regards to your father, Vicomte," Mr. Martin called after the boy. He watched Jacques leave, thinking that the boy looked poorly.

Jacques rushed down the street but was unsure where he should go. He had wanted to sell the jewels to a reputable house in the hopes that he would in the future be able to arrange something with his trust fund and buy back the family heirlooms. He couldn't, mustn't, sell them elsewhere. With his head down and his steps dragging, he made his way home, intending to return the jewels to their place. No one would know that they were missing, for no one really ever looked at them any longer, not since his mother had died. Oh God, how could he have gotten himself into such a tangle? His father would never forgive him if he knew.

Twenty-one

Madame Vassaud's was a richly appointed establishment maintained in an appropriately exclusive section of Paris. Its style, while some held to be far too ornate, was certainly designed to make a man feel like Croesus himself. Madame Vassaud had been mistress to an aristocrat for many years before she had established her little "hotel of pleasures." From him she had learned a great deal about manners, style, and what men were looking for when away from home. She applied that knowledge and hers was now considered the finest and most elegant brothel in all of Paris.

The marquis stood outside its doors, and though he had clapped Gilly on the back some twenty minutes ago and jovially announced his intentions, he now found he did not have the heart to enter. Why this was, he could not fathom. The doors opened wide, and a large attractive woman of uncertain age smiled and cooed to him, "Ah, come, dearest. That's right. Is this your first visit to us? Why yes, I see that it is. Come . . ." Madame Vassaud led him within, chattering assuagingly.

Talgarth felt like a fool. Softly he took her hand

and inclined his head. "Madame, I have made an error. I must leave."

His French was basic, but Madame thought she understood more than he said. What this Englishman needed was encouragement. She spoke in soft, halting English, "Dear, do but look." Her sweeping hand indicated a roomful of lovely women of all shapes and styles. "One of them is for you."

All at once the marquis felt ill. Cavalier rake, he told himself, don't be a fool. Here are lovelies to entertain . . . to enjoy. Indeed, he scanned the group again. A herd of women like so much livestock, treated no better than sheep being led to slaughter. Each of these young women were given to the whims of their male clients. Hell and brimstone!

He didn't want any of them, not a one, but Madame had already noticed that he and the pretty brunette had exchanged smiles. The brunette swayed toward him; he took her hand and led her to the wall table which housed a variety of wines.

She spoke in French as she poured him a glass of champagne, and a picture of Velvet flashed in his mind. He shrugged it off and whispered softly to the girl. She stroked his cheek and told him that he was very handsome. She pursed her lips and they were lovely. Velvet's lips were cherry-sweet. Velvet's green eyes glittered when she would tease. Velvet's voice tickled his heart. All at once, the marquis was speaking in English. He was pushing a handful of gold coins into the girl's hand and saying that he had to leave.

"Mais non," cried the girl in shocked surprise.

"*Non,* stay. Allow me to earn all of this." Indeed, her dark eyes opened wide at the sight of all the gold in her hands, so much more than the customary sum.

"You have already," he said, bending over her hand and turning to rush out. With Madame at his back, he hurriedly took up his hat, gloves, and cane, and a moment later he was in the cool, fresh night air. He hurried down the avenue, hailed a passing hackney, and settled against the weathered squabs with something close to relief. He only knew he had wanted out of Vassaud's, wanted away from the pretty brunette. Why didn't matter . . . or did it?

Just what was wrong with him? Velvet's giggle even in memory brought a reluctant grin to his face. So vivid was the picture of her in his mind's eye. Her pert nose, her glorious yellow hair, her soft cheeks, her smile. . . . Damn, how her smile could warm him! What was this? What was wrong with him? He caught himself; stop! What? What was all this? He was behaving like a schoolboy. This had to stop!

Louis opened his brother's bedroom door without knocking and found Jacques standing outside on his small ornamental balcony. A cool night's breeze came through the open doors, making the hangings rustle. "Jacques?" Louis called.

His brother only turned to look at him once before returning his gaze to the darkening sky. Louis went to him. "Jacques?"

"Oui, Louis. What is it?"

"Jacques, pay attention to me!" Louis took his brother's arm and angrily turned him round. "It is me—have you forgotten? Tell me, who are you? Where is my brother? Where is my father's heir?"

Jacques felt the tears which had threatened all day to explode from his throat. With a cry he threw his arms round his brother. "I am finished, Louis. My life is over! I must flee my family and my country to avoid dishonor to the name of—"

"You must stop this foolishness!" Louis shook him roughly. "I know what has happened. We must go to Father. Whatever the sum, it must be paid. Father will be angry, but in the end . . . you are his son. Jacques, he loves you."

"I cannot, and you may not without my leave. I would rather die, I tell you, Louis. You may not tell Father of this."

"No, of course I would not do so without your permission. Besides, *you* should be the one to confess to him. It wouldn't work any other way, you know."

Jacques hung his head. "You do not know the amount . . ."

"I gather it is great?"

"Louis, it is a fortune," breathed Jacques in utter despair.

"Papa is a wealthy man." Louis was frowning. "How much is it, Jacques? Will it ruin us?"

"Non, of course not. How wicked could I be? *Non,* but it is more than an entire year's allowance. It will take me nearly two years to pay it back to Father . . .

and I will be penniless at school. I am nought but a fool. You are younger and so much wiser. You were smart enough to stay away from there. You are the clever one, Louis."

Louis put a comforting arm about his brother's shoulders. "Perhaps we may take a loan from Tante Marie?"

Jacques looked at him hopefully. *"Oui, oui,* I did not think of that." He then shook his head. *"Non,* she will feel obliged to tell Papa."

"Condé, he will help us," suggested Louis, with the optimism of youth.

"It is a shameful matter." Jacques hung his head.

"I will help you pay him back. We will share whatever funds come my way," said Louis.

Jacques looked at him. "You would do that?"

"You are my brother," Louis said simply.

Twenty-two

"Her ladyship is resting, my lord, and may not be disturbed," said the small retainer blocking Farnsworth from entering the Condé house.

The small butler had spoken in French, and Farnsworth's command of the language was quick to understand the rigidness behind the words. He eyed the man calculatingly. "Ah . . . Lady Velvet is not unwell, I hope?"

The butler had been well-instructed, and he had put off more distinguished persons than an English lord. He stood his ground and said, "Her ladyship is simply resting." He offered no other explanation. It was not his place.

"Yes, I understand that," said Farnsworth, taking out a coin and passing it before the butler's eyes, "but what I want to know is has she been up and about? Will she, do you think, be up and about later this afternoon?"

"I know only that her ladyship is resting, my lord," said the butler, highly insulted. He was a loyal Condé servant. He had served the comte's father all his life, and now he served the son. He was treated with care and affection. He felt himself to be one of the family, and this . . . this Englishman dared to wave a coin at him? He started to close the door.

Farnsworth's eyes narrowed. His stare dared the butler to dismiss him, thinking, of course, that he would not. The Condé butler continued to close the door, and a moment later Farnsworth heard the snap of the bolt.

He was furious. His hazel eyes glittered dangerously. Damn the little man! He would just see about him! Yes, but he couldn't go to his cousin with such a petty complaint. It would make him look foolish, and just now his cousin was helping him with other, more important matters. There was currently a problem facing him for Nicole had not yet been able to come up with a minister of his faith . . . at least not one willing to perform a clandestine wedding. However, his cousin had come up with an excellent tale to give the next minister they found.

He hailed a passing hack, comfortable in his expectations, not realizing that his was the only name barred from the Condé house. He soothed his frustration by telling himself that Velvet had no way of knowing that he had been refused admittance. No doubt she was relaxing with a novel or getting some beauty rest. No doubt at all!

As Farnsworth stepped into the hack, Gilly, followed by the marquis, stepped out of one. The marquis was quick to notice Farnsworth as he drove by and would have run after the conveyance had Gilly not held him in check and said admonishingly, "Don't want to make cake of yourself, ol' boy."

Talgarth was impulsive, but he immediately saw

the wisdom of these words and settled for shaking his fist after Farnsworth's retreating cab to say, "Damn your soul, blackguard!" He turned to Gilly, "That's why he wasn't at his hotel this morning. We keep missing the scoundrel, for he is forever on the go! I tell you what, Gilly, think I'll camp outside his hotel room and wait for the blasted commoner!"

"Well, you could to that," said Gilly doubtfully, "but, damn, think how you would look, Dusty." He shook his head. "Won't do. Not *ton.*"

"I'm honorbound to meet him. Mark me on this," seethed the marquis.

"Aye, sadly you are, but I don't think you should do it on his terms."

"What the deuce? The devil you say!" snapped the marquis. "I mean to pound him to a pulp, I mean to beat him bloody, I mean to—"

"Have a notion he won't put up his fives. The fellow has no more pluck than a dunghill cock," said Gilly.

The marquis threw back his head with a shout of laughter. "What then? Shall I give up the fight? Not I."

"Think of a better thing to do. Something that ends the fight once and for all." Gilly shook his head. "Don't like having an enemy at our backs forever, you know."

The marquis eyed his friend measuringly. "Thought of that, ol' boy. Can't be done without killing the fellow."

"Oh, I don't know. Told you, the man is a coward.

Hold something over his head. Well . . . who knows.
Think on it some more."

"Don't have anything to hold over his head," said
the marquis gloomily. "I can't bring her name into
it. There is her family to consider. They suffered
enough. And what's more, he knows I won't bring
her name into it!"

"Well, there is his ungallant behavior with Velvet."

"Gilly, don't be a dunce." The marquis pulled a
face. "That won't fadge. Don't want Velvet's name
brought into this either!"

"Well," said Gilly tenaciously, for when a notion
entered his head, he usually stuck with it, "we know
between us that Farnsworth is nothing more than a
muckworm. There must be some bobbery we can
discover about him. Stands to reason a queer fish
like that hasn't been pound dealing everywhere he
goes."

"Aye . . ." the marquis's blue eyes were keen with
anticipation. "Agreed, my Gilly, agreed. The problem is, just what can we dig up on him?"

"We'll look about us for that. Bound to be something," replied Gilly amiably.

They had reached the Condé house, and the butler was very pleased to open the door wide for them
to enter. They had no need to inquire after Velvet,
for in a morning gown of pale green with her gold-
en curls in a flounce of cascading ringlets she nearly
threw herself into Talgarth's arms.

"Dustin, he was here, demanding to see me, but
Henri would not let him in and I was hiding in the

study, but I could hear everything, and I think I am a little afraid of him."

The marquis held her close for a long moment and patted the top of her pretty head before he held her from him and clucked, "Nonsense. What is there to be afraid of with all of us here to keep him at bay?"

"I know, but, oh, I don't know what it is. Just this feeling," said Velvet, whose hackles were up. She had an instinct that usually guided her about people, and all instincts made her wary of Lord Farnsworth.

The marquis touched her cheek, flicked her nose, and then drew her into his arms once more. The two clung together as the marquis cooed to her, calming her down.

Although Gilly's sense of romance had been heightened by his own recent experience, he knew this behavior to be quite unlike the marquis. Oh, to be sure, the marquis had always been something of a flirt, not precisely a rake, but most assuredly he had always had an affection for the ladies. This, however, was totally different. Gilly did not know why it was, he only knew that it felt different—why, the very air was sparked with the electric current that ran between these two volatile people.

"La!" cried Marie as she entered the house and nearly tore off her bonnet. She had been out doing last-minute shopping for the ball, and she was heartily sick of it. She noticed everyone gathered in her central hall. "What is this? To be certain, my hallway is designed in the first stare, but it is not for comfort.

Why are we standing here? *Moi,* I must have coffee and something sweet immediately."

She turned to her footman standing by and trying not to display interest in the goings-on. "Please bring coffee to the library and also bring that mulish tea. The gentlemen will no doubt help themselves to the other refreshments. Serve cake as well and some cheese." She turned to the assembled group and waved her hand. "Come. We shall be comfortable if you please."

As they sat, Marie casually said, "When Henri met me at the door, he informed me that the terrible Farnsworth had called. Henri does not like this Farnsworth. He does not say so, for he is too good a butler, but, well, Henri has been with my husband forever you see, and now and then he takes a liberty."

"How do you know that Henri does not like him if he didn't say so?" Gilly was curious enough to ask.

"Oh, that is very easy. He sniffed . . . like so." Marie wrinkled her nose. After some appreciative laughter, Marie shrugged and said, "We must now discuss what next is to be done."

A footman appeared at that moment with a huge tray laden with food. Some moments were spent in serving. The men poured themselves brandy from a nearby table, and Gilly sliced a piece of cheese, laid it on a biscuit, and declared it first-rate.

When all were settled with their individual refreshments, Marie picked up the former topic. "We have but two days left before the ball, only two days in which we must adroitly avoid the terrible Farnsworth. Condé believes we would all be best served to keep close to home."

"Zounds, woman!" declared the marquis, disgusted. "Do you mean *I*, er, we should let this scoundrel drive us underground?"

"He can be difficult to deal with in light of his connection to Davenant," suggested Marie tentatively. The truth be told, when her English friends left Paris the day after the ball, she would still have to deal with the Davenants!

Gilly cleared his throat and said as much. "Don't want any problems for the comte when we are gone."

"Of course, you are right, Gilly, and we won't make any problems for them, but even Napoleon himself would not allow a man to publicly insult his own gently bred females. Certainly he would find no fault in my calling Farnsworth to account for himself on that score."

"Indeed, perhaps not. At any rate, Condé has already explained to M. Davenant that under such uncomfortable circumstances, Madame's cousin will not be invited to our ball," Marie said.

"Never say so?" ejaculated Gilly.

"Well, and how did Monsieur receive that piece of news?" the marquis inquired gravely.

"He had no choice but to agree with what he called my very wise decision," said the comte from the doorway. He closed the door behind him, moved to the table, poured himself a glass of wine, and sat down in his favorite leather-upholstered winged chair to eye the group quizzically.

"Oui, oui! My Condé is *magnifique,* is he not?"
Marie jumped to her feet and ran to seat herself in
the comte's lap. He smiled at her and touched her
cheek fondly, offered her a sip of his wine, which
she took, and then returned his attention to the
young people staring after them.

"I have always been on amiable terms with Davenant. We understand one another politically and
have rarely had an occasion to butt heads. When I
advised him of Lord Farnsworth's behavior toward
my wife's cousin, he understood my outrage. I further explained that I had visited with Napoleon."

"With Napoleon?" The marquis put down his
glass of brandy and slapped his knee. "Famous!"
He turned to Gilly. "A man after my own heart."
Then back to Condé. "Do go on, Comte."

"Indeed, I had no choice but to explain to Napoleon what a dilemma we found ourselves in, you see.
Napoleon was in accord with me and said that he
had found La Colbury a delightful beauty who
should not be allowed to entertain any Englishmen
at all. He again urged me to encourage her to stay
on in Paris and marry a Frenchman."

"Enfin! My husband manages them all!" Marie
snapped her fingers. "So much for the Davenant
woman!" She turned to the marquis. "Now you have
no need to meet with Farnsworth."

"Ah, in this I must dissent, my dear," said the
marquis, his features suddenly grim. "I have every
need."

Looks were exchanged, but oddly enough Gilly
put a finger to his lips and quieted Velvet, who

would have objected. A diversion occurred at that moment as a group of young people, friends of Velvet's, arrived, and the room filled with their lively, highly spirited banter.

Later that day Jacques and Louis entered their uncle's study. Jacques met Condé's inquiring eyes and hung his head. Louis took a step forward, hand unconsciously outstretched. "Forgive us. We have a terrible confession to make . . . unforgivable. You may never wish to acknowledge us ever again. We have proven ourselves unworthy of our name."

Louis was overcome at this point and copied his brother as he closed his eyes and hung his head as well. Before Condé could speak, however, Jacques lifted his head. "*Non*, Uncle, not Louis. My brother is everything that is good, kind, and honorable. He has tried to stop me, even chasing after me. He had done everything possible that he could, but I am a fiend. I did not listen."

"*Non, non*, Jacques is all that is good—" started Louis.

The comte put up his hand. Standing, he then walked around his desk. Softly he asked, "All this drama? What then? Tell me what terrible thing you have done."

"I am so ashamed," said Jacques on a whisper.

"And you, Louis, are you too ashamed to tell me what this dreadful thing is?" prompted the comte hopefully.

"It has been a dreadful mistake. One can rectify

one's mistakes," said Louis reasonably. "We need your help, Uncle."

"Then please tell me what you have done, and we shall see how we may rectify this mistake together."

They started at the beginning, leaving out only Velvet's part in their first adventure on the town. Haltingly Jacques told his story, with interjections from his younger brother, until he reached the part about gambling with an Englishman.

The comte stood up straight. "With an Englishman you say, lad?"

"*Oui*. I knew that the stakes were getting higher than I could afford, but I was too embarrassed to pull out, and then I could not." Again, Jacques hung his head.

"What is the total sum you have lost?" Condé asked quietly.

Louis and Jacques breathed the amount together and managed to meet Condé's gaze. The comte released a low whistle and then said, "Well, a hefty amount that no doubt your entire year's allowance will not cover."

They shook their heads in unison. The comte smiled to himself. The sum was enormous, quite as much as he had paid only yesterday for a new barouche for his dear wife. It was quite within Beaupré's large fortune to manage without a great deal of trouble. However, he had no intention of telling the brothers this, for they deserved to suffer a bit more over their actions. This was an excellent lesson. He sized them up with an authoritative air and said, "Well, I take it gaming is no longer in your blood?"

"*Non*, I swear, Uncle. Only the excitement, the women, but no more. Never anything like that," said Jacques.

"Good. I will give you a voucher to take to this Englishman. Tell me, did he not realize he was playing with a minor? After all, you scarcely look of age."

"Well, as to that, he knew me—knew that I am a Beaupré. In fact, he knows my father. He threatened to take my markers to my father."

The comte was stunned, but he did not say so. He maintained his calm exterior, saying only, "Really? And who may this Englishman be?"

"I cannot say. I gave my word not to reveal his name," said Jacques.

"Of course," said the comte dryly. It was, of course, taboo socially to gamble with a minor, especially for such extraordinary amounts. To gamble with the son of an acquaintance would ruin a man's *ton*, ostracize him from the elite beau monde. How could a gentleman do such a thing? Why would a gentleman do such a thing, for while the amount was hefty, it was not as though he were taking a fortune. Who would do such a thing?

He gave the Beaupré boys his voucher and advised them who to see at the bank in the morning. He watched them go and sat down to think. A moment later he was calling for his hat and coat, pulling on his kid gloves, and taking up his walking stick. He was going to the club where he was bound to find Armand at this hour!

* * *

The marquis and Gilly parted company after they left Velvet. Gilly was off to take Miss Martin for a stroll in the park, and the marquis would not say where he was off to. As it happened, he had several stops to make, and the last one before he was to rejoin Gilly at the club was at Lord Farnsworth's hotel. This time his visit was fruitful.

Farnsworth was dressed for the evening and just crossing the lobby of his hotel when the marquis entered, spotted him, and purposely made his way toward him. Lord Farnsworth felt the trepidation he always felt whenever the marquis looked at him with that marked sneer of his. Schoolboy hates and fears are not easily discarded. Farnsworth stood his ground, feeling he was safer in the main lobby than out on the avenue.

"Well, I've finally caught up to you," said the marquis on a low controlled note.

"So you have, Dustin dearest," drawled Farnsworth. "It seems we are fated to be forever in one another's path."

"You are out there, my man. Our fates are finally going to part. You called on Lady Velvet today and were turned away. If you call tomorrow, you will be turned away. She will not see you. We stay only for the ball the comtesse is giving in her honor, and then we are off for London, where you will not be allowed within a mile of her. Do I make myself clear?" The marquis was very proud of himself for the control he was exerting. He dearly wanted to plant the scoundrel a facer as he had so many years ago. However, it had not served then and probably would not do so now.

"Given my position in London's beau monde, you cannot actually forbid me from courting Lady Velvet. It would look most peculiar," retorted Lord Farnsworth, taking a pinch of snuff to his nose and lightly inhaling. He felt himself shaking with anger.

The marquis's fist clenched and unclenched. "Your position means absolutely nothing to me and even less to my grandfather, who is Lady Velvet's guardian. Mark me: you will not be allowed to come near her now or later."

"You have more reason now than before?" Farnsworth frowned. "Or is this because of past grievances?"

"This is because you are nothing but a villain, and in this particular case, your suit is undesirable to the lady in question." The marquis turned on his heel, proud of himself for his restraint, and left his lordship seething.

Twenty-three

The Club Marsan was one of the city's finest men's clubs. It was furnished in an elegantly quiet style. Its rooms were many, providing those who needed it with privacy. There a wealthy gentleman could expect to find his friends, an amiable card game, the finest wines and liquors to be had, and, if needed, games dedicated to higher stakes. Politics, social order, philosophy, arts, theater, women, cards . . . all were discussed at Marsan's without the intervention of female relatives and lovers.

The Comte de Condé entered the main galley of Marsan's and scanned the room, as Armand was more often found there having a lively chat with one of his many friends. The comte saw his brother-in-law at a far corner and managed to catch his eye. With but a slight indication of his head, he made Armand aware that he was needed for private conversation, and the two greeted one another with quiet affection.

"What is towards?" inquired Armand, affectionately linking his arm through the comte's.

"*Tiens*, it is a most delicate matter, and, Armand, I must have your word to keep this between us just for the time being until we may discover the extent of the whole."

"You talk in riddles, Condé," chuckled Armand. "But, of course, whatever you tell me goes no further."

"It involves your sons, and you must not leave me to go and scold them. It won't do."

Armand stiffened. "What is this?"

Condé recounted the story in his own words, leaving out a detail or two which he felt Armand did not immediately need to know. However, he then stopped and said quietly, "There is more."

Armand was angry with his sons, but he still had control of himself and, as a father, was attempting to make excuses for them in his heart. At these words he put a hand to the area housing that organ and ejaculated, *Quelle horreur!* There is more?"

"I am afraid it is very serious. I suspect that Jacques has been used for some ulterior motive I can not immediately fathom."

"Of what are you speaking? I do not understand," exclaimed Armand, thinking that his sons had done quite enough and that it was time they were packed off to his aunt in the country.

"Ah, there you are!" exclaimed the marquis, coming along with Gilly in tow. He stopped short and apologized. "I am sorry; we are interrupting."

"Non, non . . ." said Armand.

Condé eyed the marquis and suggested to all, "Shall we retire to a private parlor? Armand, I should understand if you do not wish this discussed with the marquis and Gilly, but I believe the marquis has a vested interest in the story I now must continue."

"What the devil?" remarked the marquis, his brows going up.

"*Non, non,* I have no objection, though what Dustin has to do with my sons, I cannot guess."

"You will see," said Condé, leading them to a small anteroom. Closing the door at their backs, he sat down and invited them to do the same.

He had the floor, so briefly he brought the marquis and Gilly up to date on the antics of the Beaupré boys, much to Armand's chagrin.

Armand interrupted only once to say with a rueful grin, "Being a father is a terrible business—do not do it. How very uncomfortable it is to scold one's beloveds for things one has done in one's youth!" They all chuckled and then settled into comfortable silence as the Condé put up a hand and said ominously, "There is more, and this part of their tale is ugly . . . very ugly."

"The devil you say?" exclaimed the marquis. "I have seen those boys. There isn't the slightest bit of harm in them."

"No, not in them, but in the man who has used them, or Jacques rather. You see, finding a drunken Jacques in this gaming hell with a piece of muslin interested in opium was an English gentleman."

The marquis sat up with interest. "Go on."

"This English—and it saddens me to call him gentleman, so I shall not. This *man,* knowing Jacques to be the son of a gentleman he knows well enough to call an acquaintance, did not try to send Jacques home. Instead he engaged Jacques in a game of chance, and the stakes were high . . . and kept getting higher as poor Jacques imbibed more alcohol. It ended with Jacques giving his marker to this Englishman."

"How much?" Armand was frowning. "This man took my son for how much?"

He was told and all men whistled. The marquis did some quick calculation and discovered this was the equivalent of five thousand English pounds!

"Well upon my soul!" said Gilly. "But that is curst bad . . . very bad. A gentleman does not gamble with a boy . . . especially the son of a friend and with the boy in his cups! Who is this commoner?"

Condé pulled a face. "Jacques gave his word to this man that he would not disclose his name, but I have a very excellent notion."

"So do I," said the marquis grimly.

"Go on! Never say you think it is Farnsworth?" cried Gilly, shocked. "Well, what then? Is the man queer in the attic? Must be, must be dicked in the nob for that matter! Why?"

"Because he wanted a hold, a connection to Velvet," said the marquis. "I tell you the man is evil beyond comprehension."

"I don't understand," said Armand, still reeling from the knowledge that his eldest boy had gambled such high stakes.

"Armand, it is illegal to gamble with a minor—as well as unacceptable behavior from one of our own. If we can prove it is Farnsworth, we need not pay the debt."

"And we have our weapon for all time," said the marquis on a whisper. "Did you hear that, Gilly?"

"Aye, may the devil rot in hell!"

"How we shall discover for a fact that it is Farnsworth I cannot say," mused Condé thoughtfully.

"How are the boys paying him his debt?"

"That's what I should like to know," said Armand, his eyes narrowing as he scanned Condé's face.

"They came to me for help, Armand. My first obligation was to help. I do mean to keep after them to tell you the whole. I think that would be best, don't you?"

"*Oui, oui,* you are wise as ever my Condé," said Armand thankfully. "My sister is very, very lucky." Armand got up and kissed the comte on both cheeks.

Gilly pulled a face and leaned over to the marquis. "Why must they be forever doing that?"

The marquis ignored him, for he was pacing now and thinking hard. The conversation at his back scarcely was heard as Condé modestly put up his hand and objected, "*Non, non,* Armand, it is I that am the lucky one and have been since the first time I saw my dear Marie."

"Very well then, you are both lucky," said Gilly, feeling heartily sick of all this emotion. "What we have here is a curst vulgar make-bait that needs to be sent to the gallows. Short of that, at least to one of his obscure village estates, where he may rot out the remainder of his life."

Condé's eyebrows raised. "What is this, Gilly? So

much heat? I did not know that you, too, had a grievance with this man."

"Aye, for it was I that stopped Dustin from putting a bullet through his evil head all those years ago, and now look what has come of it!" He shook his head. "Only one way to handle a rum touch, and that is with his own style!"

"Right you are, Gilly, ol' boy," said the marquis suddenly as a notion came to mind. He turned to the comte. "Tell me, Condé, how are the boys to repay this gaming debt?"

"Ah, I gave them a voucher."

"You gave them a voucher? For the entire amount?" cried Armand. "Why, this is too good of you. I shall reimburse you immediately."

"Never mind, Armand, 'tis unimportant. I mean to retrieve the money from Farnsworth as soon as I may prove it was he that was involved."

The marquis exhibited great patience as he waited for the two to discuss this point out before interrupting them to pursue his thoughts. "Condé, this voucher. The boys are to present it to your bank first thing in the morning?"

"*Oui*, 'tis what we agreed."

"Well, there will be an alteration of these plans," said Talgarth, grinning broadly.

"Oh?" Condé caught the gleam in the marquis's blue eyes. "Ah, you have a plan? A viable plan?"

"Indeed, I do, and first you must immediately return home and send for Jacques!"

Twenty-four

"*Hien?* All is not well," said Nicole Davenant, clicking her tongue. "*Voyons,* what is to be done?"

"Darling, we must immediately set our plans in motion."

"*Voyons! Moi,* I am not a witch. I have not this power you seem to think," said the lady, who actually believed that she did.

"Ah, but you can do anything."

"And what is this anything?"

"*Chérie,* beloved cousin, beautiful creature, only think how romantic it will be. Velvet has agreed to fly with me. She will leave the Condé house on the night of her ball. There will be so many vehicles coming and going that they will not notice my coach waiting only a short distance off. We will go then to Villeneuve, St. George, and allow this minister you have found to marry us. After that I shall take Velvet back to England for a long honeymoon at my estate in the North Country. It will be a grand adventure. She will be thrilled."

"*Oui, oui,* it is so romantic." Davenant shook her head. "*Moi,* I do not understand how they can forbid you to court her. 'Tis outrageous. And my husband, he says you will not be invited to the ball as you allowed yourself to be seen making love to the chit in public. Very understandable, I am sure, but most unwise, *mon cher.*"

"Perhaps not. You have the Special License. What more do we need?" Farnsworth shrugged.

"Cousin, *mon cher,* you have not considered. At what hour do you think to descend on the minister? If you flee with Lady Velvet at two in the morning, you will not reach Villeneuve until three, perhaps four o'clock. How can I ask this minister to receive you at such an hour?"

"He will be well-paid."

"Do you think that will sway him? Some of these fellows snap their fingers at offers like that."

"This one will not. After all, he has already accepted an extravagant sum to marry us without the benefit of the girl's guardian being present. He will accept what I offer. Everyone, my dear, has a price!"

"This I do not argue. In fact, I think he will accept . . . but he will take an extraordinary amount."

" 'Tis nought. By the way, my sweet, I have ordered you three gowns at your modiste's. You have but to choose the style and the fabric."

Madame went and put her arms around him. "La, *mon cher,* how I adore you. Why, you do think of everything." She sighed. " 'Tis all so very romantic."

"Indeed, perhaps the last romance you will see for some years to come. War is very near."

"*Oui* . . . so sad." Doubt flickered in her eyes, for this runaway marriage still troubled her. "Lady Velvet . . . she, too, finds this arrangement suitable?"

"Lady Velvet is an exceptional young woman. She desires nothing more than to become my wife and begin our life together." Farnsworth's mind moved into another realm, and a decided sneer took over his features. How this would enrage the Marquis of Talgarth! He was outsmarting him again. Indeed, this notion was even more enjoyable than making Velvet Colbury his bride.

The marquis was at that very moment dining with the Martins and Leslie's besotted beau, Gilly. He had complained and grumbled, but he had acquiesced to his friend's request and joined them at the hotel the Martins were frequenting. His reluctance was due to the fact that although he found Edward Martin perfectly acceptable, amiable good *ton,* a silent rivalry had sprung up between them over Velvet. However, Talgarth put this aside and attempted to lead the table into witty conversation. Leslie Martin joined in, then casually asked if Velvet were at home. "Do they stay in tonight?"

"Condé seemed to think it was the wise thing for them to do until the ball," Talgarth answered on a half frown.

"You don't agree?" pursued Leslie.

"Oh well, as to that, I do; it is just that I very much feel like saying, 'Hang the ball, I am taking Velvet home.' That seems to me the only wise thing to do." He shook his head. "Have this gut feeling . . . well, never mind."

"I think, Talgarth, that you are overreacting to all

of this," said Edward Martin gently. "Don't see that Velvet should be deprived of her ball."

The marquis felt himself square off. He wanted to blister the man into oblivion. Velvet was his concern, not Edward Martin's! However, these days he had put restraints on his temper. Better to cool himself, react rationally. He settled back into his chair and relaxed. After all, Edward Martin would no doubt one day be Gilly's brother-in-law. Perhaps for Gilly's sake he answered calmly, "Well, we'll see. I genuinely hope that I am wrong."

Gilly had watched and applauded the marquis, who he felt had been goaded. He was glad that the marquis had not snapped Martin's head off, and yet he found himself coming to Dustin's defense all the same. "You are out on this one, Edward. Dustin is right. What's more, Velvet is a good little thing, only staying on for Marie's sake. Has no real taste for balls and such. Besides, give her one in London, she'd like that."

Gilly's common sense made everyone smile. He always had a way of laying things on the table in a plain manner that was infinitely profound. His beloved touched his hand and softly said, "You are ever so brilliant, Gilly."

Gilly almost shuffled his feet under the table in a dance step, he was so pleasantly surprised by this compliment. No one in his entire life, not even his dearest mother, had ever called him brilliant. He lowered his eyes and then brought them up to Leslie's face in sweet adoration.

Talgarth looked from one to the other in some

amusement and sputtered, "Good God, this is quite disgusting! What am I doing here? Well, I don't want dessert, for I am nearly sick already. I'm off!"

"No, don't leave me with them," cried Edward Martin, grinning broadly. "I am chaperon and must stay. At least bear me company."

"Can't," said the marquis simply. "You are her brother; it's your job, not mine. I have a notion, too, that Gilly is wishing you at Jericho by now. Don't see why you can't chaperon from the other gallery. It's within sight. Have a drink and enjoy the sights."

Gilly regarded his friend gratefully, for, indeed, he was wishing that he and Leslie could have a few moments alone. There were things he wanted, needed, to say to her and could not do so with her brother standing guard.

"Indeed, Edward, go off somewhere for your port . . . or whatever," Leslie chuckled.

Edward agreed that this was perhaps not such a bad notion and did take his leave of the two to take his port in the club adjacent to the dining room. He stopped the marquis at the door and gravely inquired, "Do you think that Velvet is in some kind of real danger?"

"I think, sir, that we all are," said the marquis grimly. "War is a certainty, and soon. You and Leslie are more than welcome to join us when we leave on the morning after the ball. My yacht awaits us in Le Havre."

"I thank you and will take you up on it. I know that Leslie would enjoy traveling with Velvet."

Martin inclined his head and watched the mar-

quis take his leave. Things were moving quickly . . .
too quickly, but it was just as well; he was anxious
to return to England himself.

The Marquis of Talgarth unconsciously made his
way to the Condé house. He was berating himself
for having invited Edward Martin to make the journey home with them. What, was he a fool to throw
Edward and Velvet together? It was exactly what he
did not want. On the other hand, war was hanging
over their heads, and he couldn't leave another Englishman in certain danger. Besides all that, Velvet
would enjoy Leslie Martin's company . . . as would
Gilly. Poor besotted Gilly! Confound it all! Yes, but
Gilly looked happier than he had ever seen him,
and that was saying a great deal, for Gilly was ha-
bitually sweet-tempered.

Farnsworth would have to be dealt with, and
quickly. Talgarth would not make the same mistake
he had made all those years ago. Oh no, he could
not allow that to happen again. This time he had
the man's savage measure. With a little luck,
Farnsworth would be exposed for the scoundrel he
was.

He was at the Condé door, and Henri the butler
was already opening the door wide and welcoming
the marquis in his soft French. Talgarth grinned a
greeting and was told the entire family was enjoying
a small fire in the library. The marquis said he
would announce himself and strolled thoughtfully
to the library doors, which were opened wide. He

stood a moment and felt as though he could not control the beating of his heart. There was Velvet sprawled on the hearth rug, comfortably reading a book. Her blond hair was loose, hanging in ringlet curls to the middle of her back and framing her piquant face in a tumble of glorious silk. Thick curls adorned her forehead, giving her an elfish, naughty look. She wore a simple gown of blue muslin, and Talgarth knew he had never seen any woman quite so beautiful. She was perfection. She was light. She made him feel dizzy, and he knew that all he wanted to do was scoop her up from the floor and take her into his arms! She looked up and smiled so happily to see him there, and he knew he wanted, needed, to kiss her. This left him breathless and feeling a bit of a fool.

Velvet got to her feet in a scramble of excitement. "Dustin . . . Dustin, you have come! How did you know I so wanted you to?" She went to him and found both her hands taken in his. They looked at one another in a way that made Marie's eyes start from her head.

Sensing it was time to step in, the comtesse got to her feet and called out graciously, "Dustin, how nice! Come in, come in."

Marie brought the marquis back to earth, and though he felt slightly irritated to be there, he managed to give her his gallant attention. "Dear heart, with such beauties in the Condé house, how could I stay away?"

Marie tittered, and Velvet blushed and reluctantly looked away. Condé surprised them by standing up and saying, "I, for one, am very pleased that you are here. I was going to send for you in the morning. Dustin, we must talk. Will you be so kind as to join me in my study?"

The marquis was surprised but willing. "Yes, of course."

"La, but this is too bad of you," pouted Marie, "and poor Dustin has not even been offered refreshment."

"He shall have it in the study, my love," said the comte, taking Dusty's arm and leading him from the room.

Velvet watched them go and turned to Marie. "Now why must Condé speak with Talgarth? What is toward, Marie?"

"*Moi*, I know not," said Marie. "But perhaps by morning I shall!" So saying she laughed, finding herself quite amusing.

"Of that I have no doubt whatsoever," said Velvet.

"Oh, I don't always get what I want. Condé is no fool to be manipulated by me. There are some things he just will not tell me no matter what I do, but those are usually things I have no interest in anyway."

Condé poured out a snifter of brandy and handed it to the marquis before taking a chair and inviting Talgarth to do the same. The marquis had been watching him quietly, patiently, waiting for Condé to speak and finally inquired, "Its war, isn't it?"

"As to that, I will not tell you otherwise, but we

have, I believe, still a few weeks. Your ambassador is very diplomatic. Perhaps he may yet convince Napoleon not to break the Treaty of Amiens."

"He has already broken the treaty over Malta," said the marquis gravely.

Condé shrugged. "It is not in our hands. Velvet, however, is very much in our hands, under our protection. I had both Jacques and Louis here, and we discussed everything as you wished. Our plan goes forth exactly as you laid out, and Jacques knows 'tis important to Velvet's safety. Further, we are all of us to a man ready to stand watch the night of the ball."

"I thank you," said the marquis quietly.

"I wish I knew how he means to involve Velvet by using Jacques."

" 'Tis no matter. He did not expect Jacques to come up with the money, and I believe he will not be able to turn it down once it is in sight. It will be his undoing!"

"How will you use it?"

" 'Pon rep! It will ruin him. The proof will be his signature on the voucher, the gaming voucher of a youth! I will have his soul for all eternity. The English beau monde are very hard-hearted about such crimes. He must not know that Jacques has any suspicions about him."

"Jacques means to play his part well. He will be the frightened schoolboy attempting only to discharge his debt."

"There is still the chance that Farnsworth may not accept the offer," mused the marquis. "However,

I know he thinks too much of himself to worry about such details."

"I will feel better once you have Velvet safely in England," said the comte, "though my dear Marie will miss her so very much."

"We will arrange to meet in Italy . . . or some other neutral country," said the marquis. "And perhaps if war does break out, it may not last long?"

"We both know that war with England will probably go on for years," the comte pointed out sadly. "Now, indulge me, Dustin. I have a particular desire to know what it was that Farnsworth did to you so many years ago that is still so white-hot?"

The Marquis of Talgarth eyed the Comte de Condé and bit his bottom lip before he said, "You must understand that I am honorbound to protect the name of the family that was involved. I shall not tell you their name, but in England, if this tale were to get around, well, it wouldn't take long for someone to put the puzzle together."

"Your story remains with me," said Condé.

"We were at school together, and somehow—I am not certain how it happened—we became rivals. The truth is I really didn't notice Farnsworth much in those days. We each had our own set . . . or perhaps I had my own set and he had only a friend or two." The marquis shook his head. "It doesn't matter. What does matter is that he decided to pit himself against me at nearly everything—lessons, sports, and then women! It irked him that he couldn't get the better of me, and I suppose when he started his last game he didn't really know where it was going to take him."

The marquis stopped and then eyed Condé ruefully. "That last year in school I wasn't even twenty yet, but I thought I had fallen in love . . . desperately. It was, of course, calf love with the girl of a local family. She was lovely—sweet and innocent. I sent her flowers, chocolates, and poems. As I was not the sort to make love to a girl, an innocent girl, and leave, I courted her slowly, and when she asked what my intentions were, I was young enough to be frightened into retreat.

"Farnsworth saw his chance to do me an injury and began courting the girl. When I saw her with him, I was jealous, agitated, and angry. My pride was hurt, and I stopped calling on the girl. Farnsworth gloated, bragged, but even that was not enough for him. He just couldn't leave it at that!"

The marquis's lips twisted, and his eyes of blue glinted darkly with the memory. "She wrote to me then, told me that he had used her and how ashamed she was, but I didn't find out until too late that she was pregnant. Her family had sent her away, you see, to Cornwall.

"I discovered it and went after her. I wanted to give her my name. I was no longer infatuated with her, but I felt responsible somehow. I was too late—she miscarried in her seventh month and died of complications almost immediately."

"*Mon Dieu!* This Farnsworth is of a great wickedness. Did he never make any attempt to help the child?"

"No. He denied that he was the father," said the marquis savagely.

"*Sacrebleu!* It is no wonder that you wanted him well away from our little Velvet."

"As to that, Velvet is too clear-sighted to allow the likes of such a man to pay her court; however, I don't trust him. There is no telling what someone like that can manage. You see, he doesn't play by the rules as you and I know them."

"It worries me, this business with Jacques. For certain he will use it to gain access to Velvet, but how?"

"We'll have our answers soon enough. In the meantime, depend on it, Comte: he shall not get near my Velvet!"

Twenty-five

Jacques de Beaupré was nervous but still in full command of himself. So much depended on his accomplishing what his uncle wanted. There was Velvet to be thought of in this matter. He still did not understand how she was in danger from Farnsworth, but he was not about to allow any misdeed of his to affect her!

He stood and watched Farnsworth come toward him a look of smug satisfaction on his face and felt a sense of anger tickle his nerves. Farnsworth had taken unscrupulous advantage of his youth, his uncle had said. He was underage and not responsible for a gaming debt, for it had been illegal for Farnsworth to engage him in such play! Jacques felt a fool, but at least serving Farnsworth this turn would perhaps in some manner give the man his comeuppance! He could see that Farnsworth was surprised to receive him so early in the morning.

"So, my lord, I am here to discharge my debt to you," said Jacques proudly.

Farnsworth regarded him thoughtfully, for it was true that he had not expected the boy to be in a position to repay him his gaming debt. It worried him a little. He had meant to use the situation to induce Velvet to be in his company alone as much as he could. Velvet, however, was being kept from him. Why not take the money then? Why not, indeed! He had spent quite a hefty sum for the Special License and then another for the minister to perform a questionable ceremony at an unholy hour between himself and a young woman who would be fast asleep, for he meant to drug Velvet into submission.

Well, well . . . Yes, he would take the money, and because of the timing, perhaps he could still use Jacques's problem to ruse Velvet? Of course he could. Jacques would have no opportunity to really speak about his circumstances with Velvet before the ball. Indeed, even if he did, Velvet might think he was only trying to protect her. He smiled blandly at Jacques. "Well then, I shall return your marker to you."

"Indeed, but first I must explain. I borrowed this money from an old friend. The voucher will be cashed for you at the bank. If you like, I can accompany you."

"Why could you not cash the voucher and bring it to me?" Farnsworth eyed him doubtfully.

"I am underage, a minor."

"You were not to bring my name into it!" snapped Farnsworth.

"Oh, but, my lord, I did not. As I was saying, you need only accompany me to the bank where we may sign the voucher for cashing together. I have no wish for my father to discover my foolishness, and my

friend says his man at the bank will keep our trans-
action under the strictest of confidence."

"Who is this friend?"

"As your name was kept confidential, so must
his." answered Jacques.

Farnsworth stood and pulled at his bottom lip.
This must be thought out, for he wanted no hint of
his part in all of this, yet it was a hefty sum. What
would it matter once he and Velvet were safely wed?
It wouldn't matter at all. He would take her off to
his estates and teach her how to please her husband,
and she would learn—there was no doubt of that.
Finally, his greed won the moment. "Very well. Shall
we go?"

Jacques bowed him out, and closing the door of
the hotel suite, he smiled to himself. Round one for
the name of Beaupré!

Edward Martin entered the Condé library to find
Marie and Velvet quietly seated. Marie was busy with
her stitching, and Velvet was scanning the pages of
the latest periodical. Both were heartily bored and
grateful for the interruption.

Marie invited him to be seated, and they exchanged a few quips before Marie tactfully excused
herself. "Faith, but the flowers should be arriving.
I will go and see how things are progressing. I shan't
be long, *petite,* "she said to Velvet and tripped gracefully out of the room.

Edward Martin smiled warmly at Velvet. She
looked stunning in her morning gown of pale pink

muslin. Her golden locks were tied at the nape of her neck with a matching ribbon, and her green eyes sparkled.

"I shan't ask how you are, for I can see for myself that you are absolutely enchanting." He bent low over her fingers and came up to gaze into her eyes.

Velvet looked away and began hurriedly talking about the gossip she had overheard amongst the servants. "War—is it really going to happen? 'Tis what they say, and the servants always know these things, for one's maid has a sister who works for this one or that and they hear things, know things. 'Tis so very distressing."

"Velvet, you know that war is inevitable. However, I do think we shall be in England when it strikes." He sat close to her, very close, indeed. "There is something else I wish to speak to you about."

In the year Velvet had been gadding about in Paris, she had received more than one marriage proposal. One had been from an infatuated youth whom she had kindly turned down and made an excellent friend of, and two others had proposed, she believed, because she had become all the rage. Never had she felt that any of the men who courted her were seriously, truly in love with her.

She knew Edward Martin was about to propose marriage, for she had learned to recognize the signs. She knew that here again was no love match. How could it be when she was deeply, devotedly in love with the Marquis of Talgarth? She liked Edward Martin and wanted to halt him before he could begin. She touched his lapel. "Dearest Edward, it is so comfortable to be with a man and know that we are such good *friends.*"

He understood this in a different light and took both her hands to shower kisses upon them. "Dearest Velvet, sweetest, yes, yes, such comfortable friends . . . just as it should be when two people are about to embark—"

"No!" she said abruptly, jumping to her feet. Reining herself in, she started again. "What I mean is—"

"Is this . . ." He took her into his arms and began kissing her feverishly.

Velvet managed to break free and breathlessly advised him, "Stop it, Edward. You don't want to kiss me—well, perhaps you do, but you do not wish to spend the rest of your days with me. I should prove a hard trial for you!"

"No, how can you say that? I should be enchanted to live with you."

"You are not thinking. You find yourself attracted to me . . . physically, and my grandfather told me quite bluntly once that men very often don't use their minds when they are lusting after a female. My grandfather and I had very interesting discussions." She smiled as she recalled his dear face.

"Well," she continued briskly, "you may like me, but you would not be able to live with me. I am forever jumping into one lark or another and thinking nothing of it. What would you say if I told you that I had donned the clothes of a boy and went with friends in the dark of night to the worst part of Paris just for a lark?"

This seemed to take Edward Martin by great surprise. At heart he was most assuredly a traditionalist. He believed women belonged at home with their children doing their stitching and whatever it was that women did at home. Although he enjoyed Velvet's spunk, as he enjoyed his sister's outspokenness, he did not want that in a wife. This was something he attributed to youth and hoped Velvet would grow out of in time.

Velvet knew this and said, "Aha! You see, you are very shocked. What is more, I enjoyed myself excessively and would do it all over again. What would you say if I told you that when I return to London, to my guardian, the Duke of Salsburn, I shall don my britches and scamper all over the countryside unattended whenever I can and that no one can stop me? What would you say if I told you that routing, balls, and their like bore me? I would rather be walking the hounds!"

"Never mind all that. I shan't mind it if that is what you want," said Edward.

"Oh, but you would mind it, for I don't stitch, and I don't want to have children right away, and I shall never make you the kind of biddable bride you are looking for. And besides, I am very much in— well, never mind that." She had caught herself.

Edward Martin was frowning, but he was surprised to find that he was not all that disappointed at the rejection. He had not even been sure why he had proposed to Velvet. He liked her so very much that he had been certain he was in love. He knew he wanted her: few men would not. What she had said were things that he owned were certainly true. Curiosity made him finish the sentence she had started. "You are very much in love with someone else?"

Velvet scanned her toes and nodded before her green eyes looked sadly into his. "Yes . . . madly so . . ."

"And this lucky man is the Marquis of Talgarth?"

She was surprised and blushed. "How did you know?"

"I did not. My sister thought so and mentioned it to me."

"Don't be distressed, Edward. You really do not want me," she said soothingly.

"Don't I? Well, time will tell." He took up both her hands and pressed them to his lips.

The door closed sharply, and the bang brought their heads round in what appeared to be a guilty movement away from each other. Velvet managed a welcome. "My lord, how nice . . ."

The Marquis of Talgarth was looking like the devil himself. In his blue eyes a storm brewed, and his jaw was set in a definite line. He restrained his temper. "I fear I interrupt. Carry on." So saying, he turned on his heel and left the room.

Velvet jumped to her feet and called after him but the marquis had already slammed the door in his wake. Velvet stamped her foot at the closed door and released a sound Mr. Martin thought very nearly a growl. "Oooooh! I do not believe this! It isn't fair. Why must he always think the worst?"

She turned on Edward Martin and pointed a finger. "This is in part very much your fault! I tried to stop you, didn't I? Now you are feeling hurt, my Dusty is hurt or angry or both, and I . . . I am miserable!" So saying, the lady put truth to the words by immediately bursting into tears.

Marie entered the room at this juncture. Hands to her face, she exclaimed, "So! I leave you for one minute alone with *ma petite* and this is what you do?" She went immediately to Velvet and embraced her. *"Mon ange . . ."*

"But I did nothing. I swear," Edward Martin responded devoutly.

Marie waved him off with a lax hand while the other busily petted Velvet's back.

Martin made good his escape, saying that he was very sorry for anything that he might have done to distress Lady Velvet. He hastened himself out of the house and stood in the morning's crisp spring air. Everyone in that household appeared to be mad.

A flash of what disorder his life would be like with such a volatile girl as his wife tickled his conscious thoughts. "Whew!" breathed Edward Martin as he hurried back to his hotel.

Twenty-six

Velvet stood before the gilt-framed looking glass and surveyed herself critically. Tonight she needed to look special, special enough to catch and then keep Talgarth's interest. She had not seen him since the day before when he had walked out so precipitately. She had fallen into a deep despondency and had already suffered many scolds from Marie. Well, tonight she was going to change all that! Tonight she would be ravishing, bewitching, sensual, alluring, everything a woman must be to win such a man's heart!

Her golden curls were piled in perfect Grecian style at the top of her head. Two long dangling curls twisted and tickled her ears as they bobbed with her movements. Gleaming golden curls fringed her forehead. Throughout her hair tiny white rosebuds framed in dark green satin leaves and sprinkled with silver dust had been pinned. From her dainty ears dangled pearls in a grape cluster; the same hung from a silver chain at her throat.

Velvet's gown was white organza threaded with sparkling silver. The neckline was heart-shaped, and the sleeves were short puffs that rested just below her shoulders. White rosebuds with silver dust and green satin leaves adorned the sleeves. The gown was fitted closely to her body from the empire waistline and showed to advantage her perfect curves.

The gown would have been declared quite unsuitable for a maid at her first ball in London but was certainly first-rate in Paris! Velvet smiled to herself, for though she knew this was just in Talgarth's style, for he was no prude, this gown was sure to raise Edward Martin's eyebrows! He will think himself lucky to be out of her clutches . . .

A knock sounded at her door, and to her call her cousin's maid appeared with a silver salver and a saucy smile. She advised her ladyship that this had just arrived for her. There was a posy of white roses tied with silver on the tray, and Velvet snatched at it excitedly, taking up the card that accompanied the corsage. With trembling fingers she broke the seal to read:

> Tonight is yours. I have been a fool. Forgive me.
>
> > Always,
> > Dustin.

"Yes, yes, yes!" She turned to find Marie at her door. She sent her curious maid off and turned to inquire, "Ah, from M. Martin? Very presumptuous of him in light of what transpired between—"

"No, it isn't from Edward," cried Velvet joyfully. " 'Tis from the marquis."

Marie's hazel eyes glittered. "So. This is a start, *oui? Oui!* I have known for some days now that my dear Dustin is smitten. *Moi,* I think now he knows it, too. Let me see the card?"

Velvet waved it in front of her teasingly before handing it over. Marie snatched it from her hastily, lest she change her mind. "Naughty puss, you tease your Marie so." She quickly read the marquis's short missive. "Fool? Greater than he knows, but not such a fool, for he knows it."

Velvet laughed over this logic and hugged her cousin, who made her stand still and not muss herself. She scanned her, declared her to be a daring beauty, slipped the corsage onto her wrist, and said that the marquis was awaiting them with Condé downstairs.

"What?" shrieked Velvet. "Why did you not say so? We must go at once!"

"Non, non, such a hoyden." Marie clucked her tongue. "You must not jump and prance, but glide . . . so." Marie moved accordingly.

"Oui, I glide . . . like this," teased Velvet, who dramatized the movement so that they ended in giggles. Arm in arm they took the corridor to the stairs.

The marquis had discovered many things when he walked into the library and found Edward Martin attempting to propose to Velvet. He discovered a jealous demon within himself that he never before knew existed. He wanted to take Martin by the throat and choke him to death. He had wanted to take Velvet by the hand and run with her to a quiet corner of the world where only they could thrive. He stopped himself and knew he had to escape them and the fact that she might accept Martin. His rage and his fears drove him off, and he found himself alone in some French tavern drinking himself into oblivion.

He had somehow gotten back to his hotel room and late into the morning awoke to find Gilly hovering over him with some ugly brew, demanding that he drink it. To keep Gilly quiet, he appeased him and almost immediately disgorged his insides into a handy bucket Gilly had ready. He glared at his friend. "You knew! You knew what it would do, you fiend!"

"Aye, but you'll feel more the thing now."

It was true actually. After that his head did not ache so wickedly, and though his stomach was still gurgling, he did feel rather better. He bathed, dressed, and joined Gilly in their suite to find coffee and warm bread awaiting him, nothing more, and he smiled at his friend and said lightly, "Fiendish . . . but clever." He sat with a heavy sigh and sipped at the coffee.

Gilly hesitated and then asked slowly, "Any reason for it, ol' boy? Not that a man can't get bosky now and then, but, damnation, Dustin, you didn't know who you were when you got in last night! One of the boots had to half carry you here."

"It appears that Velvet means to marry Martin," said the marquis in way of a reply.

Gilly shook his head. "Don't see that. You are

dead wrong. Can't be right. Saw Martin last night and—come to think of it, he was pretty much in his cups, too. . . . Well, never mind. Thing is he said Velvet won't have him. Seems to think she is head over heels in love with you."

The marquis jumped to his feet, held his aching head, and planted a kiss on Gilly's cheek before saying he had a few things he needed to do. Gilly brushed the kiss away from his face. "Getting as bad as these Frogs, tell you what. Good thing we are leaving in the morning!"

Thus it was that he knew himself to be desperately, wildly, securely in love with Velvet Colbury. He looked up at her now, and she seemed to float down the stairs in an aura of stardust. She took his breath away and gave it back all new and uplifting. He loved her, adored her, wanted her, and, by gad, that was a dashing gown she was wearing!

She went to him, and he saw no one save her. Their hands found each other's, and the marquis whispered, for he discovered he had lost his voice, "Beautiful little one, you do that gown justice, I swear you do!"

"Oh, you like it? Not too . . . revealing, do you think?" She peeped up at him.

"Yes, by God, damn revealing . . . but perfectly so. You carry it off enchantingly, my dear." He reached into the inner pocket of his black superfine and brought out a small red velvet box and pressed it into her hand. "For you, little one, on this special occasion."

Velvet wanted to cry, and she felt herself shake as she opened the box to find a beautiful double-stringed pearl bracelet with a diamond clasp. She gasped, "Oh, my lord, I cannot. This is too, oh, so beautiful."

He took it and started to clasp it round her free wrist at which she exclaimed, "Oh Dusty, you are wonderful, and thank you for these flowers. How did you know I would be wearing white and silver?"

He grinned at her. "I have my ways."

She flung her arms round him, and Marie felt at this point that she had better remind them of her presence. She cleared her throat and said, "I think our first guests are arriving!"

Champagne flowed, the scent of flowers filled the Condé ballroom, the fashionable set twirled about, and conversation as well as laughter was tinged with the excitement of a successful affair! Marie looked round with satisfaction and touched her husband's hand. *"Mon cher,* everything goes well, *oui?"*

"Oui, and our little Velvet is very happy."

"Oui, but not because of our ball. *Non,* 'tis for him she smiles." Marie looked in the marquis's direction, and then she sighed heavily. *"Moi,* I am very pleased. They will deal famously together, only we shall miss the wedding. This is very sad."

He stroked her cheek. "We shall be with them

in spirit, beloved, but he has spoken no word of marriage."

"Condé, you are a brilliant man, but if you doubt that they will be married, you know nothing of such matters!" tittered his lady.

"I know everything I wish to know," replied her husband confidently. He looked round and noted that the Beaupré men were managing to keep their eye on Velvet. Talgarth seemed to feel that Farnsworth would still try something this evening, and they were all watchful for any unusual signs.

The marquis waited for Velvet to be returned to him from the young pup waltzing her round the room. She skipped up to him and laughed, "Waltz with me again, my lord."

"Brat! More than one waltz per man is not permitted," he teased.

"Nonsense, this is Paris! And you and I care little for such absurdities." She gave him her hand, and he took it to his lips to say, "Salsburn knew what he was doing when he sent me after you."

He led her onto the floor and for the second time that evening beautifully waltzed her round the room. They did not speak; they did not have to as her green eyes looked up into his pools of blue.

Outside the ballroom, well down the street, Farnsworth sat ready in his coach to enact his final gambit. He had written a note and now placed it in his tiger's hand with two coins. "Give this to one of the servants who knows who Jacques de Beaupré is. Make certain he delivers it. Give him the coin when he returns to say that he has delivered it. Understand?"

The young boy nodded and hurried off to do this bidding while Farnsworth sat back and awaited the first of his plays. He did so love a good game of cards, especially when the deck was favoring him!

Jacques de Beaupré stood chatting with a young lady much his own age when a servant quietly appeared and bowed his head that he was sorry to interrupt but here was an urgent note for him. Jacques raised his eyebrows and took the note. Excusing himself to the young woman, he moved off alone and read:

Dearest Jacques,

I am distraught. You have not returned to see me. Have you forgotten your Catalina? I need you. Please do not force me to visit with your father and tell him the trouble I am in because of you.

I await you alone in the darkest corner of the garden so that we will not be seen. Please hurry.

Catalina

Jacques felt his heart sink. He had forgotten all about her. What trouble could she be in? Oh no, not a child? Jacques was still too naive to know that it was too soon for any woman to know such a thing. He was far too naive to know anything other than this girl had run him to earth and that she was his responsibility. He couldn't go to his uncle with yet another sordid story. He wouldn't go to his brother Louis, who was enjoying himself for the first time in days. He must handle this situation on his own. He quietly made his way to the garden doors and slipped out unnoticed.

Velvet waltzed now with Edward Martin, and she was peeping naughtily at him as she asked, "Tell me true, Edward. Do you like my gown?"

He answered gallantly at once, "Why, it is lovely."

"Still, you don't quite approve, do you? I see it in your eyes, sir." She smiled fondly at him.

"Well, as to that, I suppose here in Paris . . . and perhaps if you were a bit older . . . married, that is . . ."

"You still would think it far too dashing for your taste. Truth, Edward?"

"Truth then, Velvet. It's just a touch too dashing for my tastes."

"Aha! Admit to me then that you are very happy to be my friend instead of my beau, for I shall always dress myself in garments far too dashing for the average taste! Admit it, sir."

"I will admit to but one thing, Velvet. I shall always adore you," said the man sweetly.

" 'Tis the same thing. You just don't wish to say it. I accept. We understand one another."

Edward Martin threw back his head and laughed out loud. Indeed, a small part of him would always lust after Lady Velvet, but truth was they could never deal as man and wife, and this he knew at bottom.

Jacques moved into the darkness and called in a hushed voice, "Cat? Cat? Are you there? It is I, Jacques."

This was met with a blow to the back of his head, and Jacques crumpled to his feet. Two henchmen rifled him for the small amount of cash he carried and removed his signet ring. After stuffing this safely away, they roped him, covered him with a blanket, deposited him in the back of a vegetable wagon, and drove him a half-mile away. They parked their disreputable vehicle and hurried back the distance to where Farnsworth awaited them.

They delivered the ring as proof that the job was done and were paid for the first of their night's work. Farnsworth smiled grimly as the tiger left with the second note to be delivered at the Condé house.

Velvet felt her arm touched as an unfamiliar servant quietly called her name and placed a piece of paper in her hands. "This is for you, your ladyship," the youthful male servant said before slipping away. Velvet frowned, and something made her shiver as she moved aside to open the note and read its contents.

Dearest Velvet,
    I am afraid it has come to this. I have Jacques,

and I will hand him over to his creditor, who means to teach him a lesson for playing and not paying. However, I will keep him safe if you come to me. I await you in my coach down the road, and, Velvet, I have look-outs, don't serve me ill. That would not be kind to poor Jacques, who already suffers quite a headache.

Very much your loving,
Farnsworth

Velvet looked round the room automatically and did not see Jacques. What to do? She was being watched. She had known all evening that the marquis, Armand, Louis, Jacques, and even Condé were looking after her. She should tell the marquis. He would take care of her, of Jacques, but Farnsworth had him and would see if she came with anyone. She must go alone, but how? She would be seen leaving. Yes, she told herself, unless you change into a boy!

Hurriedly she told Marie she had to run to her bedchamber for a moment. Once there, she threw off her gown, slipped on her male clothing, pulled on a pair of half boots, plopped the wool cap down on her yellow curls and tucked them in. It didn't take her long, and soon she was sneaking down the servants' stairs.

Edward Martin caught the marquis's attention and met his gaze squarely. "She is quite a beauty."

"She is a goddess," said the marquis emphatically and meaningfully.

"A man would count himself the luckiest on earth to win her."

"I should think so, and more directly, I will count myself such if she will have me."

Martin grinned ruefully. "Have you? Oh, she'll have you. She made short work of me and told me that amongst other things."

"You mean she actually told you *outright* that she . . . she . . ."

"Well, only in a manner of speaking, but she told me clearly that she would not suit me. Said she liked scampering round the countryside unattended. That your grandfather wouldn't mind that. Presumably I suppose you would not either?"

"Not in the least. Don't you like riding freely?"

"Yes, but I am a man," objected Martin.

"I don't see that it signifies. Why shouldn't an accomplished rider, female or male, ride unhampered? Absurd to stop a girl like Velvet from flying over her fences, and what groom could follow her if she wished him not to?" He shook his head. " 'Tis one of the things I . . . I love about her." He said this last to himself.

"Yes, said I should never be happy about it, said I wouldn't like her kicking up larks as she did recently with her friends, and I must assume those friends to be Jacques and Louis de Beaupré."

"What larks did she kick up with them?" The marquis was grinning appreciatively.

"Velvet says she actually put on boys' clothing and

went into the worst part of Paris in the middle of the night with those two. My mind boggles."

"What? Dressed as a boy?" The marquis's mind was moving quickly. He recalled stopping an urchin when an alarm was cried. He remembered discovering the boy was a girl when he made a search of her person. It was Velvet. He could see her eyes clearly now as if it was yesterday! Velvet, you little brat! "Why, if that don't beat all!" He laughed out loud.

Martin shook his head. "I wish you happy. I see now that you two are meant for one another!"

Marie came up behind the marquis in a flurry of fear, waving a crumpled notepaper at him. "Dustin, Dustin! That fiend, he has her!" She waved the paper at him. "Oh you must read it. Read!"

"I am trying!" snapped the marquis as he snatched the notepaper from her.

While he scanned it, Marie was wailing, "Velvet's gown is on the floor. I know I saw her only five minutes ago. Oh, maybe ten . . ."

"It was five minutes, no more. I have not had my eyes off her all night," said the marquis, who touched something tucked into his cummerbund. He started for the garden doors, handing Edward Martin the note to read and saying, "If you wish to help, get Armand and arm yourself."

Gilly came up as the marquis was rushing out the garden doors. "What is toward?"

While Gilly and then Armand were being informed, the marquis was stalking Velvet. He had seen her lightly skip over the Condé courtyard wall.

He couldn't rush her with Farnsworth only a short distance off, so he crossed the avenue and vanished into the courtyards of the town houses that lined that street. He made his way to the corner where Farnsworth's hired chaise was awaiting Velvet's appearance, and he took out the small gun he had concealed on his person.

Velvet approached Farnsworth's coach cautiously. Something, she knew not what, made her feel that she was not doing the right thing for herself or Jacques. It was time to come clean, time to tell her relatives. She shouldn't play into Farnsworth's hands.

Farnsworth saw an urchin lurking about and yelled irritably in French, "Hey you! Filth of the streets! Go about your business."

"*Oui, monsieur,* I mean no harm," said Velvet, crossing the street at that point and edging toward one of the courtyard gates where she could hide herself to think.

A hand came from behind and covered her mouth as another hand went round her and dragged her backward within the courtyard. A voice hissed in her ear, "Stop struggling, you little fool!"

Velvet went limp, and the next thing she knew she was spinning round in Dustin's arms and he was kissing her fiercely, passionately. They clung together, and the marquis whispered into her ear as he nibbled its lobe, "My little thief, eh? My scamp, my she-devil. . . . How dare you go out to Farnsworth! How dare you not come to me!"

"Oh Dustin, I wanted to, but I feared if I did you

would kill him and be sent to gaol here in Paris. I was so confused."

"I am going to have his blood, but I am not going to kill him. I shall, however, clip his wings, and Lord Farnsworth shall not fly for many a year to come."

Velvet clapped her hands. "Oh Dustin, you are so clever! So very clever. How shall you do that?"

"Never mind. You shall know soon enough." He held her shoulders. "Promise me now, my love: no more secrets between us. You will always come to me?"

"If I can . . ."

"You can. I promise you that."

She snuggled her head against his chin. "Oh Dustin . . ." Then she remembered Jacques. "Oh no! Dustin, he has Jacques!"

"Not for long! Stay here." So ordering, he moved off into the shadows and slowly managed to come up streetside. Through the open window he leveled his gun at Lord Farnsworth's head. "Out, you!"

Farnsworth was taken aback but drawled, "Now, dearest, you would not shoot me in cold blood?"

"In a minute, for it will save me the trouble of ruining you, and, 'dearest,' I have in my hands the power to do both."

Farnsworth had a horse pistol on the seat, but as he reached for it, the marquis flung open the coach door and said lazily, "No, no, no. Mine is already aimed."

Farnsworth stepped out of the coach and sighed, "Now what, dear, dear Dustin, do you mean to do?"

"Where is Jacques?"

"Here!" called Jacques, staggering toward the coach. His father and brother were rushing toward him, and his brother had him in hand as Armand and Gilly leveled pistols at the driver, who had come round to hold a gun at the marquis. Edward Martin had one of Farnsworth's henchmen in hand with a gun held to his forehead, and he was saying the other one had run off.

"Doesn't matter," said the marquis. "We have who we need right here!"

Velvet had come running out and threw her arms round the marquis's waist to exclaim, "Oh Dustin, you are wonderful, just wonderful. Better than any knight any girl could ever want!"

"Yes, and what of us?" laughed Louis. "Are we not wonderful?" He had a supporting arm about his brother, whose head injury had left him wobbly.

"You are all wonderful." She looked then at Farnsworth. "And you are the worst fiend I have ever known in all my life. I wish heartily that I am never plagued with you again!"

"You will never be plagued with his offensive presence ever again, my love. Depend upon it!" said the marquis grimly. "Oblige me, little one. Go up to the house and change once more into your ball gown. Your guests and Marie await you. We shall finish here and join you."

"Ohhh," complained Velvet.

"For me, child?"

Velvet planted a loving kiss upon his cheek, threw a kiss to the assembled family of knights as she called out to tell them once more how wonderful they all

were, and scampered back up the avenue to the
Condé courtyard.

It was not so very long afterward that Velvet was
descending the main staircase looking very much
the same as she had before her little adventure. She
went first to Marie, and the two huddled to discuss
what had transpired before they were interrupted
by a guest wishing for some attention.

A moment after that, the men of Velvet's adventure returned and filtered into the ballroom. Leslie
Martin went straight to Gilly and her brother. Armand moved off to make idle conversation with an
attractive widow, and the marquis came directly up
to Velvet to take her off to a corner.

"What? What did you do with Farnsworth?" whispered Velvet excitedly.

"Dispatched him to Cornwall," said the marquis
blandly.

"What?" shrieked Velvet. "I thought you would
kill him dead." She sounded disappointed.

"Well, I couldn't do that without ending up in
prison, but, my little blood-hungry creature, I did
first draw his cork, break two of his yellowed teeth,
and severely damaged his nose. Then I packed him
off and sent him to Cornwall, where he may have
to remain for some years to come."

"Ooooh," exclaimed Velvet, touching Talgarth's
upper arm. "My strong knight, my perfect man,
but—how did you convince him to go away?"

"I waved a piece of paper with his signature on

it, a piece of paper he does not want circulated amongst the beau monde. His estates in Cornwall yield him some very fine land. They need tending. He thinks so as well."

"He accepted?"

"He had no choice."

"Tell me how."

"Someday soon, but tonight there are other things I want to—"

"Where are Jacques and Louis?" she interrupted.

"Home. Poor Jacques took quite a blow to his head. He'll be fine, though." He laughed and tweaked her nose. "From urchin to debutante. I am the luckiest man on earth. No other has a woman like you." He held her chin. "Say yes and make it official."

"Say yes to what?" asked the lady demurely.

"To becoming my bride, always my bride," he asked seriously as he kissed her fingertips.

"Always a bride, never a drudge?" she teased and twinkled.

"Forever a bride and a sweetheart," he answered softly.

"And I may don britches and ride the moors at will?"

"Britches and moors!" he retorted.

"Yes, and yes again!" answered the lady, throwing her arms round him.

"My dears," said Condé, "I am very sorry. We must have private conversation. The Martins and Gilly await us in my study. Come quickly."

He had appeared out of nowhere and looked

white. They could see that something serious had occurred, something worse than all the rest of the things that had happened already. They entered the study, where Marie went up to her husband to touch his arm. He took a moment to pour out glasses of sherry and pass them round before saying quietly, "My dear friends, it is with deep heartfelt regret that I must inform you that England has declared war on France this day, May 16, 1803, a day that I think both our countries will grieve over for years to come!"

Leslie Martin gasped and went into Gilly's arms. Her brother touched her shoulder. Velvet hugged Marie, for they were like sisters, and this would mean a long separation for them. The comte moved to touch both their heads before turning back to the gentlemen.

" 'Tis imperative that you leave France at once." He shrugged. "Who knows how the citizens of France will react to Englishmen on their soil when they hear this news?"

"Indeed, Comte, we are ready to leave. All has been packed. We have but to gather our horses," said the marquis, thinking out loud.

"Oblige me in this, Talgarth. My driver will take Miss Martin and our own dear Velvet in our barouche. The French crest on our doors will insure a safe journey. The luggage can go overhead. Miss Martin's and Velvet's horses you may tether at the boot. You three gentlemen ride beside the coach as outriders and speak only in French if you must speak at all. My driver will return my carriage on the following day."

"Yes, thank you, a very good plan, but I fear there will be no traveling until dawn, for there is very little moon tonight."

"Dawn it is," agreed the comte. "God go with you as do our hearts."

"And the wedding?" cried Marie as she squeezed Velvet's hands. "Somehow you will get word to us about your wedding?" She was looking from Velvet to Talgarth.

They laughed and hugged one another. "We shall somehow get word to you," said the marquis, "and this time next year we shall all romp together in Italy!"

Epilogue

Gilly and Leslie Martin touched fingers as they watched the receding French docks. Edward Martin conversed with the marquis's captain about the tides. War was a thing that did not seem real to any of them. They had traveled all day at a safe pace, sparing the horses, for they had to do a great many miles. They had stopped only twice for light refreshments and had noted that no one in the villages seemed to know that war had been declared.

Below, the tired horses were in crowded conditions, but they had their hay and water, and were happy enough to rest their weary legs. England was only hours away, and all of them needed sleep. The marquis had Velvet to himself at the bow of his yacht and had slipped his arms round her as she gazed out to sea. He kissed the back of her neck, her earlobes, heedless of crew and guests. He loved her with all his heart and had been so close to losing her. He sighed happily and said, "Salsburn sent me, you know, much against my will, and now methinks, my little girl, that he knew all along what would happen if he threw us together."

Velvet turned round to look at his face. "He knew that I was madly in love with you. I told him so."

"Did you, by Gad? Well, if that don't beat all! How could you? I mean, you were only a slip of a girl then."

"I was in love with you," was all Velvet said.

"And now that you know me, really know me?"

"Fishing are we?" she laughed. "I love you more than ever."

"Velvet, Velvet, I never knew what it would feel like, not wanting to live without someone . . . that one special someone. I never understood before but, Velvet, I do now. I love you . . . and I don't want to live without you." His mouth moved to hers as their yacht sliced the Channel waters leaving France behind as dusk settled. They came out of that kiss to hold each other tight and look forward to their future.